Praise for Rosemary Aubert's phenomenal debut
suspense novel

FREE REIGN

"Engrossing . . . There is a great deal to admire in this
first mystery novel by Ms. Aubert, a Toronto author and
criminologist: well-drawn characters, supple prose and
effectively delivered emotional surprises."
—*The Wall Street Journal*

"[A] gripping suspense novel."
—*The Chattanooga Times*

"Sophisticated, spellbinding . . . completely satisfying . . .
an amazing first effort."
—Scripps Howard News Service

"This excellent book's greatest strength is its portrayal of
the lives of the homeless. Without condescension or sen-
timentality, Aubert describes the day-to-day scramble of
life on the fringe as a prosperous city thunders by just
yards away."
—*Rocky Mountain News*

"[A] surprising, satisfying suspense novel . . . a mystery
story suffused with menace, corruption, personal tragedy
and natural disaster."
—*The Palm Beach Post*

continued . . .

"The more [the sleuth] digs, the more ominous his discoveries . . . [The story] is one you'll think about long after you've finished."

—*Houston Chronicle*

"Intelligently plotted . . . Sensitively details the intricacies of life on the streets . . . The author never lets the suspense grow weak. Nor does she make Ellis the most sympathetic of sleuths. The result is an unconventional mystery with moral depth."

—*The Sun-Sentinel* (Fort Lauderdale, FL)

"*Free Reign* is a wonderful roller coaster swinging through society's highs and lows, with suspense building all the way. It is intelligent, thoughtful, poignant, evocative—and compulsively readable. Your spine will tingle constantly, and you won't be able to put it down. A complete success."

—Robert J. Sawyer, Nebula Award–winning author of *The Terminal Experiment*

"Stylishly combines the suspense of a whodunit with some very current dilemmas: questionable medical technologies, homelessness and, not least, deep but conflicting personal loyalties. We can hope to hear from her fallen judge Ellis Portal again."

—Joan Barfoot, author of *Duet for Three* and *Abra*

"Aubert has a wonderful ability to create a sense of foreboding and danger in an indirect manner—the most effective manner of all to generate the shivering-hairs-on-the-back-of-the-neck phenomenon. She has proved herself a master of the obliquely angled short story and carries this same sure sense of pace and mood into the novel."

—John Lawrence Reynolds, author of the Joe McGuire series of mystery novels, including Arthur Ellis Award–winners *Gypsy Sins* and *The Man Who Murdered God*

FREE REIGN

A SUSPENSE NOVEL

by

ROSEMARY
AUBERT

BERKLEY BOOKS, NEW YORK

FREE REIGN

A Berkley Book / published by arrangement with
Bridge Works Publishing Company

PRINTING HISTORY
Bridge Works Publishing Company edition published 1997
Berkley edition / May 1998

All rights reserved.
Copyright © 1997 by Rosemary Aubert.
This book may not be reproduced in whole or in part,
by mimeograph or any other means, without permission.
For information address:
Bridge Works Publishing Company, Box 1798, Bridgehampton,
New York 11932.

The Penguin Putnam Inc. World Wide Web site address is
http://www.penguinputnam.com

ISBN: 0-425-16427-6

BERKLEY®
Berkley Books are published by The Berkley Publishing Group,
a member of Penguin Putnam Inc.,
200 Madison Avenue, New York, New York 10016.
BERKLEY and the "B" design
are trademarks belonging to Berkley Publishing Corporation.

PRINTED IN THE UNITED STATES OF AMERICA

10 9 8 7 6 5 4 3 2 1

This book is dedicated to my brother, Tony,
and to his beloved companions,
Mutley and Jayne.

I gratefully acknowledge the inspiring environmental work of David Stonehouse (City of Toronto), Helen Juhola (Toronto Field Naturalists), Charles Sauriol, and Elizabeth Simcoe.

And I thank Billie Fitzpatrick and Barbara Phillips for their excellent editorial advice, without which this book would not have been possible.

CHAPTER

ONE

MY NAME IS ELLIS PORTAL. I LIVE IN THE VALLEY OF A river called the Don that cuts a twenty-mile-long swath right through the center of a metropolis of three million people. Now I live in comfort, but not long ago, like thousands of homeless in Toronto, I managed with whatever I had on my back, over my head and in my garden. That was summer. Winter was another story, and it's not part of this one, which begins on the fifteenth of May, the May that John Stoughton-Melville, my enemy and savior, got the news he'd been appointed as a judge of the Supreme Court.

Like every story you ever heard, this one is about the teller. I am a vagrant. A voyager, a wanderer, a citizen of the kingdom of free reign.

I was once a lawyer; in fact, I was once a judge. A judge for the times. For the people. Judge not lest you also be judged.

Once I had a pager, part of my accessibility equipment. I had fax machines—some of the first—in my office, my home and my chambers. I also had a secretary, an assistant, an army of court lackies, and a wife.

But nobody could ever find me.

Available, yet not. Accessible, but not really. Ambivalence has always been a problem for me. Not because I am indecisive but because I can always see both sides of the story. How else could it be with a judge? Yet the day comes when you have to make up your mind, or, as my mother would have said, somebody is going to make it up for you.

That May I was living in a large wooden packing crate partially roofed with stolen tar paper and snugly nestled under a tree in the middle of a wood that could not be reached except by foot or horse. And the world wanted to beat a path to my door. Which is about what I expect of the world.

So it was necessary to stay hidden, which wasn't easy. The valley is a busy place: animals, insects, birds, butterflies, naturalists, joggers, picnickers, cross-country skiers, cops. I begrudged them all, though I was certainly as much an intruder in the valley as any of my neighbors—other people with no place to live except the ravines.

Like all stories worth telling, mine has its gruesome excesses, its thorny complexities, its villains, its moments of betrayal and redemption. A judge is a good storyteller. So is a lawyer. So is the son of a *brickiere*—a bricklayer—who has spent most of his life pretending not to be. My name is Ellis Portal. But that, like everything else about me, is not as it has always been.

During this second week of May, the days had finally become warm enough to encourage a pale canopy of new leaves on the trees over the box I fondly thought of as "my hut." The soil, as if awakening from its seven months of winter sleep, was still very cool to the touch. In the open meadows of the valley, early dandelions showed their bright, outlaw, yellow crowns.

Not to miss the benefit of the earliest real warmth of the year, I was working in my garden, my "encroachment," as the City Solicitor would call it. I was turning over the cold brown soil made rich by a hundred years of garbage dumping, wood-ash deposit and weed rot. It was a bright day, and I kept my eyes toward the earth.

Suddenly, I caught the glint of gold. At my feet lay

a large, solid, intricately embossed ring. Both it and the earth were moist with dew.

I reached for the gold.

Time stood still, the way it does in those moments that you come to wish had never happened. I felt the heft of the metal; I felt the gentle swell of the thick embossing. And then I felt the unmistakable texture of human skin.

The ring was on a finger the same color as the good brown soil of my garden. I lifted the ring and with it came a human hand severed at the wrist, a stump of clotted blood. A black hand—I don't mean black from decomposition; it looked quite fresh. I mean the hand of a black man, large with well-kept nails.

I had never seen such a thing, never dealt with dismemberment in all my years as a lawyer and a judge. The sight of this grim object filled me not with disgust, but with such a perfect blend of fear and grief, that I let out the sort of involuntary cry I have sometimes heard an accused utter when he hears the verdict of guilty.

The sound of my own voice so carelessly shattering the quiet of the valley stunned me. I choked back the hot threat of vomit. I dropped the hand and staggered away into the shade of the maple that guarded my makeshift hut. I thought the young leaves were trembling in a sudden wind; it was really I who was shaking, and I couldn't stop.

Then, I heard a rustling in the bushes beyond my garden. Peering out I saw something I at first took for a familiar sight, one of the mounted cops that regularly patrol the valley. Looking closer, however, I saw that this cop was one I had never seen before. I couldn't help but notice, too, the stiff way in which she sat on the horse—as if she were out of practice in her riding. My daughter, Ellen Angela, had taken up horseback riding in the days when we could afford such things. And she had sat on her horse as if she and it were a single animal. Not this cop.

She slowly circled my garden, as if she were looking for something and were determined to find it. I moved further into the shadows beneath the tree.

She stopped. Her horse lifted its head and neighed softly. Above me, a blue jay, startled by the sound, screeched and careered out of the foliage and across the garden. The horse neighed again. Its rider was slender, pale, pretty and blonde, but her hands on the reins looked strong. She took off her cap and let the breeze lift a fringe of golden hair from her forehead. It was so quiet that far, far in the distance I could hear the faint, regular beat of the commuters on the highway that ran south through the valley alongside parts of the river to the harbor on the lake.

All the cop had to do was look down as I had looked. She was no farther from the ring than I had been when I had first caught the gleam. But she didn't look, or if she did, she didn't see. Instead, she put her cap back on her young head, reined in her restless horse, and set off at a smart little trot across the valley and onto the path that led away.

I let out my breath in a sigh of relief. There are reasons that trespassing vagrants hide at the sight of the police, and they are obvious. But I had an additional reason. There was on me a sort of peace bond, an order restraining me from being found near or in the presence of certain people. One of whom was John Stoughton-Melville. I had already breached the order once. Should I breach it again, any officer in Toronto could haul me in and throw away the key.

I waited a little, until I could be sure she was well and truly gone. Then I headed back to where I had left the ring.

I wasn't going to bury gold like some demented pirate. But by the same token, I wasn't going to commit further indignity on human remains. I was a liar, a thief and a bully, but that was the extent of it. I took the cold black fingers in my own and carefully slid off the ring. I had to tug a little, and I felt a moment's panic at the thought that the hand might come apart. But the skin was as pliant as living skin and relinquished its treasure without resistance.

When I was finished, I dug a deep hole and dropped the hand into it. Then I scooped great handfuls of earth back into the hole. It wasn't until I was smoothing the soil over the place that a wave of revulsion shook me. I sat back on my haunches and waited for the nausea to pass.

I knew at once that the ring was a strange, ominous seed and that, like most things planted in good earth at a good time, it was bound to bloom into something larger than itself.

I had seen the ring before. I recognized the elaborate scrollwork that represented the scales of justice on one side and the blindfold of the goddess of justice on the other. Justice is balanced. Justice is blind. What simple notions! What innocence it takes to believe such things!

Yet on the day that ring had been bestowed, I *had* believed in these principles, and so had the person to whom this ring had first belonged. I knew this ring because I had one just like it, had had it for thirty years.

I was going to be in a great deal of trouble if anybody found out that I was involved in the discovery of part of a human body. In the ten years I had served on the bench, I had sent hundreds of people to prison, and hundreds more had taken the short ride down the street from my court to the mental hospital. But I hadn't had the least idea how hard it was for people to stay out of trouble once they'd come to the attention of the police. It wasn't until I was an ex-offender myself that I understood how visible is the mark of Cain.

Still, I had no intention of getting rid of the ring.

There were only a few people in the entire city who knew what that ring meant, and I was one of them. I put it in my pocket, wrapping it in a piece of rag so that it wouldn't fall through any holes. Then I set off across my segment of the valley, a secluded ravine of over a hundred acres surrounded on three sides by well-kept residential streets and on the fourth side by a trunk line of the railroad.

Everywhere I walked, the earth was shooting up green reminders of its own determination. At the edge of a little marsh, I saw a heron, its gray stillness a perfect match for the concrete base of the railroad embankment that abutted the marsh.

Farther on, I saw the hard buttons of ferns that would soon unfurl their lacy softness into air polluted with auto exhaust. I had often studied wild flowers close to the valley highway, where the tires of transports carried salt from the coast, and I had seen the coastal species thriving in tiny tide pools oblivious to the fact that they were a thousand miles from their real homes—the dunes and stretches of Atlantic beach. Soon the scarlet pimpernel would bloom, a tiny pink flower fooled into thinking that the vibration at its root was the sea, when really it was traffic.

When I had crossed the shallow meanders of the river, I entered a rolling section of the ravine that had once been a farm. A small apple orchard still hugged the slopes, sending the sweet, subtle perfume of blossoms over a pale green meadow, beyond which lay a thick forest of maple, poplar, beech, and ash. Before the city had allowed its renaturalization, this forest had been a mown park where, once in a while, a group of neighborhood kids would play a half-hearted game of baseball or a few women would sunbathe.

I used to have an apartment that overlooked that park. There, in an odd part of town that was neither gentrifed nor neglected, the river that runs through the heart of the city entered one of its most beautiful stretches: a wide curve of natural gravel—interrupted by a monumental outcrop—at the center of which was the swift, clean current of the river, crystal green in summer and in winter, bright blue against the snow. In this apartment, once lived my wife, Anne, my two children and myself. That was before we were rich and famous.

"It's better to be poor and happy," Anne used to say.

"It's better to be rich *and* happy," I answered. I wish I had listened to her. I wish I could hear her now. The day I found the ring, I had lived in the valley for four years. Though I tried not to, I thought of my little family often. I had not seen Anne nor Ellen nor Jeffrey for five years. The last time I'd seen them, Anne had been forty-five, Ellen twenty-three, and Jeff twenty-one.

The building overlooking the valley was where Anne had learned to cook. Sometimes, before the children came, we would take our plates out to the tiny balcony off our one-bedroom apartment and sit there in silence watching the shadows of clouds moving over the ravine. I wish now that I had asked Anne what she was thinking about. Perhaps she was considering ways to convince me that it was a triumph for the daughter of an American diplomat to learn to cook. Her family had always had a professional cook. "But I don't need one," she'd said proudly, when I promised her *we'd* have one soon. Later, when she could hire any cook she wanted, she still did all the daily meals herself. "I want to use the Italian recipes your mother taught me," she said. "And besides, your children need to know where they come from . . ."

Though the memories pained me, I loved to come to this spot, and I had made the monolith—the pile of rock in the middle of the river—my safe. This was where I headed with the ring.

I had gotten as far as the orchard when I surprised a typical birdwatcher: a slender man, with binoculars around his neck, who looked as startled as if I were a dangerous species. I could feel him try to make eye contact, but I avoided his gaze. The last thing I needed was a witness. I walked by, ignoring him completely, and I thought I heard him turn and walk off after I had passed.

I threaded my way through the orchard, crossed the meadow, negotiated the thick tangle of trees between me and the river, and sat down on the gravel beach before wading into the shallow water.

I had to take off my boots, which was not a simple matter. I seldom took them off. They were fragile, the tops held together with twine. Soon I would be going in search of a new pair, but I wasn't ready for that yet. Once I did get them off, though, the air on my feet felt so fresh and the water so clean, that I felt like singing, and I would have, except that silence was, as always, my cover.

For a fit man of fifty-five, it is perfectly possible to climb the rock monolith in bare feet as long as you go slowly, which I did. When I got halfway up, I held on with my left hand and swung my right hand around in a ninety-degree turn. Here I touched a sort of natural handle, a place where the rock jutted out. By balancing all my weight on my left foot, I was able to swing out my right leg and, switching hands quickly, change from right to left on the handle. This put me in a position on the rock that would be impossible to reach for anyone who didn't know this balancing trick.

Once in this position, I was stable enough to let go with both hands and to reach into a cleft in the rock that I had carved laboriously and with considerable injury to my fingers. That had been a long time before. On the day I'm telling you about, I had been coming to the rock for years. Never, in all that time, had I seen the least evidence that anyone but me had been there. And my hiding place would have been invisible to anyone in the apartment building because it was on the rock's far side.

In the cleft in the rock was another rock, which I slid carefully toward me. This was really a box that I had made by carving two soft stones into a top and bottom that I fitted with a hinge, also of stone. Among the few small things stored there, was a ring almost identical to the ring I had in my pocket. I took the second ring, the one from the hand, and put it into the stone box.

I took out my ring. I ran my fingers over the thickly embossed gold, over the little symbols of justice. Then I turned it so that I could see my name engraved inside. Ellis George Portal, LLB. This was the detail that was different from the ring I had found in my garden. Someone had carefully filed off the name engraved inside that ring.

Originally there had been five rings with five names. Five people. All white. My own ring had belonged only to me. But that other ring—how many hands had it passed through? And whose was the hand that I had taken it from?

It was snowing. I don't think it was winter, I can't remember anymore. Maybe it was one of those heavy snows that come too early in the autumn or too late in the spring. She was standing beside a leaded window, and its little panes were sharply edged in black against the surprising whiteness outside. The building was stone. You could see the stone through the window, and Harpur was like one of those vibrant saints whose colors burst almost sacrilegiously against the gray walls of the church. Her hair was red. Everything else about her was elegant, subdued, controlled—not by Harpur herself, but by generations of being, having, and doing everything right. Her eyes were green. Of course they were. Harpur's eyes seldom looked right at you, but when they did, you saw some kind of loss. It shocked you, and you looked away. But afterward, you were sorry that you hadn't looked longer.

We were twenty-five years old. We'd stuck together through our undergraduate work and then law school—seven years all told. We'd already called ourselves "the team" for longer than we could remember. Now, on that day, the five of us—Harpur and four men—had been admitted to the bar.

The room was full of snowlight, the soft light of expensive lamps with brass bases and green shades, the light of a fire that burned quietly and steadily in the huge fireplace. It was a rich man's room. I alone of the five could identify each of the original paintings that graced its walls, because I alone was amazed that a valuable painting could be anywhere but in a museum.

I remember that day as if it were the first day of my life, because it was. It was 1967. Perhaps it was as unusual for me, the son of a non-English-speaking *brickiere,* to have become a lawyer as it was for a woman, for Harpur. But unlike me, Harpur had been casual about it from the first. During most of her time at school, she hadn't even studied. She was like that—brilliant, instinctive, casual almost to the point of seeming lazy.

The three young men were also casual. They were, of course, finely dressed in slim gray suits, white shirts, dark ties. It was thirty years ago, before many "revolutions" in men's clothing. They were dressed as they expected to be dressed for the remainder of their professional lives. And their hair was short.

They lounged against the thick leather of the chairs grouped near the fireplace. The blaze threw warm light on their faces, but they didn't need that flattering light because they were all handsome. And most handsome of all was Gleason. He was fair in every way, his hair, his skin, his eyes. And his face danced with an irresistible animation, as if he were nothing more than a beautiful jolly child. Which was what he would remain because he would die before the night was out.

Beside Gleason, leaning close and studying his lively

motions with intensity, sat William. William, too, was
good-looking, but only for then. His auburn hair was the
type that would fade to rusty brown, his strong face
would harshen as time drew it nearer to the bone, his
slim body would become gaunt. The wiry physique he
had acquired as a member of the university sculling team
would have slackened had he not found other outlets for
his love of the outdoors.

Then there was my mentor—my rival: John Stoughton-
Melville, whom we all called "Stow."

Rare as they seem, there are men like Stow everywhere. In boyhood they are the athletes who bring pride
to their fathers and the little gentlemen who honor their
mothers. In adolescence they are sports heroes and
scholars. In adulthood they are first promising businessmen and eligible bachelors, then good husbands and
prominent citizens, then magnates, men to be reckoned
with. In old age, they become institutions. A man like
Stow is always a pleasure to be with. His command is
total but it is calm. In his company, one is intimidated,
but feels the fear is one's own fault. On the surface of
a man like Stow there is boundless hospitality, charm
and ease. Beneath this surface is something else.

I was the fifth lawyer. I was dressed like all the others,
though the gray suit was my only suit and had been
skillfully altered by my mother to hide the fact that the
tailor, who was a friend of our family, had given it to
us because the customer for whom it was intended
changed his mind. My hair was not fair. My eyes were
not light. My body was not slim. But on that day of
days, these things didn't seem to matter.

Harpur caught me watching her. She smiled. The fire-
light on her hair reminded me of a day not long before,
on which Gleason had invited the four of us fifty miles
north of the city to his family estate. We'd been
horseback riding all afternoon. Or rather, they had been
riding and I had been making excuses for staying off the

horse. Just as the sun was about to set, we reached the stable, and as Harpur dismounted, she stood between me and the setting sun. She was like an angel with a fiery halo. And I knew in that moment just how much I loved her and just how impossible it was that I would ever have her.

This realization was not exactly an act of genius on my part. How many hours had I spent plotting ways to be near her? I joined the debates club so that I could spar with her when we were the most tender of under-graduates. She outwitted me always. And even toward the end of our studies, when I contrived to be her most frequent adversary in moot court, figuring I could challenge her mind at the same time as I stupidly worshipped her body, she not only won every case, she also topped the class in her grades—leaving me a distant second. I treated her to meals that left me no money for my own and went joyously hungry. I fixed things for her—pens that wouldn't write, tires that had gone flat, even once a shoe that had lost its heel. And she laughed and thanked me and danced away.

Now she turned from the leaded window and danced toward Stow, whom she kissed on the cheek. I heard her whisper to him, "Tell them now." My breath caught in my throat, and hearing that small sound, a servant hurried to refill my glass, pretending he didn't see when I misjudged the distance to my mouth and spilled a dribble of champagne on the Turkish carpet. Were Stow and Harpur about to announce their engagement?

No one—least of all I with my futile infatuation—would have been surprised. Though I convinced myself I was not jealous of Stow, I suffered in suspecting that Stow and Harpur were meant for each other because both of them were perfect.

With his arm around Harpur, Stow moved toward the fireplace. William and Gleason, who had been deep in conversation, looked up.

Stow reached toward the top of the high mantel. The angle at which he was standing combined with the uneven quality of the light made it hard for me to see what he took down. Then I saw that it was a box from a prominent jeweler—but not the sort that engagement rings come in.

Stow handed the box to Harpur. She opened it with the air of a co-conspirator. Nestled in deep green velvet were five identical gold rings. They seemed to glow like the eyes of a tiger, and I felt a nervousness I had often felt when my mother insisted I look at relics from Lourdes and the Vatican.

"My dear, dear, friends," Stow began, assuming a posture that would soon be intimidating jurors throughout the jurisdiction, "today is not only the culmination of our shared past, it is also the commencement of our shared future. It would be easy after today for us to go our separate ways, to be nothing but people who went to school together . . ."

I shifted in my seat, embarrassed. Stow was going to do something that would make me feel impoverished— some gesture of munificence that I had no way of reciprocating. For the first time that day, I remembered that my family was waiting for me at home, that my mother had made lasagne, had roasted ham and beef, had invited the neighbors. Beyond the window, the snow was becoming heavier; the light was fading.

"Patience, Ellis, patience . . ." I looked up abruptly, caught not paying attention. Stow shook his head, laughed gently and went on. "I want us not to go our separate ways," he said. "In fact, I want our team to be linked for life."

Harpur giggled. William groaned. Gleason stared, his eyes round with expectation. I stifled anger. Nothing was going to spoil this day, not even the arrogance of my betters, especially not that.

"I want us to be a chain, and I want these five rings

to be the links.'' He reached for the box, which Harpur obligingly held up. He removed the first ring and put it on her finger. As though they had practiced this little routine, she took the second ring and came toward me. She slid the heavy ring onto my finger. I gasped, though whether because of the nearness of Harpur, or the weight of the ring, or the fact that it fit so perfectly, I don't know.

Then, she handed me the box. I knew what to do. I took the third ring and placed it on William's finger. He nodded as if accepting this gift from me, instead of from Stow. I handed William the box, and he took out Gleason's ring. As he tried to slip it onto Gleason's hand, William's fingers seemed to spasm. His hand jerked and the ring flew.

There was a moment's stunned silence. It was long enough for a few sparks from the fire to crackle into the warm dimness of the room. With a distinct "ping" the precious ring bounced on the wood floor.

Gleason jumped up, bounded over to where the ring had landed, scooped it up, and popped it on his own finger.

Then he went back to where William sat and took the box from him. He removed the fifth and final ring and walked toward Stow. As he did so, he staggered a little, and I realized just how much champagne we'd managed to down.

With a boyish flourish that would have seemed foolish in anyone else, Gleason bowed to Stow, then slipped the ring onto his finger.

The ring was wonderful. I had never owned anything like it. It was so beautiful I even forgot my humiliation over the fact that Stow could give such an expensive gift to a man who couldn't return the favor.

When we tried to thank him, he silenced us, motioned Harpur to a seat beside me, which she took. Her face, turned up toward Stow, was full of admiration. I couldn't resist glancing at the others. Each of them was listening to Stow as if he were a wizard.

"The rings we wear now," he said, "are tangible links in the chain that has bound us from the first . . ."

He was pacing now. The habit of pacing in the courtroom is a distracting annoyance, and most lawyers try hard to rid themselves of the urge. But Stow has always been a pacer, and it has always worked in his favor, capturing the attention of jury and judge the way flashes of heat lightning on the horizon catch the attention. Will this intensify? Will it strike *me*?

"These rings are meant to remind us of our responsibility to the law, to preserve all that is perfect in it and purge it of all that remains imperfect. We must know it, serve it, and change it when it needs to be changed."

I couldn't help but wonder if the others saw in this little speech the blatant ambition I saw. There are only two types of people who can change the law. Legislators. Judges. For all his respect for lawyers, it was obvious to me that Stow wasn't planning on simply remaining one.

"Those of us in this room, however," he continued, "have another responsibility. We have a responsibility to each other."

Now he was met with voluble enthusiasm. Gleason raised his glass and proposed a toast. More champagne all around. A bit of prodding at the fire. A sliver of air let in through a leaded window.

"That's why I brought these rings. I want you to take them off now and look inside."

I had to hold the ring close to the lamp to read the inscription. I saw my name—thank goodness the right one. Then I saw an expression I didn't recognize at once. I took it to be Latin. I looked closer still and saw, to my chagrin, that it wasn't Latin at all. It was Italian. "*Impegno l'onore.*" "I pledge on my honor."

I looked up at Stow, whose eyes met mine. For an

instant, the light from the low fire caught in his pupils. I looked away. The others were also studying the inscription on their rings. It didn't take much to figure out that each one had been personalized somehow but that each one also bore some form of the word to promise.

"Hey, what is this?" Of course it was Gleason who had the nerve to ask.

Stow replied, "In commemoration of this day and of the friendship that binds us, each of us must make a pledge to each of the others . . ."

"Okay," piped up Gleason, "I promise to . . ."

"Stop," Stow warned, and Gleason did, which was unusual. He sank back into his chair, like a puppy who has been reprimanded.

Stow's voice held no anger, but his tone was somehow frightening. "The pledges we make today we will carry out of this room and into our future. Today is a day of privilege and happiness, but life won't always be this good. There will be no silly promises. Instead, each of us will pledge that once and only once in our remaining lives each of us will do a favor for each of the others . . ."

"Favor, promise—what's the difference?" William asked.

"A promise is easy," Stow answered, "and it's the choice of the bestower. But a favor is different. It's the choice of the person who asks—the beggar. My pledge to each of you is this: At the single moment in your life when you most need help—when only I can do or give the thing you most need, I will give it—no questions, no refusals, no reprisals. And each of you will pledge the same—not only to me, but to each other."

Of course I thought it was a silly game. Of course I said "Yes." So did everybody else. Somebody mentioned Rumpelstiltskin and the fact that he had required the princess for whom he did a favor to promise him her first-born son.

We laughed. Servants brought more champagne, which I drank before heading for the subway and the bus to get home to my mother and her party for her son, the new lawyer.

That same night, on the way back to his estate in the country, the car that Gleason was driving skidded off the road. He was killed instantly, taking with him to the grave, or so we assumed, the four favors he had promised and the four that were promised to him.

William, who was with him, was only slightly injured, but so traumatized he had to be placed under a doctor's care.

When I heard news of the accident, I was stunned. I had thought that I would never lose touch with any of these people. They were my friends, my lifeline to the world I had struggled so hard to enter. They were a bridge out of my poor and humble past.

I was wrong of course. I was wrong about almost everything.

CHAPTER

TWO

I PUT THE SECOND RING BESIDE THE FIRST IN THE STONE box. I put the stone box back in the cleft in the rock. I pulled myself together and moved off.

There was a lot of gardening still to do, and sooner or later, I was going to have to prepare myself for a trip out of the ravine, through the valley and into the city for a visit to some shelter or used clothes bank to get new shoes and to replace a few other necessities in preparation for summer.

How did I concentrate on such things, having found what I had found? The same way I concentrated on sleeping outside when the temperature was cold enough to freeze my breath. The same way I went for five or six days on water alone. Because I had to. Because I could.

As I walked back to my hut, it began to rain. I let it wash my hair, my tattered shirt, my grimy jeans. Despite its freshness, though, rain in the valley meant danger. It brought insects, mildew, rashes and flood.

The river was calm and shallow most of the time, but it could suddenly give way to latent anger. Once or twice a year, the rain, gathering in backyards, parking lots, streets, filled it with such force that it easily jumped its banks and swept away anything in its path. The previous spring, a young couple making out near the lower reaches had been carried into the lake and drowned.

In my rambles, I had covered hundreds of square miles in the valley, and I knew that the flood-control system various city departments had worked on over the years was only one step ahead of the river. In places, the high concrete walls of spillways were eroding. In other areas, leaves and branches, the debris of many seasons, clogged drains. Sometimes rapid water skipped right over the wire baskets of rock intended to hold the river to its course.

In my old life, I would have hurried to report such things to the proper authorities, but since I had come to the valley, it began to seem to me that the river was reclaiming its territory, and that was fine with me. Though I had come as an outcast, I loved my home in the ravine, but increasingly I felt guilty there. Despite my decline in fortunes, I was a modern man, not, like the native Indians who had been there first, part of the nature of the place. My presence seemed to me more like the presence of the highway or the railroad—a convenient but costly imposition.

As I rounded the bend in the river that led to my hut, I saw that a woman was digging in my garden.

At first, I thought it was the cop—then I realized she wasn't wearing a uniform. This one had long blonde hair and the sort of sturdy build young women seem to have these days. She was using the toe of one of her heavy shoes to prod the soil I'd so carefully cultivated.

The sight filled me with rage, and I nearly shouted at her. Luckily, I restrained myself. Because I soon saw that she wasn't alone; she was with one of the very few people that I was genuinely glad to see in the valley: Tim Garrison.

"Ellis!" His friendly eyes were unhesitant to meet mine. "I thought you'd be gardening today . . ."

"I was. I took a break." I like Tim, but I hate chitchat under the best of circumstances. "Why are you here?"

"I wanted you to meet my daughter, Taylor. She's

working on her last school project of the year . . ."

A school project, I thought, *how charming! And what's it going to be about? Vagrants? Ex-criminals? Judges that live under trees?* The girl stared at me nervously, her toe still working the earth.

"It's on the insect ecology of the floodplain," Tim said, his voice full of excitement. I envied him his youth, his powerful intelligence, his handsomeness. I had lost my own good looks. But most of all, I envied the fact that he could be that excited. I figured him to be about twenty years younger than me—thirty-five or thirty-six. The kid looked about twenty but was probably fifteen. I had never sat juvenile court, but I knew that kids these days were deceptively large—not like Ellen had been at fifteen, as delicate and graceful as her mother. I dreaded the stupid questions Taylor was about to ask about "insect ecology."

"Can we sit down?" Tim asked, as if the valley were some sort of drawing room. I signalled toward the hut hidden in the trees. Outside there were rocks and a stump or two. We sat. Inside the hut was a more comfortable place to sit, but nobody went in there except me. The kid stayed in the garden, studying a leaf she'd picked up. She was making me more and more nervous.

"I don't know anything about insects," I said, but Tim's mind, I could tell, was already on something else.

"Ellis," he said softly, as if he were revealing a secret, "I've heard from the land reserve . . ."

No doubt this cryptic piece of information was supposed to mean something to me. I kept my eye on the kid. Now she was down on her haunches, poking at the soil with her finger. She was about ten feet from the place where I'd reburied the hand.

"About four months ago, I heard at work that a major foundation is offering grants for urban river conservation—the preservation of rivers that run through cities, like the Don . . ." He gestured toward the trees beyond the garden and the water beyond the trees.

"It's the usual land trust idea," he went on. "The land is purchased by a consortium that pledges to keep it in its natural state in perpetuity."

"How do you keep a river in the middle of a city of three million people in its natural state?" I asked. "And anyway, what makes anybody think this river is in its natural state? It's been used as a sewer and a garbage dump for two hundred years . . ."

"That's all changing, Ellis. Even with the remaining industrial pollution and all the run-off from the streets and parking lots, this river is cleaner today than it was five years ago."

He was right. When I first came, I couldn't camp too close to the water because of the stench. I just kept watching that kid. Now, apparently, she had actually found an insect. She was balancing it on the tip of her finger and looking at it so intently that it appeared she thought it might speak to her. All of a sudden, out of nowhere, came an image of my son at that age. Jeffrey, teetering on the threshold of manhood and reaching for the balancing hand of a father who was hardly ever home. I pushed the thought away.

"You pretend you're not interested," Tim Garrison was saying, "but I can tell by the look on your face that you've been thinking about all this . . ."

"What?"

He smiled at me the way you'd smile at an old man. "Ellis, you can't fool me. I don't know how long you've been in this valley, or even why you came here, but I do know that there's nobody in this city who knows as much about it as you."

"Sort of like a noble savage?" A look of hurt passed over Tim Garrison's open face, and I felt a tinge of guilt. "Who's got the money to buy a valley as big as this— and why would the city want to sell it?" I asked, though of course, I could guess.

"It's like anywhere else. They're strapped. The funds could be used for services, infrastructure . . ."

It was sick. The very idea that a city would sell a big piece of itself was just the sort of sick thing that I had moved into the valley to forget. No. That's not right. I moved into the valley only to hide. But once I got here, I forgot a lot of sick things.

"The consortium is all kinds of people banded together. They've done this all over the world. The land reserve has saved rain forests, deserts, prairies where the long grass still grows. And they've saved other rivers . . ."

Now the kid was digging again, using a sharp piece of rock as a tool. She was getting closer.

"Look, Tim, I've heard things like this before. A bunch of people with money get together and buy something that used to be public so they can make it private and keep it safe. That's very nice. But what happens if they change their mind—if somebody makes them a good offer? How do you think people with money got that money? By always going for the best offer, even if it means changing their philosophy—even if it means reversing it." I hoped he never asked me how I knew about people with money and power.

"Come on, Ellis, don't be so negative."

Tim Garrison worked as a lab technician at the university. I could imagine how he spent his days. He was conscientious, methodical, thorough. No wonder he devoted his every leisure hour to preserving wilderness. I was far more interested in preserving myself.

"This is very intriguing," I said. "Let me know how it all turns out . . ."

Where had the girl gone? What was she up to now?

"There's something in this for you, Ellis . . ."

"For me? What are you talking about?" I could feel the anger rising in my empty stomach, more painful than hunger.

"You could be steward of this valley," Tim said with conviction. "You could use all your knowledge to watch over it and guide others. You could be a primary consultant on this project. You could . . ."

"Become an honest man again?" He didn't deserve my cynicism. But I couldn't help it.

I stood up and walked back toward the garden. The kid was at its farthest edge, inches from where I had found the ring. She was going to find the buried hand in about two seconds.

Tim came after me. He put his hand on my shoulder. I don't let people touch me. I turned fast and his hand fell away. I looked at him, sure I would see anger in his face, but I didn't. I saw that excitement again. It made me feel eighty years old.

"You still have a lot to give, Ellis," he said. "There are still people who would be happy to accept . . ."

I just stared at him. Then I heard the kid. She was running toward us. "Dad!" she called out. "Dad, I found something in the garden, something really weird!"

I reeled. Images of jail flashed in front of me. I wasn't looking at the girl. I was looking at bars; I was hearing the slam of a cell door. I was sure I was headed back. I felt adrenaline surge. Flight.

But when I turned, I could see the kid was smiling, and the thing that she had found was small and clear and definitely not what I thought she had found.

Tim Garrison took it out of her hand and studied it. "Well," he said, in the tone of the good father, "you've got yourself a nice souvenir. It's an old medicine bottle. See these lines? They're calibrations, so the doctor or the patient would know how much medicine in a dose. And look here, at the top of the bottle. See, no thread, just this glass lip—for a rubber stopper. No screw tops in those days."

I left the two of them to their history lesson. I suppose

they were surprised when they turned around and found me gone. But I was used to slipping silently away, and I'd had enough for one day.

I moved back under the cover of my bushes. I slid down to where the thick branches with their new green leaves could hide me. I crouched there, safe and out of sight. Like an animal. I watched as father and daughter walked peacefully away.

When I was a child I went everywhere with my father. My ambivalence was well established—I thought I didn't want to go along, but I was always glad I did. Now, I would give anything to be with him, to sit with him, for example, in one of those noisy, smokey "clubs," to drink that thick, strong black coffee, to hear those endless, meaningless conversations about the soccer, and the construction and the old country. But my father is dead. He died thinking his fondest dream had come true, that his oldest son was a success in the new country. Like all good fathers, he wanted me to be something more than he had become. Angelo Portalese. "Big Angelo," they called him, but he wasn't big, he was short, wiry and strong. They called him big Angelo solely because of the existence of little Angelo—me.

By the time I was ten, I was working for him after school and during vacations. I rode beside him in the front seat of his pickup truck. We worked all year long, inside in winter, outside in summer. In autumn, we were generally busy finishing up all those things that had to be done before cold took over the city—fixing chimneys or taking inventory and making great long lists of all the tools and supplies that would need replacing over the winter—but in spring, we had time to do things slowly, and when he worked slowly, my father was an artist. Many were the neighbors whose backyard barbecues were marvels of intricately-interwoven multicolored bricks. Some homes even had one of my father's favorite structures: outdoor bread ovens.

On a typical work day, the window of the truck—my window—would be open, and I would be leaning on the edge of it, my arm half in, half out. It would be morning, but not too early because my father seldom arrived at the houses of his customers before they were comfortably up and ready to receive him. It was not an era when workers told their customers what to do.

So we would have had time for *latte* and fresh bread brought from the baker by my mother, time to inspect the garden, to check that all the tools were on the truck, to make the long trip from our own neighborhood to the one where we would work.

Our house was different from those of our customers. It was so close to the houses on either side that we could referee their arguments. It had no real front garden, just a spiky patch of grass that my father had transplanted from a park because it was the only thing that would grow in a space that was completely shaded by one huge linden tree—on city property.

For a man who has lived in doorways, it's awkward to complain, but at the time—for years and years, really—whenever I thought of that house, all I could think about was how crowded it was. Even when my two old parents were alone there, it still seemed like an awkward stack of little boxes, each room stuffed with the souvenirs of a hard, scrambling, ambitious life.

One of my father's most frequent and passionate lessons was on the "virtue" of ambition, and I was his willing student. But I hated the visibility of their ambition, the open admission of where we had come from and how far there would always be to go.

When I think of our house, I remember, too, all the Italian things in it: painted statues of the Virgin, gilt-paged prayer books, opera records, the implements of leisure and of faith. It was the archetypical immigrant house—smelling almost like the foreign country whose spirit was trapped in it. My parents, of course, saw it as the foothold of their family in the new world. They were proud of being in the new country, without ever feeling ashamed of being from the old. Not me.

So I rode with my father in the truck. We pulled away from our own tight, noisy neighborhood in the west end of the city and toward Yonge, the largest main street, which we drove on until we reached York Mills Road on the northern edge of the city. Here we turned east onto winding well-treed streets, lined with the homes of the wealthy.

By the time we'd reached Yonge, we'd been driving long enough for my father to have already warned me twice about having the window open and getting sick from the wind as well as to remind me that my arm would be torn off if another vehicle came too close. I found his concern touching but boring, so I ignored him and studied the street, watching the neighborhoods change.

I was ten years old in 1952. The war that had been raging when I was born was already being forgotten, the memory of it buried in dreams of new prosperity. Downtown stores teemed with people. My father loved to observe all this activity and to remind me as often as possible that if I studied hard and got a job that did not involve manual labor, I would be able to buy whatever I wanted when I grew up.

When we reached the customers' neighborhood on the elegant upper reaches of the river, my father often made a sweeping gesture, taking in the whole of some man-sioned street as if to say, "All this can be yours."

This was a neighborhood where bankers and the owners of department stores lived in country-like estates that seemed far removed from the downtown streets where they did business. I saw horses running in paddocks enclosed by white wooden fences. I thought the horses I saw downtown, police horses mostly, were workers but that uptown horses lived a life of privilege and ease. A smart boy like me should have figured out that anything fenced in is some kind of servant.

As we drove north and I observed the city neighborhoods change from poor to rich, my father kept up a steady stream of words. Though he did not want me to end up a *brickiere,* he couldn't resist the innate urge to pass on his skills. He knew every kind of brick there was, every color, shape, finish, composition and level of porosity. He knew the history of brick in the old world and the new and in our city and the county that contained it. He could lay them in any pattern and on the vertical, horizontal or diagonal. And he could smooth out whatever was beneath the brick to make the flattest, smoothest surface possible.

But I wasn't listening. He was speaking Italian. I'd recently decided I didn't understand that language anymore. English was now my sole language. Perfect English was not only the key to success, it was also a disguise. If your English was indistinguishable from everybody else's, nobody could ever accuse you of not belonging.

I see there was a conundrum in my life. My father encouraged my ambition without noticing how it began to put distance between us. It didn't occur to me then, and I'm sure it never occurred to my father that the more his grandiose hopes for my future were instilled in me, the more he himself came to seem wanting.

As we moved through the rich neighborhoods, I studied every detail of the mansions we passed. I dreamed of hiring a contractor to build such a house for me, of having the power to force him to do my bidding the way I understood people had the power to force my father. I already had plans as to how this might be accomplished. I didn't study only the houses of the rich. I studied the rich, themselves. Sometimes when my father was work-

ing so hard that he forgot I was with him, I sat beneath
their open windows and listened to them talk. I wasn't
above hiding in the bushes and watching as they dined
or sneaking into their garages to run my fingers along
the shiny flanks of their expensive cars.

My mother had reinforced my father's lesson in her
simple, direct way. She told me that in the new country
anybody could be rich if they tried hard enough. At ten
years old, I was already trying.

One day, when I first started working with my father,
we pulled our truck up in front of one of those grand
houses. Before we had even come to a stop, a woman
came rushing out. She spoke very rapidly, but her English was perfect. In fact, she had a recognizable British
accent. She waved at us—the backhanded wave that in-
dicates dismissal, or worse, contempt.

I was frightened and confused, but my father said absolutely nothing. He nodded at her, backed the truck
away, went down and around several long streets until
he could pull into an alley that I realized led to the rear
of the house. There waiting for us was the same woman.
This time she nodded, as if we had finally done something right.

When I asked my father about all this, he said that
laborers should always remain hidden, that he had been
confused about the address and had hoped to be able to
check it before anybody saw his truck in front of the
house. He told me it would never happen again, and that
if it did, he was likely to lose the job.

The thought of that filled me with rage. Though I
seldom stuck up for my father, I had to fight the urge
to jump down from the truck, storm around to the front
of the house, bang on the big front door and give the
witch a smack.

"Just because she owns a house like this doesn't
mean she owns *us*," I told Angelo the *brickiere*.

He started to laugh and tried to hide that laughter. No

doubt that was another thing that wasn't supposed to be seen. But before long, he was laughing too hard to stop. "That wasn't the owner," he told me. "That was just a maid—just a worker like us!"

I failed to see the humor. But I got the point—only too well. I promised myself that when I grew up, nobody would ever treat me like a servant.

My father had a specialty: a certain very complicated way of laying rectangular bricks in a pattern that looked perfectly circular. It was a good trick. Not until the last row was laid, did the circle appear in its perfection.

For a while, he was the rage among the wealthy of Toronto. The summer I was ten, he worked laying those driveways every single day from Monday to Saturday. He spent the entire summer on his hands and knees, and so, nearly, did I. But because I was so young, he let me take long breaks, which I spent where I was happiest, down on the banks of the river, which here were luxuriously landscaped, with long sweeping lawns that flowed down from the gardens of our clients, sometimes bursting into a riot of flowers at the very bottom, where a gardener had devised his own clever trick of making a bed of flowers look like water tumbling into water.

One day in the middle of that summer, as I was trespassing in the rear garden while my father worked at the front of a house, I met a pretty little girl with strawberry-blonde curls and good clothes and a precise way of speaking that let me know she was not the daughter of a servant.

I told her about the river, how it flowed from behind her house to all the other parts of the city. But I didn't tell her how I knew what I knew—that whenever I wasn't working for my father, I was wandering in the lower valley with friends whose mothers and sisters worked in the factories that lined the river toward the harbor. Those factories are long since gone—torn down or turned into studios for noisy musicians. But they gave me one more lesson in what not to be. No wife or daughter of mine was ever going to work in a factory. I didn't tell that to the little girl either.

She told me about horses. She said she had her own and that someday she'd let me ride it. All the rest of the summer, I dreamed of riding her horse. I was too polite to press the matter, but I was sure that any day would be the day she'd keep her promise and show me where the horse was and let me take it out into the meadows that still bordered her neighborhood.

I told her my nickname—which was Gelo—and when she tried to spell it, I had to admit that it was Italian and that it sounded like "Jay-low." This she found amusing, but her laughter wasn't insulting. When she said my name I didn't bristle at the Italian sounds.

At the end of that summer, the strawberry-blonde got caught playing with me and was punished, at which time she denied knowing me at all. Of course I never got to ride her horse.

So there were hard lessons of all sorts for Gelo Portalese, who, in a manner of speaking, did not live to tell the tale of his challenging early years.

When Tim Garrison and his daughter left my garden, I checked the woods for morels and had a wonderful feast. The days were lengthening, and I was beginning to be able to read after dinner, something that I loved but that was denied me in winter.

Books were always easy to get. Nobody ever throws away a book. Instead, they donate them to places like the Parke-Manning Institute—the mental hospital that Stow in his mercy arranged for me to enter five years ago. I spent six months in the Parke as a condition of my discharge for the crime of assault causing bodily harm. And when I left, one of my fellow patients pressed into my empty hands the pathetic gift of two tattered paperbacks. I hung onto those books for another six months, but I was too scattered to read them. Sometimes I just sat there holding the books in my lap, staring at them, not remembering what they were for. And when I did begin to remember, I remembered also my days among the mad—young men and women with drugged vacant eyes that didn't match the intensity of their voices as they explained over and over again what a mistake it was to keep them there; old men drooling from their medication; old women screaming in the night and setting off a chain of screams, the last of which was always my own.

I threw those books away, but I have since gathered others.

When the light of evening grew pinkish on the page, I put away my reading glasses and headed for the river to look at the sun. Over the years, I tried hard to find a clock or a watch I could keep, but they were always breaking down or getting lost. So I taught myself how to tell time by the sun, until I could tell it to the minute from any place at any time of day in any season of the year. The sun was about to slip behind the western rim of the ravine, and I stood beside the river watching it descend.

The sense of peace that always filled me at this time of evening, filled me then, too. But it was deceptive, and the calm with which I lay down was a false calm.

I woke up shaking in the middle of the night to the sound of screeching. Through the gaps between the packing-crate slats that made up my hut, I could see the light of the moon, and within seconds I realized that some animal was baying at it—a wild dog perhaps.

I turned over and tried to go back to sleep. But the trembling wouldn't stop. It wasn't about a screech or a dog or the moon. It was about the severed hand of a black man in my garden.

I found my coat in the darkness of my shelter. Once

outside, I found my shovel. And by the light of the full
moon, I began to dig.

It was cold out there, but I didn't feel it. I started at
the end of the garden farthest from where I had found
the hand. I was looking for the rest of the body. It had
to be there, and I was convinced that I would never sleep
again until I found it.

At first, my digging was erratic, my hands trembling
from cold and fear. But before long, the rhythm set in,
the rhythm of the gardener, and with it came a certain
calm determination.

I dug all night long. I felt rather than saw the moon
moving across the sky and the animals circling around
me. I never stopped to think what I was going to do with
the body once I found it. How would I explain that a
dead man with the golden ring of a secret fellowship to
which I also belonged had suddenly appeared in the middle of my wilderness?

I turned over every inch of that garden, and I found
nothing, not even the hand I had reburied.

I tried to convince myself to go back to bed and forget
about the whole thing—at least until morning. Whatever
was going on was somebody else's mystery. Somebody
else's fault. That was pretty much how I had thought
about everything for a good long time: six months in
the mental hospital, six months on the street, four years
in the valley. How else could a man live under such
conditions? To blame oneself was to go insane. Again.

Or was it?

Try as I might, I was not going to be able to ignore
that ring and the hand that had worn it. Even if the ring
was stored in a place that I was sure nobody could find,
it was there—beside my own ring, which still had clinging to it the old promises.

Yet what could I do? I had come to the valley because
I had breached the peace order by trying to apologize
for what I'd done to Harpur. As long as I was in the

ravine, I felt safe. If I left, who knew what might happen?

I put the shovel away. Later I would rake, and soon I would plant. The poor garden would actually be better for all this tortured digging.

As dawn turned to day, I turned back to my bed. Just before I entered my hut, I caught a glimpse of a silhouette moving between me and the rising sun. At first I couldn't make it out. It seemed to be a slender, agile woman on a horse. Her hair looked flaming red. Harpur!

Of course it wasn't Harpur. It was that stupid policewoman.

What was she looking for? If she was looking for me, why hadn't she found me? She couldn't be that incompetent. Tim could find me. Animals could find me.

Maybe she was looking for justice.

The thought made me laugh.

The next evening, as I watched the sun set over the rim of the valley, I did something I had not done for more than five years. When I had been on the bench, I had often thought through a case before trial began, taking each side in turn and asking myself exactly what questions each position led to. I had often found that those questions, when answered, solved the case.

On the one hand, we have Ellis Portal, a man who broke the law by an impulsive act of criminal violence, a man now free from imprisonment on condition that he fulfill the stipulations of his release. This man, when presented with evidence of violence, refrains from involvement. He keeps his own peace. He stays at home. True he is guilty of a minor theft. But since he has reason to suspect that what he stole had been stolen from someone else, he may be seen as intending to return it to its rightful owner if that owner ever makes a claim—which is highly unlikely. Ellis Portal does nothing. Is he wise?

On the other hand, we have Ellis Portal, a man who

*risks what little he has in order to right some as yet
unexplained wrong. He attempts this knowing that if he
fails all is lost. He attempts it. Is he wise?*

I stayed by the river for a long time. The sun sank;
the moon rose. A nighthawk flew up out of the brush
and was silhouetted for a brief moment against the silver
stars.

And suddenly I realized that I had asked the wrong
questions. This wasn't about me at all. It was about
truth. There *were* two questions, two simple questions
that demanded two simple answers:

Why was this hand in my garden?

Why was this ring on this hand?

Whatever it cost, I decided to go up into the city and
find out.

CHAPTER

THREE

WHEN I AWOKE THE NEXT DAY I TESTED MY INTENTIONS.
The risk of going to the city was great. But for the first
time since my exile, I felt a sense of exhilaration—as if
I could make a difference. I had once made a great deal
of difference in the lives of people. The thought that I
might again was dangerous, but I approached it with
tentative enthusiasm.

How to begin to tell you how difficult it was to go
up to the city?

Though ringed by suburban houses visible from some
sections, the ravine in which I lived was one of the wildest of the series of ravines that made up the river valley.
The Don's headwaters, still pure and sweet enough to
drink, rose twenty miles north of the city in a ridge of
glacial deposit. From there, the river flowed south
through the ravines into the lower river, where artificial
straightening of its course carried the waters to a complex harbor where the Don entered Lake Ontario.

All the ravines were linked, which meant that theo-
retically a person could follow along from one to the
next and eventually reach the inner-city neighborhoods
near the river's mouth, where the greatest concentration
of the city's street people lived.

It was to these neighborhoods I would have to head
to find the only person on the street who struck me as
caring more about others than herself. She was a na-

tive—"Swampy Cree"—of indeterminate age. Her street name was Queenie. It had been decades since she'd left her people to come to Toronto from the edge of the Arctic, nearly a thousand miles north of the city. Unlike so many who lived a hard life, Queenie was wise instead of merely wary, sensible instead of overly sensitive.

My journey to her would have to take me through the six miles of valley between my ravine and the intersection of Queen and Parliament streets where Queenie lived when I'd seen her last.

I had several choices of route, and all of them were hazardous. I could stick to the river, but the woods along its banks harbored dogs, foxes and even coyotes, whose fur-filled droppings I occasionally saw. Where rough trails existed, I would have to stay out of the rushing path of reckless mountain bikers, and on smooth paths avoid belligerent cyclists, joggers and hikers. The river route also led past golf courses and country clubs through which I'd have to trespass, risking apprehension by over-eager security guards.

Or I could follow the railroad tracks, hoping not to get pulverized by a speeding train, or the highway, avoiding being smashed by a whizzing car.

Or I could climb up the treed walls of my ravine and take to the streets. Here I would be risking mostly memories. When I was released from Parke-Manning, my brother Michele—Michael—took me into his house. But the acute embarrassment of having been in jail and the mental hospital made me so uncomfortable that I left after a few days. For a little while I lived on welfare in ramshackle roominghouses among men who sometimes beat me up.

From time to time, I retreated to the valley to get away from all that. And once, I just stayed.

No, it's not as simple as that. One night, as I said, I decided to apologize to Harpur and Stow for all the trouble I'd been. I was re-arrested outside Stow's home and held in a police station until Stow arrived. He told me that if he ever saw me again, he'd have my conditional discharge revoked and I'd end up in a federal penitentiary. I was recovered enough to recognize grandstanding. Nonetheless, I retreated to the valley for good.

Taking the street route presented one other little problem. I know of no polite way to say that I, despite my survival skills, was disgustingly odoriferous.

When I was a judge, I had my own cologne made just for me. A consultant from Paris designed the scent. He spent an entire day questioning me about my lifestyle and my preferences as well as those of my family and business associates. He asked me, for instance, whether I saw myself as someone who would be happy spending my entire life out of doors. At the time, I remember, I answered "yes" quite emphatically. "Ah," he said, "wood notes, mosses, grass . . ." In the end, he came up with a concoction that he claimed captured the essence of my personal scent. Well, sometimes I think it would be fun to let somebody like that get a whiff of what a "personal scent" really smells like!

Then there was the matter of my unshaven face, my uncut hair and my clothes. Except for my warm coat, a long, black, battered wool that must have looked quite elegant twenty-five years earlier, my clothing was treated more or less like my skin. At any given time, I had only just enough to cover my body. And like a snake's skin, every once in a while, I simply shed it and replaced it with something that looked pretty much the same. Mostly I wore what I could find. To visit Queenie, I would be dressed all in ragged denim. Which is also what I would have dressed in not to visit Queenie.

In the end I decided to get to the city by taking the path that nature takes: least resistance. It took me several hours.

I had first met Queenie the night both of us fell asleep

in separate doorways during a "save the streets" campaign sponsored by a downtown charity that had just had the good fortune—as they saw it—of acquiring a new van. We had just settled in when suddenly we were swept up and driven off to be fed soup, soap and a sermon.

Though I seldom talked to strangers, during the van ride Queenie and I found ourselves sharing stories of the street. I asked her then whether she was named after Queen Elizabeth. She laughed and said, "I was named after the spirit of the wind of the north—but they call me Queenie because Queen Street is where I spend all my time."

Queen Street runs east and west for six miles along the entire bottom of the city. It parallels Lake Ontario's shore and stretches from the lakeside beaches on one end, through all manner of city neighborhoods, to the lakeside beaches on the other. Queenie's neighborhood, an eclectic mix of roominghouses, cut-rate furniture stores, quaint restaurants, expensive antique shops and government-sponsored housing, was just about dead center.

I kept to the rear of the buildings, moving among the dumpsters in alleys, skirting loading doors and ducking down walkways.

It was late afternoon by the time I got to Queenie's usual block. I couldn't remember exactly where she lived, nor were the people I met of much assistance. I ran into some of the same problems I had in my flophouse days. Plenty of street people have fallen from elevated positions, but even so, the speech of an educated man is suspect. And no matter how hard I tried to disguise my normal way of talking, I never quite succeeded. Even my tattered appearance didn't help. As soon as I opened my mouth, I was treated to derogatory comments and gestures of contempt so eloquent they approached poetry.

I finally found Queenie by accident. Exhausted as much by my efforts at communication as I was by my long walk, I had slowed to a crawl. I had also given up slinking along the alleys and was walking right out on the street, almost amused at the wide path that decent citizens were cutting around me.

I stopped to look at some old leather-bound law books in the window of an antique store. The first indication that somebody was close enough to cause serious harm was a whispered, "Your Honor . . . ?"

I jumped and swung around. "Queenie!"

"What the hell are you doin' wanderin' around?" she asked. I don't think Queenie drinks much anymore—not since the time she was trapped in detox for ten weeks—but her speech has a slight slur.

"Queenie, I'm so lucky I found you." I extended my hand. The gesture surprised us both. I hadn't shaken hands with anybody in years. It was not part of the street's social amenities to offer one's hand to another since either might carry a weapon or a disease. I withdrew my hand before Queenie had to suffer the embarrassment of letting me know she preferred not to take it.

There was an awkward pause. Despite all I wanted to tell her, I couldn't think of what to say next. Like a bad comedian, I missed my timing, and when she spoke, I found myself also speaking—two at once and incomprehensible.

We both laughed and started up the street together. The laughter relaxed us, and I found my tongue, though I reminded myself to go slowly. I needed Queenie. I felt she always gave good advice. I didn't want to scare her by saying too much too soon. "It's been a long time since I've been up here."

"Yeah," she answered. She brushed a strand of hair away from her eyes. Her hair was long and had a beautiful silver shine to it that I didn't think was the result of cosmetics. Maybe she still had a room with a bath. Maybe her hair was just clean. "I'm glad you came up. I needed to see you. Somebody's been asking around . . ."

The late afternoon sun had grown warm, but I felt a chill of alarm. "Asking for me?"

I waited for her answer. The air smelled of the street—dusty and oily, with a human undertone that I found myself drawing into my nostrils as if I needed to stock up for the hours—the weeks, really—when the only human smell was my own. Why did I suddenly seem to crave human company?

"It was a young woman," Queenie finally said. "Nice looking. Said she heard I was a friend of yours . . ."

"And . . . ?"

"I told her I didn't know where you were—that I didn't see you since last fall."

"Did she say why she was looking for me?"

"No. But when I said you didn't make it up to the community center for Christmas she did look concerned."

"Some do-gooder volunteer—or a social worker? They still get after me sometimes."

"I don't think so . . ." There was a note of hesitation in her voice, as if she had something more to say about this woman, but she clammed up and I didn't press.

Again we walked in silence for a while. Queenie was wearing a long shawl and she adjusted it so that it fell off her shoulders, revealing a clean white tee-shirt underneath. "Nice warm evening . . ."

"Yes."

"What are you doing up here, Your Honor? Are you going to tell me or do we need to beat around the bush for a while?"

"Oh, Queenie," I gushed, "something awful has happened and I need your help."

She looked stunned at this little outburst, but she calmly gestured to a nearby streetcar passenger shelter, and we entered the glass enclosure and sat down on the bench. On winter nights each shelter on this stretch of Queen Street would be a spoken-for sleeping spot, but at other times a private conversation could be held there without interruption.

"Let's have it, Your Honor."

The whole story of the hand and the rings came out all in a rush, and Queenie just sat there until I was finished. The first thing she said was the thing I was most afraid she'd say.

"Your Honor, you're crazy."

"No, Queenie. I know what I saw. And I have the ring. Only I have no idea whose it is. Nor do I know how it could end up on a black hand when all the lawyers were white. Unless some pimp stole it . . ."

She gave me a grave stare. "Why would you think it was a pimp, first off?"

"Only because of all the black pimps that came before my bench. They had so much gold. But come to think of it, so did my Italian aunts!"

Queenie smiled at that. "Well, a pimp could be black or not. The only way you're gonna find out about a pimp is to talk to hookers. But I'll tell you right now, I never heard of a hooker in this city killing her pimp—even if a lot of them deserve to be knocked off."

She was quiet for a minute. "You know," she resumed, "when I said you were crazy what I meant was, you got it okay down in the valley, living in nature and all. Why give it up just for a chance to get in trouble?"

"I don't know. I just feel like I owe it to myself and to the victim to find out what happened. If there's a murderer, he has to be brought to justice."

"Yeah?" Queenie said with a smirk. "And how do you plan to do that?"

"First I need to know who that hand belongs to. Then

I need to know which lawyer lost the ring . . ."

"I don't know anything about lawyers . . ." Queenie
interrupted defensively. As if that was all she cared to
say about the matter, she rose. We left the streetcar shelter and as we walked on, a few of the street people
greeted her.

Despite their dishevelled appearances, their staggers
and their slurs, the respect these people showed Queenie
was genuinely impressive. I felt something tugging at
me I couldn't recognize right away. When I did recognize the feeling, I didn't like calling it by name. It was
envy.

We came to a little park where we sat on a stone
bench. There were children playing, and we watched
idly as they climbed up a slide, slid down, climbed up,
slid down.

"If you want to learn about pimps, you could do me
a little favor at the same time, Your Honor . . ."

"Of course, Queenie. I'd be happy to. What can I
do?"

She hesitated. "I need you to check on somebody for
me."

"Sure, who?"

She didn't answer right away. We walked again until
we reached the community center. Queenie wanted me
to go in with her to get some supper, but I had been
kicked out for inappropriate behavior during Thanksgiving dinner, so I decided I'd better wait outside. Social
workers have long memories.

When Queenie came back out, she handed me a sandwich and an orange. The food here was carefully ra-
tioned, but Queenie knew lots of ways to get around that.
Sometimes she bartered for extra, sometimes she bar-
gained, sometimes she stole. I didn't ask any questions.
"Thanks."

"I need to find a little Cree hooker—a friend of mine.
Her people come from up by Moosonee near James Bay.

The kid's got a few problems—a little into drugs, a little beat up by her pimp now and then, too fast to shoot off her mouth—the usual. I like to keep an eye on her.''

When I asked the girl's name, Queenie smiled. "Last time I talked to her, she was calling herself Moonstar. She's just a kid, so who knows what she's thinking about right now? She's probably got some other name cooked up." She hesitated. "I don't know what her real name is . . ."

That sounded like a lie, but as far as I was concerned, it was Queenie's right to lie about something like that. If I had wanted her to protect me, she would have, even if it meant lying. I would lie for her, too. The reason Queenie and I stayed friends was because she didn't ask me how I landed on the street and I didn't ask her how she did. Whoever Moonstar was and whatever she meant to Queenie, I wasn't going to learn by prying.

"You'll have to wait a while," Queenie reminded me. It would be hours before there would be any action on the strip of Queen Street where prostitutes strolled—the "Track." "You're gonna have to get over to the West End. I'd go myself but my legs ain't so good and I'm right out of streetcar tickets." She pulled her shawl tighter. "Tell Moonstar I'm thinkin' about her . . . And Your Honor . . ."

"Yes?"

"About those lawyers and their rings? You're gonna have to figure that out for yourself or get your fancy friends to help you. Nobody on the street is gonna tell a judge anything they know about lawyers . . ."

By the time I got to the Track, my feet were killing me and my boots were totally hopeless. They flapped with every step I took. I killed some time looking for something to fix them, and I was lucky to find a roll of duct tape in the garbage outside an office building. Not only was it long enough to wrap around my boots several times, it would also render them fairly waterproof.

One of the secrets of living on your own is never to turn
your back on anything that's warm, waterproof or legal
tender.

When the sun finally went down and the street lights
came up, I studied the main stretch of the Track for good
surveillance points from which to keep an eye out for a
girl that looked Cree. I didn't know the tribes that well,
but I could tell the difference between the native peoples
of Northern Ontario and the ones from out west, such
as those of British Columbia.

Every spot I picked seemed to have somebody in it
already—a cop or a pimp or a drunk.

A lot of what I saw out there made me sad, despite
my many years of experience on both sides of the
bench—and on park benches, too. I don't know what
was sadder—the young girls who looked like babies or
the older girls who looked like wrecks. And I don't
know what made me more angry—the arrogant johns in
their good suits and expensive cars or the pimps in *their*
good suits and expensive cars.

Once in a while, I could see a girl who had the light
of intelligence shining out from behind her heavily
made-up face. When I encountered a girl like that in
court, I never knew what to expect. Often, they were
quiet and respectful, but sometimes they made smart re-
marks, too. Worse, sometimes I would find myself wanting to question them or lecture them about things that
had nothing to do with the simple, easily-disposed-of
charges they were usually brought up on—shoplifting or
writing bad checks. I guess they made me feel fatherly—
which, watching them now from the shadows—made
me feel sick, too. The kind of father I was, they were
better off with their pimps.

It took four hours before I found Moonstar—who,
luckily, still used the same name. If I just walked up to
her, she'd refuse to speak to me. I was obviously not a
john, but I might be a cop. So I slipped into a narrow

space between two stores and watched her.

The rules of the Track are the same as the rules of a royal ball. For every pretty girl, there are two not so pretty, and they all hang around in clusters with the pretty one in the middle and the other two flanking her like ladies in waiting around the princess at the ball. On the Track, the middle one is the pimp's "wife" or main girl and the others are the "wife-in-laws." The princess gets picked to dance first. The others take her leavings—if they get to dance at all.

To my eye, Moonstar was a beauty, with the same thick hair and black eyes of Queenie, who, it suddenly occurred to me, might be her grandmother. But Moonstar did not possess the slim, long-legged, blonde good looks the average john considered highly attractive. Moonstar seldom got the best tricks. Even I could figure that out. So she was left standing there alone like a wallflower, giving me the chance to talk to her.

She was leaning toward the empty street and her hair fell in a black mass over her shoulders. She was intent— as if by staring she could conjure up a car with a good trick in it.

I walked up silently behind her, to give myself the benefit of surprise. As it was, she wasn't surprised. I was. Because when she turned to see me, the light caught her young, smooth face, and on it I could read a combination of emotions that touched me in a place I didn't know still existed. Her face showed disgust combined with hope. As if it would be better to have a dirty, awful old trick like me than no trick at all.

"Moonstar?" I asked softly.

The disgust changed to fear. She turned as if to run, but the second she took a step away, the intensity of the shadows in one of the doorways behind her changed, and I realized her pimp was back there and had his eye on her. To run would have looked like she was afraid of a trick—a pimp would surely beat her for that.

She smiled, just an awkward crack across her pretty face, but enough to show me that one of her front teeth was missing. "Looking for a date?" she asked, with about as much feeling as the Clerk of the Court used when he said "All arise." Formality.

"Moonstar," I said, keeping my voice low and trying to look like there was at least a chance that I might have some money, "Queenie said it was okay to talk to you."

Her face softened, but not much. "I'm going to get beat if I talk to Queenie's friends. You gotta leave . . ."

"I just need to talk to you for a second. I need to know if everything's okay with you. Queenie's concerned."

"I don't need Queenie to look after me. I got my man," Moonstar said without emotion. She hesitated. Behind her, the shadows shifted again. "But maybe old Queenie would rather see me back in that damn hostel . . . Listen, next time you see Queenie, you tell her I got a better chance of staying alive out here than I ever had in there."

I wanted to ask her more, to really talk to her so I could tell Queenie how she sounded, but I could sense the impatience of her pimp even if I couldn't see him.

"Second Chance," Moonstar hissed contemptuously.

"What?"

"That's what they call that stupid hostel, as in second chance to get killed, which is what I'm going to be if you don't get lost."

I didn't know what she was talking about, but I certainly wouldn't be helping Queenie by getting her friend hurt. So I backed off. But I decided to take a look at the hostel if it wasn't too far away—in case there was something about it Queenie needed to know.

Second Chance Hostel for Women was a lot easier to find than Moonstar. I just looked it up in the phone book, finding it between Second Chance Clothing and Second

Chance Mission. There are a lot of second chances on the street. And a lot of last chances, too.

It was, appropriately, not far from the Track on one of the side streets that provide such a dramatic contrast to the main streets in some parts of this city. All the houses here were huge Victorian family homes, and only their nearness to their neighbors prevented them from being considered mansions. That and the fact that one or two of them had been turned into roominghouses.

Second Chance Hostel for Women was pretty well disguised. I only knew it by the street number; there was no sign outside. The house had the same wide verandah, the same stately windows, the same well-tended lawn and landscaped garden as the other houses on the block. I could tell just by looking at it that it was the beneficiary of some major funds and that its board of directors was probably some well-to-do citizens who were absolutely thrilled with themselves to be working on a project like this.

I had never actually sentenced a girl to Second Chance, but many times I *had* sent a person to a hostel or a halfway house or some other program that helped them without costing the taxpayer an arm and a leg and without making a criminal out of somebody whose main problem was a lack of luck.

My support of places like Second Chance was one of the things I was noted for in my judicial decisions. I was a great favorite among the executive directors and board members of such organizations because I made it clear that I would rather send someone to a halfway house than to jail. But when my own time came, I would rather have died than suffer the humiliation of being an inmate of a halfway house run by a director with whom I had once socialized.

There was an alley running alongside Second Chance house, out of the view of the sidewalk and away from the light of the street. I slid into the shadows there onto a curb about twenty feet away from the window of a recreation room. I could see inside without being seen.

At first, the room was empty, but then a number of females drifted in together, as if for a final visit with each other before heading to bed—by then it was after eleven.

' Most of the girls seemed to be teenagers—rather well-dressed, I thought. Only one or two were obviously pregnant. There were no babies visible, but perhaps they'd all been put to bed.

The girls looked quite content. They laughed and smiled. Nice. I thought about Moonstar and her pimp, and I had to be realistic. This comfortable home was a far cry from the fear and the filth of the street.

But I had to be honest, too. The mood in the room seemed far from relaxed. Two or three of the girls seemed withdrawn. And the minute an older woman—obviously a counsellor of some sort—entered, all laughing stopped. The scene made me tense with the unease you feel watching young animals and their keeper in a zoo.

I was musing on this poetic thought when I felt a hand on my shoulder.

I jumped a mile, astonished that I had been so careless. That was twice in the same day that I had let somebody sneak up on me. Being back on the street was starting to take its toll. This time the person behind me wasn't a friend—it was a cop.

"Let's move along, Dad," he said. "The show's over."

He could have been rough or unkind. He wasn't. Of course I moved along. I'd had enough.

I went back home, even though it took me almost all night to get there.

I was sick the next day—or maybe just exhausted. I slept until late afternoon, roasted some potatoes for my dinner and ate them with a salad of early dandelions. Then I went back to sleep and didn't wake up until it was already dark.

I made a fire, which I don't usually do after sunset, since it can attract attention. But I was cold and I needed to sit up for a while and think.

Talking to Queenie had made me feel hungry for companionship. I thought again about my early days with Anne. Before our marriage I hadn't known how comforting it could be to have somebody to talk to on a regular basis. I hadn't married for companionship. Nor, I am sorry to say, had I married for love. I married Anne because she was suitable, because I was a twenty-six-year-old lawyer who needed a wife, and because Harpur had married Stow. In fact, I met Anne at their wedding and married her seven months later. Anne's family had followed her diplomat father around the world from the time she was born. But she had insisted on staying in Toronto when his posting as consul had ended. When I met her she was finishing her last year at the Ontario College of Art.

Of Anne I expected propriety, faithfulness and children. But she always gave me so much more. In return, I had given her public disgrace.

It was hours before I got around to thinking about Moonstar and the hostel. By then, the embers of my fire were long extinguished and the night had grown cold under the clear and distant stars. I hoped the little hooker had a decent place to sleep.

I didn't really have much to tell Queenie, and I didn't know when I'd see her again. I thought about her suggestions. How could I possibly find out anything about the ring? The whole thing was hopeless. Maybe her best idea was the one about it being stupid to give up my peaceful home in the valley. Well, not peaceful now, considering, but certainly more peaceful than the back

alleys off Queen Street, the out-of-bounds community
center or the sleazy strip of the Track.

As I pondered, the moon rose, and by its diminishing
light, I could see the vague outline of my garden. It was
exactly as I had left it after my night of frantic digging.
It was time to get to work.

The next day I raked the entire garden. Since my only
tool was the discarded tines of a leaf rake abandoned by
a homeowner in the fall, the work was slow. When it
was done, I rested for a bit. The sun was moving toward
the summer solstice and there must be about a month to
go—just the right time to begin planting.

In a small sunlit clearing deep in the woods, I had a
greenhouse that vandals hadn't wrecked. I made it out
of windows I found in the garbage, and it housed the
fledgling plants I'd nursed mostly from seed. I had also
stolen a few plants from people's gardens on the edge
of the valley.

I spent the entire afternoon setting out the plants, patting the soil around them into firm mounds that would
support their roots as they grew. Kneeling on the earth,
feeling it in my hands, letting the sun warm my back
through the rag of my shirt, I felt like a free and peaceful
man.

When I finished planting, I carried water from the
river and carefully watered each row.

I rested again. By now it was nearly time for dinner,
so I ate several apples and some greens.

There were still a few hours of light left, which made
me happy because I knew I'd have time to read. But it
also reminded me of the day before and my long trek
across town waiting for nightfall and Moonstar.

To chase away the disturbing images of the girls on
the Track and the captives of Second Chance, I got back
to work. I took everything out of my hut, including the
loose slats on the bottom that had served all winter as
the base of my bed. Beneath them, I surprised several

families of beetles, an entire civilization of worms, and even a pregnant vole—which made me feel guilty.

I burned the worst of the old blankets and shook the others, happy to find no insects in them except the odd ant—a sure sign of impending summer. I encountered no rat droppings and no lice, proof that life alone in the wood was more vermin-free than life in the flophouses.

It took me only a couple of hours to rearrange the hut, to make it new for spring. When I finished, I felt new myself.

I stepped outside. I was surprised to see that the day was nearly over and the sun was about to set.

I had had the luxury of a fire the night before, and I had a treat planned for myself on that evening, too. One of the treasures I kept hidden nearby was a stash of tobacco and a pipe. I sat down to smoke and contemplate the passing of a perfect day.

But I knew—of course I did—that this peace was an illusion, that I would have to return to the city. I felt an emotion that had been growing in me: not a desire but a need, the need to right a wrong. I felt I was about to kiss peace goodbye.

My name was still Angelo Portalese, but I was practicing different names, trying them out in secret, the way I was also trying out cigarettes, scotch and sex.

I was fifteen.

I was first in my class and first in my father's heart. Though his pride was pleasing to me, I was beginning to feel the burden of it. I couldn't help but wonder what would have happened if I hadn't come in first, hadn't been the best. I found it easier to love my mother than to love him.

One day I came home late from school and found her in the kitchen, as I had expected. But instead of cooking, she was crying. I dropped my books and ran to her. ''Gelo,'' she sobbed, ''oh, Gelo!''

"Mamma, what's wrong? Where is everybody?" I was terrified, but I could feel power stirring in me.

I ran to the sink and pulled from a rack one of the spotless linen towels she had washed and bleached and dried in the sun. I soaked it in cold water, wrung it out and hurried back to her. "Tell me what's wrong."

Unlike my father, my mother always tried to speak English, even in distress. "Michael is gone get your uncle and Father Giuseppe."

Gone to get the relatives and the priest—the worst. What could be wrong?

"Is it Papa?" I asked.

She nodded. I had never realized how small she was. I wiped her face again. Now I was kneeling on the floor beside her chair, reaching up to her, an absurd pieta on her shining linoleum floor, the roles reversed, she the sufferer, I the consoler.

"Mama, please," I said, "if you can't tell me what's wrong, I can't help. Has there been an accident? Has Papa been hurt? Is he sick?"

"No, no hurt, no sick," she managed.

"Is he here in the house?" Perhaps they'd had a fight, though that would have been very unusual.

Stifling another sob, she took such a deep breath that the chair she was sitting on shifted and I almost fell. "The police is take your father."

"The police?"

She nodded again.

And now her fear finally made its way into my blood. Like all immigrants in those days—and many now, I suppose—I was paralyzed with fear at the thought of involvement with the police.

It wasn't the police themselves. Individual officers were sometimes the butt of jokes and pranks in the neighborhood. No, it was their connection to immigration officials that scared us. For my parents, though legal immigrants, were not citizens, and they lived in mortal terror of being sent back to the old country.

All of us, all our lives had been as law-abiding as human effort could allow people to be. Why then, could the police have taken my father?

Fortunately, I was spared from having to get anything more out of my mother by the arrival of my sister Arletta with our Aunt Mary, my mother's sister, who had been able to find out where they were holding my father. I told Arletta and Aunt Mary to stay with my mother, and I set out to find him.

Of course I had to take the bus. My father was being held not in the local police station, which was within a few blocks of our house, but in a station near our fine customers with their horse-riding daughters and their circular drives.

The night I was arrested myself, some thirty-five years later, I was taken to one of the newest of the downtown stations. I remember thinking then that I had been there before, but I hadn't. What I was remembering was the station where my father was being held that night. In 1957 it was very new. There were no laser fingerprinting, no police computer, no DNA typing in my father's day. But there were shiny police cruisers and a fancy camera to take my father's picture, left, front, right—if it should come to that—which it didn't. Through the grace of Stow, it didn't come to that for me either.

The station was on a busy corner of Yonge Street. Going up on the bus, shame overtook me. Whatever my father was accused of, he had almost certainly not done—or at least not done on purpose. He seldom made mistakes. He was a clever and careful man. He was also a pleaser, a man who would bend over backward to ingratiate himself to his customers. But his English had never much progressed from what it had been when he had stepped off the boat.

The closer I got to the police station the more embarrassed I became. What if my father had to stay in

jail? Would *I* have to explain to his customers why their
jobs were undone? And if my father couldn't work, what
would we do for money? It was an era when every shop-
keeper we did business with knew us personally—and
we knew exactly which families on our street couldn't
pay their bills on time. Would I have to tell people that
we couldn't pay?

But as I walked through the elegant doors of the station, shame left me, and so did fear. I saw my father
being led in handcuffs down a long hall, and without
thought, I ran after his captors. Unlike my mother, however, I was not hysterical. Unlike my father, I was not
inarticulate. Something told me what to do, and I did it.

I asked on what grounds my father had been arrested.
I inquired as to whether he had been advised of his right
to remain silent. I asked whether he had been allowed
to consult a lawyer. I asked whether charges had been
filed.

I only knew about these things from reading, yet, as
would happen to me from time to time in my life, it was
as if I could see the books in front of my eyes.

The result of this surprising performance was that the
police confided they were relieved to have somebody
who could get my father to talk. Words had failed him
completely, they said. Of course it wasn't words that had
failed him. It was his dysfunctional English that had
failed him.

As I translated, the story came out that one of my
father's customers had accused him of stealing a valuable piece of statuary from their garden. When the ac-
cusation had been leveled, my father had gone to his
truck and produced the stolen statue. What he had neglected to do was to explain clearly that the statue had
never been stolen. It was under canvas on his truck because the gardener, a Scotsman whose English was completely incomprehensible to my father, had put the statue

there to keep it safe while he was working on the nearby hedges.

A simple phone call produced the gardener and an apology from the customer—which, to my disgust, elicited further apologies from my father, who begged me to render them not only to the police and the gardener, but also to the customer who had wronged him.

My father must have been frightened by this ordeal, for he said not a word on the trip back home.

I, too, was silent. All I could think about was the feeling that had come over me when I had seen him in handcuffs. It was related to the feeling of strength I had felt in my mother's kitchen. But it was different, far different from the feeling of maturity I felt when I sat behind DiFasio's garage and smoked cigarettes with my buddies. And it was also different from the sensation of power I felt when a jolt of scotch hit my stomach and exploded in my brain.

What I had felt in the kitchen and the police station was a kind of authority too rich for the blood of a fifteen-year-old boy, just as it was to prove, ultimately, too rich for the blood of a fifty-year-old man. It was the authority of those who hold the fate of others in their hand, not by chance, or by violence, but by the power of their knowledge of law.

I was not a forgetful lad, and the feeling stayed with me until I could do something with it.

As for my father, his silence left him the moment he entered the welcoming arms of my hysterical mother. I, his first born, his namesake, his son, had brought honor to him and to our family. He thanked me, he blessed me, he toasted me.

Now recovered, my mother cooked my favorite meal. And all of us, so relieved, so happy to be safe, headed down to the local coffee bar for *gelato*.

There we ran into several of my father's cronies, who had to hear every detail of the awful day.

It was like a bad dream, my father said, but thanks to his own little Angelo, all was well once more.

He put his arm around my shoulder and toasted me again.

I accepted his thanks and his love. But at the same time another part of me was angry, embarrassed and ashamed. Why didn't he learn to speak English? How could he let himself get into trouble and then make sure everybody knew it?

My father was a victim. Nobody was ever going to make a victim out of me.

That night when I got home, the name Ellis Portal came to me as if, to use one of my mother's phrases, whispered by an angel. I wrote it down. I tested it on my tongue and in my ear. There was nothing foreign about it. It was a good strong North American name. An appropriate name for a powerful man—a lawyer for instance. Maybe even a judge. I decided it was just right.

I have called myself Ellis Portal ever since.

CHAPTER
FOUR

BRIGHT AND EARLY THE DAY AFTER MY SPRING PLANTING and my spring cleaning, I hiked to a grassy slope in the northeast corner of my ravine. Here, a little park opened onto streets of suburban houses, leading to a shopping plaza in which was located the area Welfare office.

The arrogance I had displayed when I was a powerful man didn't go over very well when I was a powerless one, and combined with my anger and shame, made me a hard person to "help." I had worn out a lot of welcomes among the social service agencies of the city. There was hardly a worker who didn't cringe when she saw me coming. Nonetheless, by acting as if I'd turned over a new leaf and could now grovel with the best of them, I managed to score four subway tokens.

After sitting on the subway for ten stops, I realized I was starving. I decided that since I had begun my day grovelling—and had had such good luck at it—I might as well grovel for lunch.

Not wanting to risk showing up at the community center, I decided to give the Good Hand food kitchen a shot and I arrived just in time for the noon lineup. I have to admit, I was a little surprised at the quality of the clientele. In the old days, the Good Hand had been one of the roughest, most violent soup kitchens. But now, some of its patrons chatted amicably with each other about the economy and the stock market. Some sounded

educated, and their clothes were shabby Club Monaco
and Gap. And they carried newspapers. I had never
known people who bought newspapers when they
couldn't afford food. Clearly these were people to avoid.
I didn't want to run into some lawyer who had fallen on
hard times and have to chat about how I, too, had fallen.

It didn't bother me though that some of the old regulars recognized me and didn't hesitate to let it be
known. "Your Honor!" one old reprobate called out.
He was Johnny Dirt, a man who got his name because
many decades before, he had come down off some farm
north of the city and told people about it and they named
him and it stuck. Not that city life had made the name
in any way inappropriate. Johnny Dirt had dust caked in
his hair, and his clothes were obviously out of the nearest trash can.

"John!" I said. "How are you keeping?"

"Well, I'll tell you, Your Honor, it's getting hard out
here—harder and harder . . ." He shifted from one foot
to the other, taking a remarkably long time. As with a
lot of ex-boozers, the old ways of moving and talking
had stuck as fast as his name. "You," he said, making
a weak fist and very slowly moving it toward my shoulder in some half-remembered gesture of camaraderie,
"we been worried about you. Thought maybe you died
over the winter . . ."

"Not that I know of," I said. Johnny Dirt had enough
life left in him to laugh.

"So who else is around these days?" I asked. Johnny
took another chance at shifting his weight. He lurched
toward me in a bizarre gesture of confidentiality that put
his mouth near my nose. I held my own breath, which
was probably a mercy to him, too.

"See a lot of hookers in here, now. The girls didn't
used to come in these places, but things is gettin'
bad . . ."

"Ever see a little Native girl named Moonstar?"

He screwed up his face in an effort to think. I felt grateful that he was willing to try so hard. After what seemed quite a while, he came to a conclusion. "Yeah," he said, "I seen her around here. Friend of Queenie's, ain't she? By the way, Queenie's been asking after you. Seems some woman is looking for you. You done a flit from some sweetheart?"

Johnny Dirt laughed again and a little gust of spring wind whistled among his remaining teeth.

I was just about to ask him what he knew about Moonstar when I heard the cowbell.

I suppose the sound of a cowbell has a certain rustic charm to a social worker who spends his weekends by the fire in his vacation cabin up north. That would explain why the head social worker at the Good Hand used it to summon us to our lunch.

I, however, didn't get that far.

Just as Johnny Dirt was about to reach for a battered red plastic tray, one of the new people cut ahead of him. Nobody used to breadlines would ever have made such a stupid error, but this guy didn't look like he'd been down and out for long, and we, Johnny and I, were willing to tolerate a little inexperience.

I merely said to the man, "I believe we were here first."

With that, Johnny elbowed the guy and took a step toward the food. The guy grabbed out at Johnny, caught him by the shoulder, swung him around and spit in his face.

That was all I could take. I went after him. I had no particular love for Johnny, but he always played by the rules, and so did I. I decked the newcomer and sent him sprawling. I didn't break skin, I didn't draw blood, I just knocked him down.

It was, however, enough.

Within seconds, one of the social workers was standing beside me eager to practice his latest skills at crisis intervention. "You realize," he said very calmly, as if talking to a two-year old, "that you have breached the rules here, don't you?"

I wanted to deck him too, but I just stood there, trying to make my heart stop pounding.

"Here, when we've hurt somebody, we apologize," the social worker went on.

I ignored him. I had to keep my eyes on the guy on the floor and his friends, in case they decided to retaliate. They were helping him up, treating him like he'd been mortally wounded, though it was easy to see that nothing was wrong with him.

"So," the social worker insisted, "will we have an apology here?"

I turned to look at him, and all of a sudden I was looking at every self-righteous idiot I'd had to beg for a bite, a bed or a Band-Aid for the past five years. I felt myself slipping into the anger that seemed always ready to welcome me. "Apology?" I said in almost a whisper. "You're asking me for an apology?"

Out of the corner of my eye, I saw Johnny Dirt and a few others move away. They saw what was coming and so did I, but I was powerless to stop.

I moved closer to the social worker. He moved back. I moved again. I was very close to him now, and his eyes were locked into mine in a way that made all his lessons in calming clients fade from his memory. He couldn't have taken his eyes from mine had he wanted to. The anger—my anger—was holding him like an animal with one paw in a steel jaw.

I smiled. He opened his mouth, but nothing seemed to come out of it. I could feel his fear as if he were vibrating and my whole body was an antenna. When I opened my mouth, the voice that came out of it was the voice that used to be able to reach the farthest spectator in the largest courtroom. "An apology? Who's going to apologize?" I yelled. "Who's going to apologize for the fact that we sleep in the street while you sleep in luxury?''

"Leave the social worker alone," I heard somebody in the crowd say. "He's not bad . . ."

"Not bad?" I asked. "He's not bad?" I swung around and tried to catch the eye of the person who'd had enough nerve to speak. Wisely, he had slunk back into silence and the safety of the crowd. But my eye fell on the stack of red plastic trays. I lunged for them. The anger was like neon running through me hot and steady. It was so energizing that my movements were the fast, sleek movements of the dancer—of the young. I grabbed an entire pile of trays—dozens of them—and flung them toward the crowd with all my might.

The slabs of red plastic sailed through the air like missiles. Some of the men ducked. Some were hit. One actually caught a tray and threw it back at me, missing wildly.

All the time this was going on, the voice was screaming out of me. It was saying, "I'm the one who should be apologized to. Me. Me. Me."

Nobody tried to fight me or stop me or come near me. I could feel my mouth working, and I could feel that foam was coming out of it—something that had happened to me before, something I had thought was a myth until it happened the first time. But even the shame of that didn't stop me.

I was also moving—stomping and circling and waving my arms.

Then suddenly, I heard the cowbell. Not far away as it had sounded when the chief social worker had rung it for lunch, but right in my ear. Over and over, clanging until I couldn't stand it anymore. Until I sank to the ground.

The social worker was standing over me with a rolled newspaper in his hand. Seeing it from the vantage point of the floor, the same vantage point that a dog would

see it from, was all I needed to snap out of my spasm
of fury. Shame blinded me. I literally lost my powers of
sight for a second, and when they returned, all I wanted
to look at was my ravine, my garden.

I knew he wouldn't hit me with the newspaper if I
could let him know I was back to my senses, but I dared
not open my mouth to try to tell him anything.

So, just like a dog, I crawled away from him on all
fours. At the door, I had to stand, of course, and the
moment I did, I felt the newspaper hit the middle of my
back and fall to the rear of my heels. I stooped, picked
up the paper, walked out the door and closed it behind
me. And then I ran as fast as my fifty-five-year-old legs
and lungs would let me.

In a few minutes, I had reached the same park I'd sat
in with Queenie the day before. I sank down on the
grass. I pulled my knees to my chin. I crossed my arms
over my knees. As if part of my body belonged to somebody else, I stared at my hands. One of them was still
holding the newspaper. I put it down on the grass. I
rested my head on my arms.

Anger, the old enemy, was still there, always ready to
attack me. But now there was a far worse enemy, a person capable of mutilating other people. If I could not
control myself, how could I hope to outwit a killer?

My father stood with the check in his hand, a look of
puzzlement on his face. "I thought this was what you
wanted," he said. As always, he spoke in Italian and I
answered in English.

"I *wanted* to do it on my own. I *wanted* to accept the
scholarship—it's a big honor to get a college scholarship."

"But Gelo, the scholarship isn't enough. You'd have
to work and go to school at the same time. Your grades
would suffer. If you accept your uncle's gift, you can

be a proper student—get to the head of your class like always.''

"If I have any outside financial support, I'll have to turn the scholarship down. I'll lose it. Don't you get it? Can't you understand?'' I yelled.

"Why are you mad? A person does you a favor and you get mad. What's the matter with you?''

"You. You're what's the matter with me—always telling me what to do. Why don't you get off my back?''

"Don't talk to me like that, Angelo, I'm your father.''

"Don't call me Angelo.''

I was seventeen. In a few months I would graduate from high school. I'd already been told I'd be valedictorian. I had been accepted at the University of Toronto on a scholarship that would pay for all my courses. All I needed was money for books and personal necessities, which I could earn if my father would pay me for working for him. But no, he wanted to do it the old way, have me concentrate on my studies courtesy of his well-off older brother. There was no way I was going to be the dutiful nephew of an Italian uncle who would waste no time, I was sure, in taking a personal interest in my courses and my grades for future return of favors granted.

I grabbed my uncle's check from my father, crumpled it into a ball and threw it at him.

It hit him on the forehead, then dropped to the floor. We both stared at it in astonishment. I had never felt that angry before, never openly defied my father, never struck out against him.

He bent down, retrieved the check and uncrumpled it. He walked over to our dining room table, put the check down and smoothed it with the heel of his hand. He looked at the check and not at me as he spoke.

"Any other man would slap your face right now, Gelo. But you're the one with the temper, not me. A man with a bad temper can never be a free man. Remember that, Gelo. Just remember that.''

Thank the Lord, nobody in the park came near me. After a while, I must have slept. Since I was by no means the only derelict sleeping there, it didn't matter that I was stretched out on the grass.

When I woke up, I saw that it had started to rain, and I was fairly soaked. So was the newspaper, but I picked it up anyway, and I walked out of the park.

Even though there was no sun, I could tell by the quality of the light that it was now late afternoon. I hadn't yet eaten anything. I was relieved it was raining. It would make it less likely that anybody would be in the back alleys to compete in my search for edible garbage.

As it turned out, I was lucky. I happened along the rear of a McDonald's just as a kid was emptying the trash, and I found a few nearly whole burgers, quite a lot of fries and even some milk. I covered these things with discarded wrappers and put the whole thing in a bag. Then I headed for a sheltered spot I knew under a loading platform behind the train station. It was a bit of a walk, but I was as hungry for calm solitude as I was for food.

The walk did no harm to the food, which was cold anyway, and the newspaper dried a little after the rain let up. I looked forward to the pleasure of my usual routine—dinner and a quiet hour of reading. Like any traveller, I tried to maintain the comforts of home while away.

Nobody had beat me to the spot, and the workers had probably called it a day because of the rain. The sun was returning, and there was a sort of dim glow in the corner I settled into. I unwrapped my meal and ate.

When I finished, I carefully folded the wrappers and put them in my pocket—out of habit because I never knew when a bit of paper might come in handy, especially if it was waxed.

Then I carefully unfolded the newspaper. The outer pages were useless, so wet they were transparent. Even if I'd had better light, I wouldn't have been able to read them. Toward the center, however, they were drier, and I pulled out a few that were clearly legible.

Like most street people, I took certain precautions when out of my own domain. Before leaving home, I had tied my glasses to a loose thread inside the pocket of my shirt, and they were still there when I reached for them.

Almost at once, my eye fell on the headline, ''Prominent Businessman Feared Missing.'' I scanned the article for details, captured by the accompanying photograph, which was of a middle-aged black man who appeared to be expensively groomed. In the photo, one of his hands was visible.

Straining in the uncertain light, I studied the picture. Was that a gold ring he wore? Maybe. I just couldn't tell. I was concentrating so hard that I was suddenly startled to hear footsteps above me on the loading platform.

Hunkering deeper into the corner, I tried to arrange the newspaper over me so that if the intruder looked in, all he would see was a pile of garbage.

The footsteps stopped for a minute. Two strong feet hit the pavement right in front of the opening to my hiding place. I felt, rather than saw, the quality of the light change as the intruder leaned down to peer in. Then I felt the swipe of a cop's baton against the thin soles of my done-for boots.

But I didn't cry out—or even let my breath out. Maybe he didn't feel like hauling me out and forcing me to move on—or worse. Maybe he really thought I was a heap of trash. Either way, he left without harassing me any further.

I was getting shakier by the minute. For all I knew the soup kitchen might have reported me for assault. The cop might have been following me, though it seemed unlikely.

Still, my safest bet was to wait at least an hour to make sure he was gone. A bum like me wasn't worth an hour's surveillance, but I wanted to be safe. I waited for the hour, and then I crept out, stiff from head to toe.

I still had three subway tokens left. I used one of them to get myself home well before dark.

I had had it with the city. Enough was enough.

I even threw away the newspaper with the article about the missing man. It was useless anyway. Just as that cop had showed up, I had glanced back up at the top of the article to see who'd written it. That's when my eye had fallen on the date of the paper.

The thing was eighteen months old.

I hoped the man in the picture was safe and sound in his own home as I was safe and sound in mine.

I spent the next two days on my hands and knees in the garden. Even though the plants hadn't grown an inch since I had planted them, the weeds had multiplied.

It sickened me that my ancient anger was still so virulent—so close to the surface. I thought my peace in the valley had gotten rid of some of it. But the injustice to Johnny in the soup kitchen had set me off. There was that word again—injustice. Suddenly I remembered the evening in which I had been presented an award by one of the city's civic organizations like the Rotary. The presenter had been Stow himself. He had said, "My colleague Ellis Portal is a passionate man, and we are all fortunate that he turns his passion against those who harm society and society's most vulnerable . . ."

Well, be that as it may, it would be the last time the guy would push ahead or spit on somebody else without a serious reason. I'd helped him to advance a grade in the school of hard knocks, and someday he'd tell the tale as part of the personal myth that every loser writes about himself.

I wasn't sorry about the social worker. I should have been ashamed of my attitude and ashamed to have so incensed a professional that he would actually throw something at a client, but the thought just made me laugh.

I was sorry I had blown my chance to talk longer to Johnny Dirt. Who was the woman who had gone to Queenie looking for me? I wondered whether other people ever asked Queenie questions about me—but why would they? And anyway, she couldn't tell anybody where I was. She didn't exactly know.

I thought about the newspaper article I'd read. It couldn't have anything to do with the hand I found in the garden. For one thing, it would have been just too much of a coincidence to have found a real clue to this mystery in a newspaper somebody shot at my back!

More importantly, the time was wrong. Eighteen months—an eternity. I hated to think about it, but that hand had not been decomposed. It seemed perfect except for the clean sharp cut that had severed it from its owner.

But maybe seeing the article had served one purpose. When I'd read the byline, I'd recognized it—Aliana Caterina.

As a judge, I always got good press because I welcomed the media into my courtroom. They were, in my opinion, the eye of the public, and I wanted the public to see how the courts were becoming more and more crowded, how cases were taking longer and longer to come before the bench because there were so many of them, how the middle class was joining the poor in the glassed-in lock-up beside the judge's dais.

After my arrest, I wanted only to avoid the press. But Aliana was more than just a reporter. When I went to the university, my father hired a worker to help him with the driveways. His name was Vincent Caterina. Working for my father gave Vinnie the financial security to marry, and when I was about twenty, he and his wife had a little girl, Aliana. By the time I was elevated to the bench, she was working part-time as a reporter for the largest of the Italian-language newspapers in the city. I used to see her in my courtroom all the time. And she was in the press box the day I was arraigned on the assault charge. By that time she was about thirty and as well-known as some of the writers on the major dailies. Now, I noticed, she was writing for the biggest paper in the city—one with a daily circulation of half a million copies.

All of the other reporters at my arraignment were scribbling away, as anxious to get the dirt on me as they'd once been to praise me. Only Aliana's head was not bent over her notebook. Hers were the only eyes meeting mine. And in them, though I did not realize it until later, I saw not disgust, but compassion. She wasn't a stranger. But she wasn't family either. In her there was familiarity, but not enough to excite the intense shame I felt when I thought about my family. Aliana became the only reporter to whom I granted an interview when I was inside, but after she came to the mental hospital and I spoke to her, I never saw the interview, never saw her again.

Was she still a reporter? Was she still kind and sympathetic? More importantly, was *she* the person to help me find out why one of the lawyers' rings had been found on an unknown hand?

She would surely know whether the man she had written about eighteen months before had been found—and whether any others were missing under similar circumstances. She might also know something about the community from which the black businessman came. At any rate, she had covered the crime beat, so she had ways of finding out what she didn't know both about lawyers and about the victims of crime.

Besides, in talking to her, if I could get to her, I wouldn't have anything to explain about my past. She would know it all already.

I felt exhilarated by the notion of finding Aliana, as if I were about to set out on a quest, which, of course, I was.

Like every quest, this one was going to require some sort of armor. My everyday rag-tag appearance might be good enough for a social call on Queenie, or for luncheon at the Good Hand cafe, but it was by no means suitable for an appointment with a noted journalist, nor even for the research I must do to get to that journalist.

After dinner, as I sat by the river and watched the nighthawks circle the meadows before they headed for the city and their flights over the darkened backyards, I thought about what I would need and how I would get it.

The most basic thing I needed was a clean-up, but not my daily sponge-off with collected rainwater or my occasional dip in the questionable waters of the river. And I couldn't count on rainfall, which would provide a strong cold shower, but only at its own discretion. No, I needed a take-all-your-clothes-off, get-right-into-the-water kind of clean-up.

Then I needed a haircut and a shave.

And then I needed my suit.

I would have to go after the suit first. If it was still where I'd hidden it, I was in business.

The sense of exhilaration stayed as I walked back toward my hut. If I could get myself fixed up enough to move freely in the city even for a single day, I might move closer to answering my two questions. Why was that ring with its many promises on that hand and how had it come to be in my garden?

•   •   •

The suit was in a hollow in a tree in a plastic bag from
the Parke-Manning Institute. Or at least it had been when
I'd last seen it. It had a shirt and tie that went with it,
as well as a pair of dress loafers.

The history of the suit was intimately connected to
my own history. Immediately after my arrest, I had been
taken before a Justice of the Peace, charged with assault
causing bodily harm, and remanded to the Don Jail,
which was another structure built on the banks of my
beloved river. I had been in the Don Jail only long
enough to turn over my own clothes, suffer the humiliation of a delousing shower, and notice that rats shared
the jail with the rock music that thundered day and night,
when Stow rescued me.

He managed to get me sent—as I had sent so many
others—to the City Mental Hygiene Unit for psychiatric
assessment. I was deemed fit to stand trial and booked
for arraignment at Old City Hall, the very courthouse at
which I'd sat for the previous ten years.

On the day of my arraignment, my brother Michael
brought the suit to the courthouse lock-up. As if I were
a child, he dressed me. At the arraignment, I pleaded
guilty, but was given a discharge conditional on the
peace bond and on spending six months at the Parke-
Manning mental hospital, to which I was hustled off in
a police van.

Six months later, on my discharge, Michael came to
take me to his house. The suit, shirt, tie and shoes were
handed to him by the discharge nurse. They were still
in the same bag when I carried them out of Michael's
house two days later. It was a miracle that I managed to
hang on to them during the next six months in roominghouses, shelters and hostels, each one worse than the
last; but I did.

In the four years I'd been in the valley, I'd worn the
suit three times. First to sneak back to my own house at
a time when I knew it was unlikely for Anne to be there,

in order to bully the maid into giving me back my judge's robe. Then to my mother's funeral, though I had to stay so far away from everyone that all I was able to see was the crowd as they surrounded her grave. She had had a stroke shortly after my father died eight years earlier. She'd been in a nursing home and, mercifully, had known nothing about what happened to me.

The third time I wore the suit was to see if it still fit before I wrapped it up tight in many layers of plastic and slid it into its hiding place in a large dead elm near a meander—a bend—in the river on the farthest western boundary of the ravine, the wildest and most inaccessible section. I had just discovered the art of creating hiding places, and I was like a squirrel, secreting things away, then going back to see if they were still there, which mostly they weren't.

So maybe the suit was gone, but I had to find out. Because I had to wade across the river and make my way through thick woods and into a clearing, it took the whole morning to get to the elm, which stood near a spot where the river made a wide loop, leaving an area of meadow surrounded by river on all sides, like an island, but not completely cut off.

The old elm was still standing. The suit was still there, too. In fact, it was in perfect shape. As I pulled the shirt from the bag, though, I could see that it had not fared as well. Something had eaten part of it away. The collar was fine, and so was the front of the shirt, but the back had gaping holes in it.

And one of the cuffs was ruined, too—frayed and stained at the edge.

This was a disappointment. I did have a needle and thread, but I certainly didn't have the kind of cloth I needed to patch a shirt, nor could I think of a way to get any.

But still, I had something to work with. I reached into the bag and pulled out the tie and the shoes. They hadn't been harmed by their odd hibernation. I blessed my old self for insisting on quality. Anything cheap would have disintegrated.

My steps were almost light as I carried back this treasure—this ticket to—what?

I worked on the shirt all afternoon. I closed all the holes in the back, which left it with only half a back. And I took a piece from the shirt-tail in the front to rebuild the cuff. It still had frayed edges, but I was sure that the sleeve of the jacket would come down far enough to cover it.

I couldn't cut my hair myself, but fortunately, I didn't have to. One of the inhabitants of the valley was a man I always called Pete the Shears, because he had somehow managed to keep—through all his difficulties—a pair of barber's scissors that were his most prized possession.

Pete the Shears owed me a favor. He had once needed to write a letter to the government about a small pension he had coming. The letter had taken me five minutes, but he was convinced that it was a masterpiece and I had saved his life. The only way he could repay favors was to give haircuts. I took him up on this once a year. Though I would now be anticipating by about six months, I was fairly certain that Pete would oblige.

An hour's walk brought me to his camp. It was poor—compared to mine—his shelter was only pieces of canvas, but cutting being his trade, he'd decorated with rough artwork, valley debris in the shape of birds and butterflies.

"For party?" he asked, as he unwrapped the precious shears from the tattered rag in which he kept them. This was his standard joke, and I politely laughed.

"Yes, Pete. For a dress ball. Just a little off the top and sides, please." This was my joke. He'd have to take off a good six inches just to get to the point where he could start his real work.

I was fairly sure that Pete the Shears had learned his barbering skills in prison. He had probably come to the valley because he had neither the ability to work nor the understanding required to get adequate assistance from the government. Whatever his background, though, he was a pleasant man. Once our little conversation was over, I was free to sit back, close my eyes, give myself to his hands.

When he was done, I said to Pete what I always said, "Come by my place whenever you like, and we'll work on your reading . . ."

"Yes, thank you. To read . . ." he answered, with a smile and a little bow.

Of course he would never come by or start to learn to read. But it was a socially appropriate way of acknowledging our mutual concern for each other, and we never failed to engage in this exchange.

On one of the streets outside the south side of my ravine, there was a fancy restaurant with a reflecting pool in front, sheltered from the street by a series of elevated walkways and decorative planters holding trapped fir trees. In the middle of the pool, a fountain spurted freshly aerated water into a shallow pond.

By calculating back to the day I had been thrown out of the soup kitchen, I was able to figure out that it was still a weekday. This meant that two o'clock should be late enough to start up out of the valley, in order to bathe at about 3:00 A.M.

By law, the restaurant would have to close at one, and the staff would surely be gone by three.

I planned to wear my ragged old clothes and to wash them before I washed myself. If I could wring them tightly enough, I could put them back on wet and let them dry on the way home.

There wasn't much of a moon, but the cloudless night had its own clarity. As I made my way south through the ravine, I could feel small animals scurry out of my path. All the birds were still, and no fish leapt from the shadowed depths of the river. But the night was far from silent. A cacophonous chorus of frogs seemed to shrill from beneath every shrub, every clump of grass, every wild flower on the banks.

Leaving the valley for civilization, I kept as much as possible to the side streets where the good citizens slept in the security of their homes. Closer to Eglinton, the major east-west artery on which the restaurant sat, there was traffic, including a police cruiser. I stepped well out of the glare of the streetlights until it passed.

When I was sure the cops were a good distance away, I moved toward the far side of the fountain, completely out of view from the street, and prepared for the luxury of my shower.

First, I took from my pocket a large hunk of soap I had made by collecting scraps from public washrooms over a long period of time—a bar more luxurious to me than hand-milled French soap. I took off my shabby things, handling my shirt and pants, my socks and underwear with caution, so they didn't tear. I washed them, watching the swift drainage system of the pool carry away the soapy water. I wrung them out and spread them at the side of the pool, where I could reach them easily when I got out. Beside them, I put my towel, a clean rag that I'd washed in my rain barrel earlier in the day.

The water was cold and my whole body shook as I negotiated the pond and made my way toward the curtain of water that formed the fountain at its center.

It was wonderful to get that clean, to have gallons and gallons of water falling over me all at the same time, washing away the silt of the valley, the dust of the city, the excretions of my own body.

Because I was splashing and singing and generally being stupid, I once again failed to stand guard, failed to keep track of time, failed to realize that I might not remain alone. For I suddenly realized that in the small silences between the phrases of my song, another sound had begun to intrude. At first, I thought it was just the water. Then, with a start, I realized it was weeping.

I was stunned.

As long as I stood behind the curtain of water, I was safe. But how long could I do that? And what might happen to my clothes?

I had to escape. The weeping sounded not like a crazed man, but a heartbroken woman. This meant a lower likelihood that I would be physically assaulted, but a much higher danger of being accused of sexual assault if I were to reveal myself in my state of undress.

Cautiously, I moved through the curtain of falling water. Peering from behind its edge, I saw a young woman sitting on a bench near the pool. Her clothes were business clothes, her hair was clean and stylish. A briefcase and a good leather purse lay on the ground near her feet.

She wasn't looking at me or at anything near me. Her head was bent, and her shoulders shook in compulsive sobs. She didn't seem to notice, or to care, that my laundry was spread only a short distance away.

Despite my primary concern—my own safety—I was moved because the woman's misery seemed so total. No woman her age, dressed as she was, would allow herself to be in so deserted a spot at three o'clock in the morning unless she was so desperate that she didn't care anything about her personal safety. Betrayed in love? More likely betrayed in business.

I moved back into the water. My feet were now numb and my shoulders had begun to ache from the pressure of the fountain. I tried to judge from the sound whether she was wearing down—the way I used to listen to my own children as they screamed their rage over having to go to bed.

I heard the ragged intake of her breath. I took a chance at looking out again, and I saw that she had indeed stopped crying, though she was still moving in jerky spasms.

I watched as she reached for her fine briefcase, fumbled with its combination lock and wrenched it open. Grabbing handfuls of papers, she began to toss them wildly in the air. Before long, she was laughing hysterically, and she was moving closer and closer to the edge of the pool, to the place where my clothes lay in their embarrassing display.

The toe of her smart pump was nearly touching the taped toe of my own footwear when both she and I were distracted by the sound of running feet.

The cops!

I couldn't waste a second. As quickly as I could, I ran straight at her.

The shock was more than she could take. Her screams tore through the night.

As if I didn't even notice her, I bent down and scooped up as many of my clothes as I could. I got my shirt and my underwear and both my shoes. I lost my pants, my socks, my makeshift towel and, of course, my soap.

Now her screaming was focused. She was yelling to the police to catch me.

And I'm sure they would have. Running with bare wet feet down Eglinton Avenue, stark naked, chased by two people whose combined age was less than my own, I was an easy target.

But I was saved by two things.

The first was that I was running for my life.

The second was that Miss Business Failure fainted dead away, distracting the cops long enough for me to make good my escape.

I won't bore you with how I made it back through the residential streets in my underwear, how I stole new pants and socks from a jogger who had carelessly left his gym bag under a tree, how I slept, then rose, splashed my face with rainwater, shaved, dressed in my suit, checked my appearance in a scrap of mirror, admired myself, and set out once more for downtown Toronto.

CHAPTER

FIVE

PROMINENT JUDGE BEGINS SIX-MONTH SENTENCE

BY ALIANA CATERINA

Judge Ellis Portal has meted out to himself a sentence more severe than any he ever imposed on another.

The first time I saw him, I was so intimidated by the grandeur—albeit faded—of the courts of "Old City Hall" that I stood outside the heavy wooden door of Judge Portal's courtroom, afraid to go in. Each time a lawyer, a cop, or some stunned citizen went in or came out, I peeked through to get a glimpse of the man who, at the age of 40, reigned like Solomon from the high, ornate bench.

Even peeking through the door, I could see that Ellis Portal was exceptional. The black silk judge's gown seemed to sit easily on the shoulders of this stocky but handsome man. As he surveyed the crowded room, his facial expression was one of calm al-

ertness, as if he could be counted on
to hear and remember every detail of
the testimony of the desperate people
who came before him, people whose
one goal was to stay out of jail.

Now, his personal life in tatters
around him, Ellis Portal is in custody
himself . . .

Aliana Caterina's interview with me had catapulted her
directly into the big time, I found. As soon as I asked
the librarian at the reference library how to find Aliana's
work, I was led to a computer. Aliana's name was
punched in and a chronological list of her articles
jumped onto the screen. The first one she'd sold to the
Toronto Daily World was the one about me, and apparently she hadn't looked back since.

As I read her piece, the words swam before my eyes.
I wasn't ready to face her quick rundown of my rise and
fall. Nor could I yet bear to learn how I had answered
Aliana when she had asked the good reporter's—and the
good judge's—only real question: "Why?"

Instead of reading any further, I studied the icons at
the corner of the computer screen and managed to click
on one that looked like a picture frame.

Suddenly, without warning, I was staring myself in
the face. It was like peering into some sort of magic
mirror because I wasn't looking at a shabby valley bum
with a haircut done by a well-meaning ex-con, I was
looking at an elegant man of forty-five, his hair not gray,
but black and coiffured, his face unlined, his opinion of
himself high, to judge by the self-confidence of his expression.

I clicked again. There on the computer screen, as clear
as if it had been on television, was a picture of Stow.
He was presenting me with a plaque. This looked to be
about the same vintage as the first picture, but Stow

looked little changed from how he'd always been: slim, tall, not so much handsome as commanding, impeccably tailored. Just over our shoulders, I could make out two other figures. One was Anne; the other was Harpur. I clicked away from even that shadow of their presence.

And now I was looking at Anne and me in evening clothes at the opening of some new theater or at one of the endless galas and charity balls that we frequented in the eighties.

The next click brought another personal shot, perhaps from one of those "personality profiles" newspapers are so fond of. It showed me and my son and daughter on a winter outing. We smiled from between our skis, which were planted ends-up in a snowbank in one of those studied but casual poses so appropriate to the mood of après-ski.

Where were we? *Who* were we?

Ellis Portal at the age of forty-eight. Married for twenty-two years to Anne Miller-Smith, daughter of the late Allan Miller-Smith, retired U.S. diplomat. Father of Ellen Angela, twenty-one and Jeffrey Allan, nineteen. A man who would never again be so svelte because every morning in 1990 he rose at five-thirty to work out at a gym near Old City Hall courthouse. A man who dressed in his chambers in order to have time to read case law for two hours before court was called to order. A man who skipped lunch to meet with the members of the Law Commission—headed by Stow, of course—to work as a volunteer advisor on legal reform. A man who skipped dinner in order to work with a tennis pro—indoors and out, summer, spring, winter and fall.

And then back to my chambers to write decisions, sometimes so far into the night that there was no point in going home at all, which, if it bothered Anne, was never a matter of contention between us. After the many years of our marriage, we seemed to have come to a number of understandings. She always had volunteer work of her own. She always had friends. And she had family, though now that I think of it, she was closer to my family than her own. Closer, I sometimes thought, than I was myself. "I spent all my formative years among foreigners," she told me once. "I always just wanted to settle down. Yet to remain among my own staid New England relatives would have been unbearably mundane after the life I'd led. Your family has all the stability I crave—and all the warmth and color I've come to love among those from other cultures."

Our marriage had its physical side. Of course it did. But it could not be described as passionate. The main passion I felt for Anne by the time I reached forty-eight was gratitude—that she had never made on me the profound emotional demands my father had made on me. She did not cling. Her dependence on me was financial, which I considered appropriate. She was cool, elegant and distant. I thought that those three things were the same thing. And I thought that coolness was her nature. Sometimes I glimpsed a surprising warmth in her, but it was always when she was in the presence of my mother and my siblings, and I thought she was acting like them to please them, which I found a further mark of her elegance.

Nowhere was this more evident that when she spoke to them in Italian. At their very first meeting, Anne and my father chatted for nearly an hour. Afterward he said to me, "She is as kind as she is beautiful." I was charmed to see the old man so smitten.

She *was* kind. And I was grateful that she was a good partner, a person with whom one could set goals and have a reasonable expectation of meeting them without resistance or interruption.

And she was a good mother. As the years went by and I became more and more successful, she uncomplainingly took on more and more of the duties of parenting. It was Anne who arranged appointments and lessons, who spent hours ferrying, toting, paying and listening. It was she who met with teachers, monitored friendships, imposed curfews and meted out punishments.

I had long felt that a woman like Anne was my due. It never occurred to me that the only reason she put up with my arrogance was that she truly loved me. "I've never known anyone like you, Ellis," she always said with such mysterious fondness that I never had the courage to ask her what she meant.

As I sat there in the library, I remembered an occasion, not long after the death of my father, on which Anne had reached out to me in a simple, exceptional way.

She was lovely that evening, dressed in a gown of black velvet that set off the pale creaminess of her shoulders. I was in a tuxedo, my tie lovingly arranged by my daughter. "You look like a movie star, Daddy."

It was a gala, the opening of a new mounting of Beethoven's *Fidelio*. I loved opera, but I was usually so tired that I had to fight sleep or so preoccupied that I had a hard time paying attention. That was not the case that evening, however. I was fully involved in the music and the story—watching as a long line of chained convicts snaked their way across a sparsely lighted stage, when suddenly I felt a wetness on my cheek and realized to my shock that I was weeping.

Deeply embarrassed, I raised my hand to wipe my face and found Anne pressing into my fingers a handkerchief that bore strong traces of her cool perfume. "It's because of your father," she whispered. "It's okay, love. It's okay . . ."

But it wasn't because of my father. The old man had loved *Italian* opera. I doubt he'd ever heard *Fidelio,* may not have even known it existed. No. What struck me as I watched the imprisoned characters was the futility of

my own life. No matter how hard I worked to change
the law and to change the society it was supposed to
uphold, nothing ever changed. New laws sprouted new
criminals to break them. New procedures multiplied.
Every effort to unclog the courts resulted in more back-
logs and longer delays.

I was tired of the courts. I was tired of the law. I was
tired to death of the unending stream of hard-luck cases
that I had to sit in judgment on day after day. Was there
no bottom to the vipers' nests that people could throw
themselves into?

At intermission, Anne insisted that we take a cab
home, that I go immediately to bed, that I not work out
in the morning. Exhausted, I acceded to all of this. And
the next day, I woke up quite refreshed. Yet something
had told me the incident was the beginning of some new,
awful period in my life.

For a while, all went on as before. Anne and I and
our children lived in a large center-hall Georgian with a
broad verandah that overlooked the valley's vista on one
of the wealthy streets on which I had once worked with
my father. Our household included a gardener, a house-
keeper, and several maids (whom we called "assis-
tants").

It wasn't until some months later that I again felt stirring in me the terrible desperation I'd felt the night of
Fidelio. Again, it was a time of high stress. The Law
Commission had just released its report, and the tough
measures we'd proposed for making the courts more accessible had met with resistance from most of the senior
judges across the country. Stow had asked me to see
what I could do to soften up a couple of the local old
boys. In order to make this easier, Stow had obtained a
guest pass for me at the Windsor, the exclusive club to
which he belonged. I was spending what seemed like
endless hours there entertaining the judges, cajoling

them, treating them to drink after drink—all on Stow's tab.

So again I hadn't spent an evening at home in longer than I could remember. And when I did get home, I wasn't exactly sober.

Which was why I missed my daughter's university graduation, including her valedictorian address, for which she'd prepared for months and which I had promised—over and over—to hear.

When I got home past midnight and found Ellen waiting for me, she told me in her serious way that she was very disappointed. That she considered a promise a sacred trust. She took great pains to explain that her valedictory speech had gone very well and she'd been publicly praised by the president of the university, but that my missing her address was not the point. The point was that I had promised and not delivered. She also said that she wasn't angry, just very hurt.

But I was angry. Instead of apologizing to her, I yelled. I told her she had no right to make such demands. What was the matter with her, anyway? Didn't she know how hard I had always worked so that she and her brother could have a comfortable future?

"You're a sick man, Daddy," was her reply. She had always surveyed me like a solemn little analyst, as if she were the parent instead of me.

She was right. I was sick. Over the years, I had resorted to anger the way a progressing addict resorts to his fix. A little here and there just to keep going, just to keep things on an even keel. And I used with myself the addict's arguments. It was not interfering with my daily life. It was not causing me the loss of anything I valued. Shortly after the incident with Ellen, though, anger nearly cost me the loss of something I'd wanted for years—to be interviewed as an applicant to the Windsor Club.

It was a rare day off for me, and Anne and I had

breakfast together. "I don't like the fact that they still don't take Jews there . . ." she said.

"Anne, please. It's illegal to exclude people from any organization on the basis of religion . . ."

"They may not be particularly interested in Italians, either . . ."

"The vice-president of the board is Italian," I snapped. I really didn't want an argument just then. I couldn't admit to myself that I was nervous. And I was uncomfortable thinking about the clothes I was going to wear, which I was afraid were too casual.

Stow had told me that the interview would be informal, that it would take place not in the board room of the club but in the tennis lounge during lunch and a game. He told me that there would be four interviewers among the seven men I'd meet. That I would have no way of knowing which of the men were actually interviewing me. That I needed three votes out of four to be admitted to the club as a probationer and that in the event that anyone voted against me, I would have to find out within one year, on my own, who that party was and convince him to change his vote, or I would never become a permanent member.

I now had a driver who negotiated the busy streets of the city with the professional's ease in my Mercedes, so I was free to think about my interview all the way to the club. How would I present myself? I wanted the interviewers, whoever they were, to be aware of my connections, but I couldn't drop names. I wanted them to consider my accomplishments, but I certainly hoped that they would not dwell on the fact that I was sometimes called, "The little guy's friend." And I wanted them to have no question about my taste. That would have been so much simpler if I'd been able to wear a dark suit.

In the end I decided it would be easiest just to act as much like my nominator as I could. Like Stow.

As my driver pulled up onto the vast stone-paved

drive of the club, circled past the imposing marble facade of the building with its columns and its bas-relief
portico, slipped under an arched canopy and deposited
me into the hands of the rear doorman, I tried to clear
my mind of everything, to relax, to let the day unfold
as I so hoped it would.

Gathered near the steps of a formal garden were eight
men—Stow and seven complete strangers.

We shook hands all around. "Let's head down to the
lounge," Stow suggested, leading us along an avenue of
trees toward a sheltered spot between the club's formal
grounds and a wilder section where trees and shrubs
grew in a tame approximation of the northern wood.

The walkway was rather narrow, and the line of men
naturally narrowed to accommodate it. I found myself
walking beside a man somewhat older than myself. "I
know your face," he said, squinting a little as he studied
me.

I smiled and reminded him smoothly that I'd been
leading quite a public life lately. I hid my disappointment at having to do so. If he didn't already know who
I was, what chance did I have for his vote—if he was a
voter . . . ?

"No, no," he said. "I mean I know that face from
elsewhere." He studied me some more. I fought to hide
my discomfort, reminding myself that everything that
afternoon was designed to be a test.

I was saved from further scrutiny, however, by Stow
who was suddenly at my side. "This way," he said amicably. "I've asked for something very light for lunch
so that we can have our game afterward. I know you
never eat before you play, Ellis, but the others . . ."

"Of course," I said, and I followed him into the
lounge, an airy room surrounded on three sides by
French doors and open toward the tennis courts on the
fourth side.

I would not have eaten much under any circumstances, but knowing my every move was being minutely observed by at least four of the seven, I couldn't touch a thing on my plate.

Across the table from me sat the man who was sure he knew me. He watched in silence while the others asked me countless questions about my background, my work . . .

I answered with ease. I was, after all, an accomplished public speaker, and this was no different from any other presentation. The men were so cordial and relaxed that I soon relaxed too.

It wasn't until lunch had been cleared and coffee was brought that the man across the table spoke up.

"You used to work in construction . . ."

I stared at him in astonishment. "I beg your pardon?"

"That's where I know you from . . ."

I heard Stow clear his throat. "Let's get over to the tennis courts . . ."

But the man would not be interrupted. "I thought I recognized that face. You look like your father . . ."

"What?"

"You're Angelo Portalese's boy, aren't you? The bricklayer's son . . ."

Dead silence. Seven men waiting.

"I'd prefer not to talk about my family," I said, fighting to hide my shock.

"A man *is* his family," my tormentor replied arrogantly.

"Gentlemen, this way, please . . ." It was Stow.

"Portalese was a decent man. You don't need to be ashamed to be his boy . . ." the man persisted.

"I'm not his son!"

Judas. Oh, Ellis, you Judas.

There was a yet more complete silence. Into it came the mocking sound of a sweet bird singing in the wood beyond. But that was all. Nobody said another word about my family. We proceeded to the courts. I played a good hard game. My anger lent a passion to my playing that allowed me to win rather impressively. After the game there were drinks all around. Release. Good cheer.

Three of four people voted me into the club.

But I never became a permanent member because before my year was up, the fragile scaffolding of my life came tumbling down around me.

From the time of that incident at the Windsor Club, I felt as if I were leading a double existence, confused between the self I had created and my allegiance to the family I had come from. My temper seemed to become shorter and shorter though my conduct on the bench never varied from the calm, compassionate, competent work I was known for.

Which made it all the more shocking when, in a moment of fury, I attacked the last person on earth I ever thought I would harm.

The library was growing warm, but of course I couldn't remove my jacket.

I got up to breathe, to stretch. I left the computer and walked toward one of the doors, which looked out onto a busy street. As I stood there, I realized I wasn't far from Stow's office.

Perhaps it was the suit, but for one fleeting second, I actually entertained the notion of dropping by for a visit, despite the restraining order. In the old days, Stow had always welcomed a visit from me. I thought it was because he enjoyed my company, but now, after all that's happened, I realize the real role I've played in Stow's life. I am a reminder of all he never has to be afraid of being.

Though I ran the risk of relinquishing my place at the computer, I strolled out onto the sidewalk. It felt so good to walk freely. I wished that each time I came up to the city I could dress like this, but I had long ago accepted the probability that this suit would have to last me the rest of my life. My mother had always talked about things that would last for the rest of one's life. I should have listened.

The fresh air perked me up a bit. I returned to the computer, which was still available, fully intending to go back and force myself to read the rest of Aliana's article. In order to get to the article, I had to figure out how to get out of the file of pictures. I clicked one more time.

Another picture flashed up. I stared at it in bewilderment. There I sat beside my hut in the valley! I was reading a book. My ragged clothes were visible in every tattered detail. The tar-papered shack I called home looked little different from when I'd left that morning. Across the bottom of the picture was a caption: "Sign of the times? Among the recession-ridden of the city, the Don valley has become a sort of country retreat. Even the mighty—like fallen judicial star Ellis Portal—can be found 'down by the river . . .' "

I hadn't the least idea who had taken the picture. Who had found me in the valley? Why should anybody care what I was doing down there? What was this picture doing in Aliana Caterina's file? That was just one more question I had for her, and I wasn't going to waste any more time researching. The *Toronto Daily World* was near the harbor. I could walk there—even in my dress loafers—in less than an hour.

Soon, I was at the bottom of the city. The traffic near the harbor seemed to come from every direction, and though there were clearly marked places for pedestrians to cross—and traffic lights, too—I was suddenly immobilized. From where I stood I could actually see Aliana's tall building, with the letters TDW emblazoned on top.

As I was studying it, a car careered around the corner

and nearly knocked me into the street. I retreated farther onto the sidewalk.

I was shaking. The building was so close, yet I had to make my way through this dangerous intersection before I could get to it. Another car, wanting to turn but waiting for me to cross, honked loudly. I tore across the street.

But my shoes were slippery—and just before I made the opposite side, I went flying, sliding along the pavement and hitting my shoulder hard against the curb.

Pain and shock shot through me. As always, my first impulse was to get up and run, but I couldn't make my body respond to my will.

Eventually I managed to move. The pain in my shoulder took my breath away. I staggered up. Nothing was wrong with my legs, I was grateful to discover.

There were no other pedestrians around, so I was spared having to pretend that I was okay. In fact, I was badly shaken. I could, however, walk without too much difficulty, and I kept going until I got to a narrow park that ran along the water, and a line of smartly-painted benches where passersby could sit and look out over the water.

My shoulder was throbbing, but I could tell already that no serious damage had been done. I was far more worried about my suit. I couldn't take off my jacket to check what harm had come to it, but I reached along the shoulders and across as much of the back as I could to feel whether it was torn.

It wasn't. Once again I thanked my insistence on quality and resumed my quest for Aliana Caterina. I had to sign in at security. This proved remarkably easy. I just wrote my name on the sheet of paper the security desk clerk shoved at me. He didn't even look at it. But he did press a button that activated an elevator across from the desk.

I figured that with all the security, the elevator must

lead directly into the newsroom, and I was right.

I'd never been in a newsroom before, but it was as I had imagined it would be—a large open space crammed with desks, computers and overflowing paper, crowded with people.

I hadn't been standing there more than a few seconds when one of those people caught sight of me and politely asked me who I was looking for.

"Ms. Caterina."

"And you have an appointment?"

"Yes," I lied.

"Come this way and I'll see if she's in." I followed her as she made her way through a maze of desks toward the farthest reaches of the room, where I saw that cubicles had been set aside for various reporters, of which Aliana was one. Her name was engraved in white on a small black plaque affixed to the wall beside one of the doors. Just outside the door was an upholstered chair and beside it a table on which sat a copy of the *Toronto Daily World*.

"Have a seat," the woman said, "I'm sure Ms. Caterina will be with you in a short while. Is it about an interview?"

I nodded. Sure it was about an interview—about an interview she had done with a mental patient five years before. I was glad of that newspaper on the table. I picked it up and pretended to read it. It would hide my face from Aliana as she approached her office. That gave me the advantage of surprise.

It was the only advantage I had.

Glancing across the room, I saw that it was after three. I wasn't sure how long I would have to sit in this position of ambush, but I was prepared to do it as long as necessary.

I sat for two hours. At five, some of the workers packed it in and got ready to go home. There was a general shuffle of papers, chairs and people. I took the opportunity to disappear into the washroom and take a good look at myself and my suit. Once again, I brushed off the shoulder where it had come into contact with the street. The fabric was bruised, but okay. My shirt had not fared so well, though. Some of the stitching I'd done had come loose.

I splashed my face with water, and I ran my fingers through my hair.

When I got back to Aliana Caterina's office, she was sitting at her desk.

Compared to what the years had done to the person I'd just been looking at in the washroom mirror, the years had been very good to Aliana. In the old days, I had noticed only her kindness. Now I could see that she was one of those polished women who, by their mid-thirties, attain a maturity and personal attractiveness that seems part physical beauty and part intellectual power. Aliana had olive skin, delicate features and raven hair. Seeing her study her papers, her head bent, the fluorescent light adding blue highlights to the smooth black curve of her hair, I felt I'd made a terrible mistake. One word from her and I'd be out on my ear—charged with trespassing or worse.

I tried to move soundlessly away from her door.

But I failed. She looked up and saw me standing there. And I could tell that even in the first seconds, she knew who I was. I could see, too, that for all my fine toilette, Aliana wasn't fooled. The last time she had seen me I'd been down on my luck. Now I was down and out. She was subtle enough to know which was which.

"Ellis . . ." she said, rising from her desk and extending her hand, which I took. "Do we have an appointment?"

"No, Aliana, I don't have any appointments these days."

The hint of a smile crossed her lips. She was quite a beautiful woman. "Wise," she said, "very wise. I, myself make far too many appointments . . ."

The brush-off. She glanced at her watch.

"Aliana, I've gone to some difficulty to find you to-day, and I only need a moment of your time . . ."

"Look," she said, "I'd like to talk to you, I really would. I'm sure that whatever's happened to you in the last few years is something I'd be interested in. But you understand how it is. I'm pressed . . ."

I waited for the old fury, the only slightly submerged anger, to come over me. I waited for the rumble in my chest that would burst out as my own voice yelling that I didn't care what her schedule was. That I wouldn't make an appointment with her if my life depended on it. That her interest meant nothing to me. Never would. Never had. I waited for the anger to open its arms and embrace me.

But it didn't. Nothing happened. I looked at Aliana Caterina. She was even still smiling. So I smiled back.

"What I can do," she said, "is set up a time for us to get together." She shuffled through the papers on her desk and from a small pile extracted a leather-bound daybook.

I, who hadn't voluntarily kept an appointment of any sort since the day I was arraigned, waited patiently while she searched through the little squares on her calendar, looking for one with enough room left in which to write my name.

"Thursday the fourteenth of June be okay? About three o'clock?"

"Certainly," I responded, not adding that I'd be fine about the three o'clock if somebody could just let me know when it was Thursday the fourteenth.

But in the mysterious absence of anger, I had nothing left to go by except whatever remained of those luxuries called manners. So I reached out as if to shake her hand.

As I did so, the piece of cloth I had used to repair the cuff of the shirt came completely undone, slipped out of my jacket and hung in a ragged, dirty patch, dangling over the desk.

Shame overtook me entirely. Silenced even my inner voice. I just stood there. Devoid of everything but the desire never to have been born.

"Listen," Aliana said, in the tone of somebody who's just had a brainstorm, "I've got a better idea. It's after five. I haven't eaten all day. What say we go down to the ground floor to the Press Box and have a bite? That way I can pick your brain and buy you supper—you know—payment for your cooperation. Not that I offer bribes, don't get me wrong."

I found the strength to look at her then. I felt only gratitude. "Fine," I said. "I'm hungry, too."

The Press Box would not have been the cafeteria of a major metropolitan daily if the food had been any good, but that didn't matter to me. I was ravenous, and even my sudden nervousness at talking to Aliana didn't prevent me from eating a bowl of soup, a salad, a sandwich and ice cream. Nor did my eagerness to know what that picture of me was doing in a file with her name on it prevent me from gulping down three cartons of milk. She seemed to have a pretty good appetite, too, despite her slimness.

Over coffee, we slowed down, and she started in on the questions.

"So, tell me, Your Honor," she began, "how are you getting along these days?"

A thousand fancy phrases went through my head, but why bother? I was past trying to hide who I was—especially from her, considering.

"You should know—you've seen the picture. Maybe you even took it yourself . . ."

"What?"

"This morning at the library I did a little research. In a computer file under your by-line I found a picture of me outside my hut. Did you take that?"

"Ellis, I have no idea what you're talking about. I don't even know where you live."

"I live in the valley," I said simply.

She stared at me blankly. Her puzzlement seemed genuine. I could see her shuffling through her mental rotary file. "Is there a facility down there?" she asked. "I wasn't aware . . ."

"A facility? How genteel you are, Aliana," I said without rancor. "Do you mean a hostel? A shelter? A group home?"

She looked hurt, and I felt like a fool. "I'm sorry," I said.

"I'm sure the picture was in that file because it's connected to you—not me," she said. "So where *do* you live in the valley?"

I told her about my home in the ravine. I told her about the seasons. About the river. About Tim Garrison. I told her about Pete the Shears. I told her how I sometimes nursed sick animals back to health, and also how I always carefully avoided having them attach themselves to me emotionally.

"Animals do have very obvious emotions, don't they?" she answered thoughtfully, at which moment I felt an emotion myself, one that I hadn't felt in a long time. I think you'd call it fondness.

"In the valley—as in jail and maybe even in the media—emotional attachment is a danger," I said.

I felt like asking her whether she was married, whether she had a family.

When I had talked for almost half an hour—without finding a way to tell her what I'd really come for—she reached out and touched me. "Ellis," she said, "I've heard enough to convince me. I'd love to do a story on you. I'll give it any slant you want: Fundraising for the environment of the valley, more shelters for the homeless—you name it."

The mysterious refusal of my usual anger to kick in

persisted. Instead of railing at her jumping to conclusions about my intent, I felt relaxed. "No, wait," I said, "I haven't told you why I came . . ."

"I've got a few more minutes," she answered, looking at her watch again. "Let's get more coffee."

For a minute, I forgot I was penniless. I made a move to stand, but she touched me. "Hey," she said, "my treat—remember?"

When she came back and set a steaming mug in front of me, I got to the point. "Aliana, there is something you *can* do for me, but it's not to write about me or the homeless. I want you to help me solve a mystery."

"Solve a mystery? What do you mean?" She looked a little shocked, and I hoped she didn't think I'd relapsed into the unreality of the mentally disturbed.

"Aliana, I'm afraid somebody may have been murdered. I've found tangible evidence of it in my ravine. I have no notion who the victim might be. But I do have a clue to the mystery, and I want you to help me follow it. What I need from you is very specific. The victim— an adult black male—was wearing a particular piece of jewelry that I suspect belonged to one of three lawyers here in town. It may have been stolen. It may have been a gift. You're a crime reporter. You've got sources all over the city. All I need you to do is find out whether one of those lawyers is in some kind of trouble."

I could see her stiffen. Now she was all reporter. Her sources were inviolable. Even her posture was their guard. "I can't reveal anything confidential about anybody to anybody," she declared.

"I know. What I'm asking may not even involve confidential matters. It might be public record—a bankruptcy, an illness, an unexplained purchase or sale."

A startling thought occurred to me. "It might even be a divorce . . ."

She held up her hand as if to stop me before I said something she didn't want to hear—the way I used to

stop a witness from inadvertently incriminating himself.
"Let me make sure I understand this," she said. "You
find evidence that leads you to suspect somebody may
have been murdered. I can only conclude that you came
to me instead of the police. Now, Ellis—Your Honor—
you're asking me to be an accessory after the fact—an
accessory to murder."

She was sharp. She was fast. She was wrong.

"No. You could only be an accessory if I had committed the murder . . ."

She played with the handle of her mug. Her fingers
were long and slim. So were her nails. I wondered how
she spent hours typing on her computer with nails like
that. Maybe they were stronger than they looked. Maybe
she was.

"How do I know that, Ellis?"

"Because that's the law."

"That's not what I'm talking about," she said, her
eyes suddenly catching mine and holding. I could see
how she must have got her stories. There was no compassion—no softness of any sort—there now. "How do
I know you're not telling me about somebody you killed
yourself?"

"Why would I be that stupid?"

She took a breath. Behind her, the door to the cafeteria
swung open and a laughing group of people burst in.
Aliana moved closer to me. Her hair brushed my face.
Her perfume smelled like lemon and spice. Her voice,
when she finally spoke, was a whisper. "Ellis," she
said. "You may be a man without control—and without
luck—but you aren't a man without a conscience."

She took me aback. It was almost as if she had
thought about me over the years. Though I didn't want
to be touched by anything now, I was touched by her
concern.

"All right, Aliana. You're correct in all your assump-
tions, except one. I didn't kill anybody. I'm aware

there's no reason in the world for you to trust me or
help me . . .''

"That's not . . .''

"Let me finish. There's no reason for you to be interested in this story without details. It's the least you
can ask. So I'm going to give you details. I'm also going
to trust you. Because there are only four people who
know what I'm going to tell you . . .''

She looked at me without emotion. How many times
does a reporter hear a line like that?

But she was still listening, which was good. Because
I had decided to tell her the story of the rings.

"Twenty-five years ago," I began, "there were five
of us just starting out as lawyers. We were pretty sure
of ourselves and almost sure of our future. However, one
of us, John Stoughton-Melville, whom I'm sure you
know, decided we needed something to remind us that
the future would not be without its difficulties, the kind
of difficulties with which friends can help friends.''

I spoke slowly, drawing her in. It had been a long
time since I had held an audience spellbound, and despite the grim urgency of my mission, I found myself
enjoying her attention. I told her about Stow and his
little speech in the drawing room before the fire. I told
her about Harpur. I described William in his already
staid demeanor and Gleason in all his golden charm. I
told her how William and Gleason listened, and how it
was the last speech of Stow's that Gleason would ever
hear.

"How tragic," Aliana said softly when I got to that
part of the tale. I felt as if I were telling a fairy tale to
a child. Soon, however, I would get to the part where
something evil comes out of the wood . . .

I told her a little about how I was then. How I had
felt about my prospects, what I had hoped for. It wasn't
really necessary to my story, but it worked itself in, and
she kept on listening. I even told her about my mother

waiting for me with a good, old Italian dinner the day I was called to the bar. "Your parents were the sweetest people . . ." she said.

"So, if you think of it," I pressed, "there were twenty promises exchanged that night. Stow was adamant that we take him seriously. He didn't let anyone offer a favor right there on the spot, but he, himself, promised us a sort of carte blanche assistance should we ever need it . . ."

"And did you?"

"Yes."

How was I going to tell her about the rings without telling her about the hand? She'd think I was making it up—that I was insane. I couldn't risk it. "Less than a week ago, I saw one of the five rings on a person to whom it could not legitimately belong . . ."

"Which ring was it—I mean whose?"

"I don't know."

"But you saw it up close enough to be sure that it was one of these rings?"

"It was unmistakable."

"So," she said, "these are the people you want me to check up on—and you can't do it because you'll be arrested if you go near them. . . ."

"Yes."

"But any one of the three could have given the ring away, or sold it—or even discarded it. People get rid of very valuable things sometimes, just to get rid of the memories. How does your seeing the ring on somebody's finger have anything to do with murder—unless you saw it on a body? Is that what you're saying?"

"Not exactly."

"But you think that somebody was murdered because of this ring . . . ?" She paused. "Where's your own ring?"

"I have it."

"Even after everything that's happened?"

"Yes."

"Stow—Stoughton-Melville—he's been named to the Supreme Court, and he'll be sworn in in the fall, but I suppose you know that?"

I laughed. "I read about it through the window of a newspaper box. I know I should have bought the paper . . ."

Aliana didn't smile. "He was your lawyer when you got into trouble." She paused. "That's how you got out of going to jail, isn't it?"

"I did go to jail . . ."

"But only for a little while, right? And that was his favor to you. He pulled some strings behind the scenes. He massaged the Crown attorneys. He got the charges dropped on the condition that you undergo mental assessment . . . You got him to fulfill his promise."

Impatience was beginning to make me nervous, not angry, just nervous. She was interested. I was close. I was so close to getting her to do the simple thing I needed done.

"I need another coffee," she said. "Can I get you one?"

"No thanks," I said. "You go ahead. I'll wait."

Who was I kidding?

Sitting there without her increased my nervousness. The noisy crew who were the only others in the cafeteria glanced my way now and then. They probably thought Aliana Caterina was doing another bleeding-heart story. Maybe she thought that, too. Just when I'd about decided I'd wasted the whole day, she came back with a look on her face that I recognized. It was the look I'd seen on the faces of jurors in the opening hours of a trial—when they are first beginning to weigh the evidence, first beginning to understand how much is at stake. First getting hooked on the mystery . . .

"Did anybody ever ask his favor of you?"

"No, but there was one other favor that I called in,"

I told her. "I asked Harpur—before she married Stow, of course—if she would go out with me. She did."

Aliana smiled. "An act of desperation?"

I smiled back. "You could say that."

"Happens to the best of us," she replied. "Look, Ellis, the ring might have been given in fear—a bribe of some sort or a warning. It seems to me that what's confusing you about all this is that it turned up on the hand of a black man. I take it all your lawyer friends were white. Could it be Harpur who gave the ring to the man you think was murdered?"

"Harpur? As a bribe?"

"No," Aliana replied cautiously, "as a token of love."

"As a token of love!" The thought shocked me. But not because of the racial implications. It shocked me that I could still, after all this time, feel a jolt of jealousy at the thought that Harpur might have been unfaithful to Stow with someone and that that someone was not me.

"Ring sizes can be changed by jewelers, so we have no way of knowing whether it was her ring," Aliana said. "If it wasn't given as a love token or as bribe, it might simply have been stolen or pawned. If so, then it wouldn't be much of a clue at all, would it, Ellis?"

"It might be a big clue, if someone were to check out a few pawn shops to see if one of our lawyers ever visited them . . ."

At that suggestion, Aliana shook her head and glanced at her watch yet again. "This is all fascinating on a personal level, Ellis, but it's not news. I don't really see why you think I'd be interested in this . . ."

"Look, Aliana, I'm asking a simple favor. You could just check around while you're doing your other work . . . Something's going on with those lawyers. It *has* to be."

I was getting too excited. "I've got a deadline," Aliana Caterina said in her best reporter voice. "I think we've spent enough time discussing this, don't you, Mr. Portal?''

Across the space between us and the table where the others sat, there was now a bridge of silence over which our words were marching. I struggled to keep my voice low.

"Aliana, all I'm asking for is a little harmless information . . ."

Her voice was low, too. Almost like a hiss. "Look, Ellis, I'm getting scared. You're talking nonsense. If you've got a problem, go to the police. I'm not a detective. I'm a reporter . . ." She stood.

A story. She needed a story. All right, I thought, I'll give you a story. "Aliana, please, sit back down just for a minute. I haven't told you everything . . ."

It must have been another of those lines that reporters hear all the time, because it had an instant effect. She sat back down—only on the very edge of her chair, as if she were ready to bolt instantly if the story weren't good enough.

"The reason I think there may have been a murder is I found the ring on a severed human hand . . ."

Her mouth dropped. She stared at me dumbfounded. Then she glanced over at the next table. The people there were laughing and chatting. They hadn't heard a word.

Aliana looked back at me. Looked down. Seemed to think about things. Looked back up.

"Listen, Ellis," she said not unkindly, "I don't know what you've been through since I saw you last, but obviously it hasn't been easy for you. I'm sorry about that. I never thought that what happened to you was fair. But that's life. I guess when you first came in here today, I thought you wanted me to tell the public a little more of your story. Well, I would have been willing to do that, you know. And help you out a bit—get you some food, some clothes . . ."

She stopped, and I looked up at her. She was blushing.

"I think our readers would like to know what happened to you," she resumed. "After all, you used to have a lot of supporters." She paused. "But, I could only do that if we did an interview—just a regular, ordinary . . ."

"Forget it," I interrupted. "I didn't come here to get my name in the paper. Or my picture, either, by the way."

"That picture had nothing to do with me. I can imagine how a man in your position would feel about going to the police. But I know for a fact that a lot of them would remember you—I mean remember the good things."

She wasn't finished. "Whatever's going on down in that ravine is a matter for the police. Don't waste any more time. Don't jeopardize the hard-won freedom that you've got. Come back to my office. We can call them together. I can do that much for you."

I thought about it. I decided to go with her.

We left the cafeteria together and headed for the elevator.

But by the time Aliana Caterina got back to her office, she was alone. At least I assume she got back to her office. I don't know for sure because I ducked out an exit so fast that she didn't realize I was no longer behind her.

When I left the *Toronto Daily World* I discovered I had lost my one remaining subway token—probably in my fall. But I wasn't concerned. A public trail led out of the downtown streets into the valley and followed the river for several miles before disappearing into parks and ravines with paved paths.

I usually avoided this route. The trail was frequented by bicyclists, hikers, joggers, naturalists, families. They did not consider vagrants to be a welcome component of the scenery. There were also police down there all the time.

But on this night, which mercifully was one on which the dark would come late, I was dressed no differently from some of the businessmen who regularly walked home from work through the valley at that time of year.

There, at the heart of the city, the river was like a trapped animal. Its banks were encased in cement. It had been artificially restructured, which disturbed its dynamics, making it too deep in some places yet so shallow in others that its bottom was exposed.

To the west of the riverside trail ran the railroad. On the east the high-speed parkway siphoned cars from the highways south of the city and sucked them up in a racing stream toward the suburbs in the north.

Old factories, run-down and empty government buildings, boarded-up warehouses, stark parking garages—these were the neighbors of the river in its lowest reaches, and the water ran between them with the silent resignation of the has-been.

But I loved the river even here. I loved how dark it was, how it held its secrets with the dignity of the damned. I loved how grass and even small trees managed to sprout out of the concrete that held it captive. I loved how the old bridges spanned it in graceful arches that were duplicated on its surface in light reflected from the evening sky.

I loved the trees that still grew as close to it as they could get. I loved the Canada geese that settled beside it and somehow found food for their young in the murky water.

And I loved the sounds, even if they were the sounds of man rather than the sounds of nature. I loved the rattle of the old bridges as the streetcars went over them. I loved the lap of the water as it licked the concrete. I loved the wind in the slim weeds that grew between the railroad ties. I even loved the sound of the rush-hour trains, the buzzing traffic, the sound of my own feet on the asphalt path.

I think what I really loved in those moments when I was cupped in the hand of the city was life. But I could never admit such a thing to myself.

After a few miles, the old buildings disappeared. The river and its valley widened. Now it was ringed by high-rise apartment buildings. The banks here were high and wide and covered with smooth lawn.

Then it all changed again and I found myself walking through a series of lovely parks. The further north I went, the wilder and more deserted the valley was, but the path was still paved and I was still seldom alone as I walked.

When I'd been walking for nearly two hours, I entered the final park of the public valley system. This was a park of unnatural beauty—I mean artificial beauty. Every inch of it was manicured to perfection. The trees that lined the river here were willows, each branch of which swept down in a graceful curve that seemed eager to embrace the waters where white ducks swam beneath bridges of rounded stone.

The city cultivated this park as a showpiece—with great success. Even then, late in the evening, a gaggle of foreign tourists—using their flash apparatus to make sure—were busily snapping photographs of the flower beds. On weekends, there were so many brides and grooms who came here for wedding photographs that it was hard for the photographers to keep other brides and other grooms out of the background.

At the northernmost edge of this park was a path that led almost directly into the ravine in which I lived. It was easy for me to find because I was used to reading the lay of the land. But the path itself was invisible to anyone who didn't know it—who hadn't been shown it by someone else. It was highly unlikely, though certainly not impossible, that a person could stumble upon this path. Even if he did, he would still have at least an hour's hike through tangled brush before he reached my section of the valley.

As I approached the hidden path, I began to feel a sense of foreboding. Maybe there's a scent left when someone trespasses. Maybe the whole forest knows when part of it is violated because of air currents or a change in light—who knows? All I know is that evening, I felt more afraid the closer I got to home.

As I rounded the last bend in the path, I saw that my compound was in a shambles.

Of course, I noticed the garden first.

It was completely torn apart. Every plant had been pulled from its place, and the tender leaves ripped from their slender stalks. Whole rows had been scraped away, and even in the now-failing light, I could see that the seeds I'd planted had begun to sprout, small white tendrils reaching out of their casings.

My hut was smashed—just a few planks propped against a tree remained—and my belongings were scattered in front of it, my blankets resting in the dust.

They had even found my books, which were lying on the ground, the soft rising breeze of coming night riffling their pages.

I looked around me in despair—a despair too deep for anger. This was the second time. I couldn't ignore the danger anymore. I needed to think about my safety. I needed to move to an even more remote part of the ravine.

But before I could do a single thing, I had to take off my good suit. I had to wrap it and put it where night could not dampen its fine cloth. I had to take off my shoes and wrap them, too.

When I had done this, I meant to try to save some of the plants, but I was too tired.

With what little strength I had left, I pulled a scrap

of blanket around me and lay down on the ground. Above me, the stars of the city gleamed with a pale distant light.

They seemed small and cheap and mean.

CHAPTER

SIX

ONE THING MY LIFE IN THE VALLEY HAD ROBBED ME OF was my previously inexhaustible energy. After a long day in the city, I usually would have fallen asleep instantly and for a good long time. But this night, I stared toward the sky as I lay in the open air under the trees. I could hear the sounds of the night birds, and once in a while, the cry of some larger animal—a fox or a stray dog.

Who would have torn my place apart? Was someone looking for the missing hand, and had they become enraged with *me* when they hadn't found it?

Whatever was after me was not an animal. Nor was there any reason to suspect the usual inhabitants of the valley—no others living in the ravines had cause deliberately to harm my home.

As I lay in the darkness, fragments of images flickered behind my closed eyes until all the fragments gathered into one image—that shadow behind the shoulder of Stow—Harpur.

I must have been at the university for only a few days when I caught my first glimpse of her. The University of Toronto sprawled through many blocks of the city, but concentrated at its center was a series of stately neo-Gothic gray stone buildings that circled a grassy playing field called King's College Common. I was crossing the common one bright September morning when I looked up and saw, floating through one of the buildings' stone colonnades, a slender girl with red hair the color of the leaves of autumn. She was alone and seemed deep in thought as she drifted into an arched doorway and disappeared.

A few days later, I was late for philosophy class. I gingerly approached, hearing the class already in session. Someone as speaking. The voice was laughing, lilting. But challenging too. "You're the professor," it said, "and it's your obligation to convince me not only that I should be studying this topic, but also that I should accept your view of it as being in some way superior to my own."

Now, I knew that the university was a forum for open discussion and intellectual freedom, but the thought that anyone—especially a woman—could speak to a professor in that bold way filled me with such a rush of excitement that I stumbled, hit the doorway with my shoulder, dropped my books and startled the whole class, including the professor who, perhaps already rattled, stood there frozen. I hurried to gather my things from the floor.

I heard the lilting voice tease, "Come in, it was just getting interesting."

I looked up and saw the red-headed girl. In a flash I realized that though her lovely voice laughed, her deep green eyes did not.

That was the first day of the seven years I spent close enough to reach out and touch Harpur but never able to because of my feelings of inferiority. And also because the only person not subject to her teasing, tempting, confusing contempt was Stow.

These shards of memory pursued me into my dreams, where Harpur and Stow—now young, now old, now happy, now not—danced before me in impossible scenarios, each of which served to remind me of my self-imposed exile from their golden lives.

I woke up, startled. It was early morning, the sun just rising over the edge of the valley. I couldn't figure out why I was outside instead of in my hut, until, slowly, the truth dawned on me. I lifted my head and looked around. A fine mist of dew had settled on the heaps of rubble that had been my home. I closed my eyes again.

The first day Harpur ever singled me out for special notice was the day we buried Gleason. William was so distraught that he had to be led sobbing from the funeral. The rest of us—Harpur and Stow and I—were too shocked by Gleason's death to be embarrassed by this show of emotion.

It was Stow who went to look after William, which left Harpur and me alone, and after the funeral, she invited me back to her house. At any other time, I would have been so overtaken with anxiety at being alone with her that I would probably have refused, but subdued as we were by sorrow, we simply went together as friends. I had never been invited before.

My parents had surprised me with the gift of a car, and, though it was only a Chevy, I was almost proud to be driving it behind her Bentley, following her north up Yonge Street into her neighborhood. We had gone quite a way before I realized that we were headed for one of the streets on which my father had worked.

To this day, despite all that has conspired to turn me away from pride, I recall how proud I felt that those streets, down which I had once ridden in a pickup truck, were the very streets that held the home of my friend and colleague, Harpur Blane. I was no longer the uneducated son of a laborer who couldn't speak English. I was an educated man, a lawyer, the personal friend of a woman whose wealth was so obvious, her place in the establishment so assured, that she wore it with the ease that my mother might wear an old coat. Harpur's coat was mink.

She had, in a very Harpur-like way, forgotten her door

keys. A maid let us in. What struck me first was not the pale carpet that covered what seemed like acres of floor, not the white marble fireplace that dominated the reception room, not the winding staircase that led to a wide landing on which sat a white Steinway grand piano. Not the paintings, the flowers, the accents in silver and brass. No. What struck me first was the complete absence of clutter. So powerful was the impression of all that space with nothing much in it, that I came to associate empty space with expensive taste. Even a woman as fastidious in her decorating as my wife Anne, who never left a room without putting everything in it away, couldn't ever empty our house enough for me.

"Let's have some tea . . ." Harpur said, handing her coat to the maid and nodding to the woman.

I didn't know whether her statement was an invitation to me or an order to the servant, so I said nothing. I stood awkwardly near the front door, waiting for some signal.

Ordinarily, Harpur would have laughed pleasantly to see me confused, but it was a very sad day for both of us, and her spirits were very much dampened. She smiled softly and said, "Please, Ellis, come in. Have a seat. Shall I have Matthew light us a fire?"

I don't recall the day of Gleason's funeral to have been especially cold, though the snowy roads were the cause, at least in part, of his death. Nonetheless, I agreed to the fire. "Fine," Harpur said. I half expected her to ring a bell in order to summon Matthew, whoever he might be. But she didn't. She excused herself and disappeared.

I sat down. The furniture in the reception room was upholstered in beige silk. It was early afternoon, and the light, as I recall it now, was quite strong. It came through two huge windows, each swathed in curtains of the same soft fabric, and as it caught the sheen of the chairs and the couch, they almost glowed.

Over the mantel was a painting—a very modern painting, I thought—of what I at first took to be Harpur. But as I studied it more closely, I realized that it was neither as modern as it seemed, nor was it a very good likeness. Puzzled, I stood up and moved closer.

"It's Mother—when she was young—in the thirties. I don't mean her thirties," Harpur said with a rippling laugh, "I mean the nineteen thirties."

I turned abruptly, ashamed to have been caught studying the picture, which seemed very bad manners, but Harpur was still smiling. "She looks just like me—doesn't she?"

No, I wanted to say, *no, Harpur, no. For all her beauty, she's nowhere as beautiful as you—you standing there with your face as pale as all this silk and even your hair subdued by this flooding light . . .*

Of course I said no such thing. I just nodded.

Harpur laughed again, softly, quietly. "Come and sit down, Ellis, please. Make yourself at home. Matthew will light the fire in a moment, and tea is just about ready . . ."

I took a place on one of the couches and, to my pleasure and surprise, Harpur sat beside me.

I cannot after all these years remember what we talked about. I assume we shared our sorrow over the loss of Gleason. We must have commiserated over the sad state of William, too. He and Gleason had been "thick as thieves," as my mother would have said, had she ever met them. Despite being with him on nearly a daily basis, I knew little about William's background. In many ways his personality was as much a mystery to me as Harpur's—only less fascinating.

I suppose Harpur and I would have taken the tea brought by the silent servant, would have moved, perhaps, to a general discussion about our own plans. The five of us had spoken about this at length over the last year. Though Harpur mentioned assisting her father in his banking business, I had the feeling she really wasn't interested in her plans. She seemed more interested in talking about me.

The very idea filled me with a painful shyness. "I've joined a local firm," I said evasively.

"In Little Italy?"

Today, everyone would cringe at such a description of the upstanding Italian community in our city. I cringed then, too.

"Yes."

"I'm glad to hear that, Ellis. You're sensitive to the needs of people—kind. I can tell that. I know you're impatient and that it hasn't been as easy for you as it's been for the rest of us . . ."

Perhaps she sensed me stiffen at the suggestion that I might be disadvantaged. She rushed to make sure I didn't misunderstand her, and in so doing, she touched me, the first time she ever touched me on purpose. The feel of her hand on my arm distracted me from her words, but I forced myself to listen. I didn't want to miss any word of hers, even if it was an inadvertently hurtful word. "Our parents—Gleason's and Stow's and mine—they've been throwing money at us all our lives. We're bums, really . . ."

It was 1967, a time when the rich, as they had been before and would be again, were suddenly unfashionable.

"Harpur," I answered, laughing a little. "You are the last person in the world anybody would think of as a bum."

"But I am. For all my fine insistence on being treated equally all through school, I'm happy that my father paid every cent of what my long, long education has cost."

I didn't have the nerve to tell her that my education had also been paid for by a relative. How could my Italian uncle compare to Harpur's father, a banker whose family had helped found the university more than a century earlier?

I tried to pay attention to what she was saying, but as we sat there, she seemed to be moving closer. Though everything in me longed for another touch, I looked for an excuse to move away. In front of us, on a low table, sat a small round marble object. As if to study it, I bent forward.

So I wasn't looking at her when she said, "I've wondered about you, Ellis, for a long time . . ."

I was glad that I had not extended my hand to touch the object. Because then she would have seen my fingers tremble.

"What do you mean, Harpur?" I said, keeping my voice steady—my new lawyer's voice.

"I've wondered how a man like you keeps going."

Was she insulting me? All through university, my temper had been held in check simply because there was so little pressure on me. All I needed to do to please my father and satisfy my uncle was to get good grades.

"And why," I said, still not facing her, "do you think I need special effort to keep going?"

"Oh, Ellis," she said, genuinely surprised, "I've hurt your feelings! And it's absolutely the last thing on earth I would ever want to do. I just meant that for a spoiled brat like me for whom everything has been so easy, the struggle of a man like you is inspiring."

"Struggle?" I turned to face her.

In my too-brief, but still long, career, I have only once in a while seen a facial expression of such innocence that I believed it totally and at once. That was how Harpur looked in that moment. And so, it was I who apologized, not she.

"Forgive me," I said. "I'm too touchy."

"Oh, Ellis, I'd never forgive you if you were less touchy," she declared, moving closer still. I could feel the depression in the couch from the weight of her body.

She was a slender woman and it was firm upholstery.
The thought of her that close was unnerving.

So I stood up and moved toward the wide windows.
I could see trees, a hedge. But everything was as if
through a fog. Why was I here? How could I escape?
As if I really wanted to escape.

The expensive carpet muffled her movements, but I
was not surprised when I felt her hand on my shoulder.
"I only wanted to tell you how much I admire you,
Ellis . . ."

I turned. All I knew was she had said my name, her
hand was still on my shoulder, her perfume was like a
cape that she had drawn around the shoulders of both of
us the way my childhood picture of guardian angels had
shown them drawing capes of magic safety around their
charges.

When I turned, the hand that had been on my shoulder
was suddenly at my nape. Without another thought, I
put my arms around her. It was like holding air. It was
as if she weren't really there at all. Insubstantial. Nothing but an idea, an energy, a compulsion. I kissed her.

Her kiss was like her subtle, insisting perfume—rich
and exclusive. I wanted more. I wanted to forget the
tragedy that had brought us together. I wanted to forget
that I was here in her domain. I wanted nothing to distract me from this moment of rare and unexpected luck.

We kissed again and again. It seemed a very long time
until either of us needed a breath. Still, I was surprised
when Harpur pulled away. Feeling her withdraw, I was
released from the spell. My eyes had been closed. Now
they shot open. Though her face was upturned, I was
too overcome to look at her.

I looked past her. Beyond the window I saw a complicated brick driveway that curled from the street,
around the front of the house and toward the back. There
were only two people in the entire city who knew how

to create that pattern, and I was one of them, I, the son of the Angelo Portalese, the *brickiere*.

I made my apologies to Harpur, explained that I was so shaken by what had happened to Gleason that I must have lost my head, asked her for my coat, and left.

Was she hurt that I was so casual, so apparently dismissive of her feelings? I don't think so. Didn't dare to think so at the time. But to make sure, I mustered all the courage I had and called her the next day. "You're naughty, Ellis. Kiss and run. And now what, back for more?"

"No, I . . ."

"Tell you what. I promised you something. Let it be this: I promise to allow you to take me out to dinner—but no more kissing."

She laughed her rippling laugh and I laughed, too. Though I must have realized my golden moment of the day before was now most certainly over.

She kept her promise. She dined with me. She was as delightful and inaccessible as ever. Whatever our kiss had meant, it was never to recur. In fact, I was never alone with her again.

It was only a little past dawn, and I was dreaming about a persistent hand shaking my shoulder.

I awoke startled. I was staring right into the eyes of the young blonde police officer. Her pretty face was contorted into a grimace that I took for anger. I sat up, and her hand fell away. For a moment, I was frightened that that gesture might be construed as assault. To be arrested for trespassing—which I figured she intended—was bad enough, but to be arrested for assaulting a police officer would have finished me off.

"Easy," she said gently, as if she were concerned for me. "Take it easy."

She glanced around the site. "Looks like you've run into a little trouble down here . . ."

I knew better than to answer.

"Listen, oldtimer, I'd be happy to take you to a shelter." Her eyes were a clear blue, like the river on a winter day. I thought about my daughter, Ellen, who as a baby had her mother's coloring—Anne's silky blonde hair, her pure skin, her startling blue eyes. I remembered that when Ellen was an infant, I used to check from time to time to see whether her eyes were beginning to darken. One day, as I gazed at her, she blinked and smiled. It was the first time she ever communicated with me. I felt like bursting into song. Instead, I had patted her little head and left the room in satisfaction. It was hard to imagine never seeing Ellen again. No.

"No," I said.

"No shelter?" The policewoman shook her head, as if I were passing up some wonderful opportunity that would never come my way again. I wished every tender-hearted do-gooder in the whole city could be treated to a night in a shelter—just so they would wise up.

"Why don't you think it over . . ." she said with exasperation. Giving somebody the opportunity to "think it over" was a police officer's way of saying, "I don't feel like taking you in right now, but next time I might be in a different mood." I didn't know why she was giving me a break, but I wasn't in a position to ask questions. It would take me at least a couple hours to move my stuff, and I knew I better get started as soon as she left. I had to get her off my back. I *did* need to think about things.

"This is public property. Illegal use constitutes trespass. I'm sure I don't have to explain that to you."

"What?" How did she know I was likely to know the law?

Her little cop face was perfectly unreadable. "We're through with this conversation, sir. You belong up on the street. I don't want to see you down here again."

I decided to move my stuff immediately—across the

river, through the woods on the other side, and closer to the tree where I had hidden my suit. I'd only be able to take essentials, including the suit, which I could put back in the tree when I had time. I also had to take my judge's gown, which I kept in my hut and which, mercifully, had escaped the notice of the vandals.

Besides those precious items of clothing, I took blankets, my few tools and utensils, a couple of books, and as many planks of wood as I could carry. I had to take things an armload at a time, and it seemed to take forever.

The new site had water and cover—everything I needed, except my garden. As I surveyed the set-up, it occurred to me that this was more accessible by water than the old site. But in all my time in this ravine, I had never seen a canoe on the river.

Each time I returned to the old site, I sneaked up on it because I was afraid the police or the vandals might come back. Finally, after several hours, everything was moved, and I had rebuilt a fair approximation of my packing-crate mansion in the new location. Once more, I felt safe.

I found some mushrooms and greens in the wood and made myself supper. I thought for sure that the moment I finished eating, I'd fall asleep.

Instead, I felt overcome by restless frustration. I hadn't accomplished a thing by talking to Aliana. I thought that maybe I should have pursued the pimp angle by talking further to Queenie.

Late as it was, I decided to go back to the Track. It had only been a couple of nights since my bath and haircut. Of course the good effect of my shave was long gone, but by the dim light of the Track, I must not have looked completely destitute because a number of girls approached me rather hopefully as I walked down the street.

It was while I was distracted by thoughts of avoiding

them that I bumped into Moonstar. Despite the relative
warmth of the night, she was shivering, as if she'd been
working her corner for a while.

"Hi . . ." I said tentatively.

She looked me over with the hooker's quick, assess-
ing glance. Her eyes widened, and I knew she thought
I was a trick.

"Looking for some company tonight?" she asked.
Her voice was low, husky. I hadn't remembered that,
and for a minute, I thought I'd made a mistake. But then
she tossed her head and her beautiful hair caught the
low gleam of the streetlight.

At the same time, she recognized me. "You . . ." she
said. "I been looking for you. We gotta talk . . ."

I thought she might have some sort of message for
Queenie—or from her. I looked around. There was nobody. No customers. No cops. No pimp.

"I could take you for a coffee," I offered, "if you
have a minute."

She laughed, shivered again, and pulled her thin
blouse across her chest. I saw that she had on a delicate
silver necklace with an unusual pendant of turquoise and
coral. Under the blouse she wore a tight top of some
other flimsy material. It matched her short skirt. No
wonder she was so cold. "I got the time if you got the
money."

"I have enough to buy you a coffee," I lied. "Your
man allows you to have a coffee now and then, doesn't
he?"

"Only with him."

"But he's not around right now is he?"

"No," she said carefully. "He's not here tonight.
He's . . ." A car went by, close to the curb. As if remembering what she was supposed to be doing, she
moved closer to the street. She leaned over a little and
again let her hair fall in front of her shoulders so that it
swung over her breasts.

Thinking fast, I slipped into the shadows behind her. Whatever I might feel about prostitution, I didn't want her to suffer from missing a date because of me, and she didn't. The car slid to a stop, she leaned further, negotiated for a minute, then slid in beside the driver.

I used the time well, hitting strangers up for a few dollars. I seldom begged, but I figured nobody would recognize me in this part of town.

When Moonstar got back, I was waiting for her. "What's on your mind, Moonstar?" I asked when her trick had pulled off into the checkered darkness.

"The other day I seen Johnny Dirt. He says he knows you."

"Yes, he knows me."

"He says you used to be a judge."

I hesitated. Once in a while somebody asked me to help them or their relatives or friends out of some legal fix. And when I refused, which I always did, there was sometimes a big argument. Had Moonstar's pimp been picked up? Is that what this was all about?

"So," she persisted. "*Are* you a judge or no? Because if you are, there's something I gotta tell you about Second Chance."

"Yes. Yes, I'm a judge, but . . ."

"Okay then, let's go for that coffee."

We headed for the nearest donut shop, where I bought her a coffee, which she gulped down, hot as it was, so I bought her another. I didn't buy one for myself. I'd run out of cash.

"What's the matter, Moonstar? I thought you'd left that hostel."

For a minute she just sat there sipping her coffee. She turned to face me, and I could see something of the real Moonstar behind her heavy make-up, for her eyes were full of such a combination of weary sadness and youthful vulnerability that I felt like hugging her.

"A judge is a person who finds out whether a person is guilty, right?"

"Well, yes. Sometimes. Often you need a jury, too."

"But a judge could do it alone—like a detective or something?"

"What do you mean?"

She thought for a minute. On the paper cup that her coffee was in, her lipstick had left a garish red imprint. It looked like half of a sad, tired smile. Her hands seemed to tighten around the cup. They were scratched, and I couldn't tell what from—drugs, a fight, the passion of a client? Her skin was pale bronze, and in the web between her left thumb and forefinger, she had a tattoo— a black spider so realistic that I fought the urge to tell her to brush it away.

On any Saturday morning in Old City Hall court, I might have seen a dozen girls like Moonstar. And if it were a holiday, or tourist season, or any other time when the police were instructed to "sweep" the streets, I might have seen a lot more.

Communicating for the purposes of prostitution was a relatively minor criminal offense under our law. I always thought it a much greater offense to put a kid like Moonstar behind bars—even for the hours between being picked up on Friday night and being shoved into court lock-up on Saturday morning, preparatory to being released on recognizance and back on the street in time for the Saturday night shift.

Once or twice, a girl seemed in such bad shape that I sentenced her to detention just so she could have a shower and a warm place to sleep. I wished I could do it again so I could help this girl. I couldn't even scratch up enough money to buy her something decent to eat.

"I mean," Moonstar said, "that somebody who knows how to find out whether somebody has killed somebody needs to know about Second Chance because it's not a safe place; it's not a safe place at all."

"What?"

She looked at me with a sidelong glance that made her look over forty instead of under twenty. "People have been missing from there . . ."

"People, you mean more than one?"

She didn't answer at first. She knocked back the dregs of her coffee. The lipstick smile was blurred on its rim. "People," she repeated.

She swung around on the donut shop's patched red stool. Now she was facing a smudged window that managed to give a pretty clear view of the street. She studied the sidewalk for a while.

"It's real slow out there, tonight," she observed. "Business is rotten." She swiveled around so that she was facing me, "You know what that means," she said matter-of-factly. She drew her fingers across her neck in the classic throat-slit gesture.

I swiveled on the seat, away from her old, innocent eyes.

"You're really, like, a bum, aren't you?" she asked.

"Yes," I answered without looking at her.

"But you used to be a judge?"

"Same difference!"

She laughed a sweet, soft laugh.

"Well, Mr. Judge Bum, could you beg me some supper so I can eat and still have something to give my old man when he comes back to town?"

"Yes," I said. "Yes, I think maybe I could do that."

"I could tell you more about that hostel."

"It's a deal."

CHAPTER

SEVEN

IT TOOK ME ONLY AN HOUR TO BEG ENOUGH TO BUY Moonstar's supper. She chose a submarine shop, and to spare her the embarrassment of having me watch her eat, I waited outside until she finished.

Gratitude—or perhaps just food—made her friendly, almost effusive. "So," she said, "I'm ready if you are."

I smiled. "Let's just walk and talk, shall we?"

She smiled back and shook her head, tossing her lovely hair. "You really talk like a gentleman. You walk like one, too."

"And how does a gentleman walk?"

She did a creditable imitation of Charlie Chaplin's strut, which left both of us laughing.

When the breeze died down the night was pleasant, and a few turns brought us to neighborhoods less noisy and bright than the streets of the Track. The relative darkness hid the fact that we made a straggly pair indeed—a voluptuous girl in tight clothes and a tattered man past his prime.

Yet, as we walked, we became so engrossed in our conversation that we gave no thought to who might see us and what they might think.

"That hostel," she began, "it has a name . . ."

"Second Chance . . ."

"Yeah," she answered, "that's right. And I think that name is a—what do you call it when something means

more than one thing—like two things at the same
time?"

"A double entendre?" I suggested.

She stopped in the middle of the sidewalk, laughed,
shook her head and said, "Are you kidding? Nothing
fancy like that!"

"All right, let's think again. Maybe you mean a pun."

"Yeah. That's it exactly. A pun. Like you say one
thing, but really you mean something else. Well, the
people at that hostel, the social workers and them, they
make this big deal about how when you go there you're
getting this second chance. You're getting to start all
over and make a new life and all that . . ."

"I'm sure that's what the hostel intends to do . . ."

"Yeah, well that's what they want you to think. That
it's your second chance. But the way the pun comes in
is this. It's not really your second chance at all. It's
somebody else's second chance."

"What do you mean?"

She leaned closer and put her hand on my arm. Her
fingers were long and slender, but her nails were bitten
to the quick. I recalled Anne's nails. They were smooth
and shapely and always subtly colored to coordinate
with her elegant clothes. She spent more in a week to
keep them that way, I was sure, than Moonstar spent on
herself in a year. "They sell something there—something rich people can't get anywhere else. I'm sure of
it."

"What could they possibly sell in a hostel? Not drugs;
certainly not guns . . ."

Moonstar's low voice was suddenly even lower. I had
to lean very close to hear. "No," she said, "anybody
can get those anywhere—can't they?"

"I guess so."

"No. What they sell is babies . . ."

I stopped in my tracks—sure she was fooling me, trying to make me look like a sucker for believing that even

if she did know something, she'd be stupid enough to tell it to somebody like me for the price of a couple of coffees and a submarine sandwich.

"Weird, isn't it?" she said with no mockery, no malice. "But I thought about this all for a long time, and I think I got it figured out . . ."

Moonstar began to present her case to me. As with my learned brethren in the law, so with Moonstar. I kept quiet and listened respectfully to her submission.

"First of all," she said, "rich people run these places. I mean real rich people. The nicer the hostel, the richer the people that run it. If a thing is run by the government, then everything is just as good as it's supposed to be—no better. But rich people, they can't stand to have their name on stuff that isn't nice. You get me?"

"Yes."

"And another thing about rich people is that they don't ever do something for nothing. They only do stuff when they're going to get something out of it, something more than what they put into it, like, you know, profit."

"I'm sure Second Chance is a nonprofit charity," I objected.

"Yeah," she said, with that little note of triumph of one who is using her opponent's point to bolster a point of her own. "So if they aren't getting profit out of Second Chance, what are the rich people getting? Now, before you say they're getting money off their income tax, which I know they are, answer me this—aren't there easier ways to get money off your income tax than helping pregnant girls?"

"Maybe," I answered, "and maybe not. What do you think, Moonstar?" I was coaxing her, just as I had so often caught myself coaxing young, promising lawyers. Not right. Not fair.

"I don't think it's enough," she replied. "I don't think those people would go to all that trouble just to get money off their tax. I think they're getting something else. If they're not getting it for themselves, then they're getting it for their friends and relatives. And what could they be getting? The only thing is babies.''

"Look," I said patiently, wanting to let her know that what she was saying made sense only in a limited way, "what you're saying seems logical, but there are some other things that maybe you haven't thought about."

"Yeah, like what?"

"Well, there are other benefits to becoming involved in a person's community as a volunteer at a place like Second Chance. You can have a say in how things are done. You can help people . . .''

"Oh yeah?" she said belligerently. "Well, Mr. Bum on the Street, just how many people do you run into that want to help you for nothing?"

"None."

"Right. And anyway, I'm not making this up. I know because it happened to me."

"What?"

"I was there myself. I was, like, a customer or whatever you call it there at Second Chance."

"A client?"

"Yeah. I was a client and they took my baby. I think they sold it."

I started to feel dizzy. Whether it was because I hadn't eaten much in the last few days, or the running around, or the having to move my home, or the disrupted sleep, I didn't know.

"Hey—you okay?" Moonstar said. "You look sick or something."

"I'm not sick. Just tired. I need to sit down."

"Can you make it to the parkette?"

Across the dark street, I could see trees outlined against a streetlight. It was dangerous to sit in places like that after dark, regardless of the neighborhood, but in that moment it seemed that neither I nor Moonstar had much to lose. "I'm about ready to fall down, but let's try."

She put her hand on my shoulder, as if to guide me. As physical support, the gesture was useless, but there was an unexpected comfort in her touch. Was that what men paid her for?

I considered telling Moonstar just to leave me alone in the parkette, but somehow the words failed me. We found a bench and sat down. I rested my head against the hard wood and closed my eyes. There were more stars in the constellations behind my eyelids than were visible in the downtown sky.

"You any better?" Moonstar asked. "This ain't exactly an excellent place to hang out . . ."

I opened my eyes. My head was clearing. It was time for me either to go home or find some spot to sleep in. And Moonstar had already lost at least an hour's work. The situation was growing rapidly more unsafe for both of us.

"I just need to sit here for a few minutes. Why don't you talk to me some more? Just keep telling me about the hostel. What did you mean when you said that you knew about babies because it happened to you?"

"Like I said, I was a customer at the hostel a couple of years ago. I was fifteen. I wasn't working the street then. I was at home and my parents were on my back all the time. 'Go to school. Get a job. Stay away from drugs. Stay away from boys.' I got pregnant and I ran away. One day I really needed something, like a lipstick or a bottle of aspirin. Anyway, I lifted it from a drugstore."

"Yes . . ."

"The store guard sees me and does this big routine. Next thing I know, I'm at the police station. It was Sunday—no courts are open or anything. They find out I ran away and they make me this offer. I can stay in jail overnight or I can go home to my parents. Some offer. I picked jail.

"On the Monday, I went to court. Somewhere along the line, they got to asking me about being pregnant, which it was obvious I was—seven months. Then, one thing sort of led to another thing and I got sent to the hostel.

"I was mad at first, but to tell the truth, it wasn't so bad. The food was good and the counsellors weren't the worst I ever saw. I didn't get along with the other girls, though. They were all stuck-up types that accidentally got in trouble—not street kids at all. And everybody seemed kind of quiet, like they always wanted to keep their mouth shut. Well, that's okay, I understand that scene.

"Another thing I noticed was that there were a lot of rich people visiting all the time. Sometimes we had to talk to them—tell them about ourselves and our lives. Every time a rich person asked to talk to one of the girls, they went in a little private room or alone together out on the patio. After I was there for a month or so, one of the rich people asked to talk to *me*. She told me that I was lucky to be at Second Chance. As soon as she said the name of the place, I got this funny feeling, the feeling that made me think of that pun thing—that the second chance wasn't for me or my baby at all.

"Anyway, in the end, it didn't matter. Something went wrong."

She looked down at her fingers as she spoke, as if searching for a new nail to bite. Not finding one, she rubbed her hands together and resumed her tale without looking up.

"One day, just out of nowhere, I got this pain. It was like totally unbelievable. I knew it was too early for the baby, so I knew something was really wrong. I was scared—no, terrified. But what happened was something even worse than if I had had to put up with the pain for a long time, the way the other girls said I would."

"What happened?"

"I don't know. I mean I never actually found out. It was like all of a sudden it was all over. One minute I had this awful pain, and the next minute I woke up from, like, sleeping for a long time, and I wasn't pregnant anymore. It was just all over. At first, I was real happy— man, you can bet on it!

"Then I thought about my baby. Where was my baby? All the time I was pregnant, I never thought about the kid, even when I felt it move inside of me. But when I woke up, and it was gone, I all of a sudden wanted it more than anything in the world. I tried to figure out where I was. It looked like a hospital. I started to get out of bed, but somebody must have been watching me somehow, because the minute I moved, the door to the room opened up and somebody came in. I just heard it, I couldn't really see the door from where I was laying on the bed. 'Where's my baby?' I asked. I turned around. It wasn't a doctor or a nurse. The person who came in the room was one of the counsellors from the hostel. She goes, 'I want you to be calm.' Then she tells me my baby is dead . . .''

I wanted to reach out to her and touch her, but I forced myself to stay still.

"I was real sad at first. Then I figured it out. My baby wasn't dead at all. That woman, the one that told me I was lucky, she bought it. She paid money to that hostel and she bought my baby . . ."

"Moonstar, even if the hostel lied to you, isn't it more likely that someone just adopted your child?"

She stiffened, anger contorting her face. "No!" she cried. "No. No. If a baby is adopted, they don't tell the real mother that the baby is dead, do they?"

I was afraid to say anything else. Her mood swing was rapid and dramatic. I just wanted her to calm down.

"Do they?" she demanded.

Before I had a chance to answer, I heard voices behind us—strong young male voices punctuated with hard laughter. I sat up straight. Moonstar also stiffened. "A gang . . ." she said softly.

A Native hooker and an old bum sitting together on a park bench in the middle of the night. What could make a gang member happier? Ten or twelve of them entered the park, keeping to its perimeter, the way I'd seen foxes keep to the perimeter of my compound in the ravine.

They kicked over every trash can in their path before selecting a picnic table to overturn. When they took out lighters, I thought they intended to set it on fire. Instead, without righting it, they sat on and around the table, pulled out cigarettes and commenced to smoke. They talked, but they were too far away for us to hear what they were saying, though we did catch periodic bursts of laughter that sounded threatening.

"They're like dogs," Moonstar whispered contemptuously. "If you stand still, they could sniff you and walk away, but if you run, they're going to chase . . ."

"We better stay here."

"Yeah."

I thought about what she'd said about her baby. I couldn't think of a way to restart the conversation, but I didn't need to. Moonstar wasn't finished.

"Even though they told me that my baby was dead, I was one of the lucky ones."

"What?"

"Yeah. Some of the girls didn't just lose their babies, they lost worse."

"What do you mean?"

"I was in the hospital for a couple days and I had time to think. If the hostel sold my kid, then they must have sold other babies, too. So when they took me back there, I started to ask around. At first, everybody told me just to shut up and forget about it. They said I was lucky to get rid of it and that if I didn't quit asking questions, I'd get thrown out. Big deal.

"One night, after everybody else was asleep, I got to talking to one of the girls and she told me her best friend used to live in the hostel. She got a pain just like me. The next day, the baby wasn't just gone—*she* was gone, too!"

"The mother was missing?"

"All her things were gone, too. All her clothes, everything. Even her stupid Second Chance environment mug with her name on it.

"I got kicked out the next day, but I didn't forget what happened. I sort of kept asking around. I found another girl that disappeared—I mean I found out her name and all kinds of stuff about her. Then I heard it happened again—to the girl who talked to me that night. I made the stupid mistake of telling my pimp about it. He beat me good for not minding my own business."

Another burst of laughter erupted from the darkness. Out of the corner of my eye, I saw one of the gang members lift his heavy boot and give the nearest overturned trash can a kick that sent garbage flying across the grass.

"Moonstar, why do you think all this means that people are selling children?"

"You take the baby and get rid of the mother. It's like getting rid of that chicken that lays golden eggs or whatever."

I suppressed a groan.

"You don't believe me, do you?"

"Yes, I do."

"It wasn't only babies and mothers that disappeared," she said. "I heard there was also a pimp."

"A pimp!"

"Yeah. They're like, you know, businessmen. They move around a lot. The good ones, they have girls in more than one city. Like my man. That's where he is now. In Detroit checking up on my wives-in-law. But usually they come back. I can't think of any pimp that ever disappeared except Solomon.''

"Solomon?'' It seemed an unlikely name for a pimp.

To my surprise, Moonstar laughed. "Yeah,'' she said. "We called him that from the Bible. One time this woman came and gave us Bible lessons—until she got caught by the social workers because nothing's supposed to be about religion at that hostel. But the woman, she already told us about King Solomon and that he was real wise—which meant he always could tell other people the smart thing to do. Solomon the pimp was like that. He was a pimp, all right. I even met some of his girls. But he was real smart, and he liked telling other people what to do. I knew him from the street. I used to see him hanging around outside the hostel a lot too.''

I felt my heart start to beat faster. Two from the gang had broken away from the group and were headed right toward us.

"What did the pimp look like?'' I asked Moonstar. Maybe gang members *were* like dogs. I pretended I didn't see them.

"He looked like a pimp. Big. Cute.''

"Black?''

"Not all pimps are black, you know.''

That reminded me of Queenie. "Was *he*?''

"Yeah.''

There wasn't time for another word. I smelled sweat, stale cigarette smoke, urine, aftershave. I looked up expecting to see evil-looking, scowling teenagers.

But these were men, and one of them was studying me intently. "I know you,'' he said.

"I don't think . . .''

"Yeah. You're that judge—Portal.''

"Yeah,'' Moonstar said unexpectedly. "He is—so what?''

"I owe you one, man, that's what. I did an assault

when I was sixteen. Got tried in adult court. You gave me a break, man. Can I buy you a drink or something?''

''What goes around, comes around,'' Moonstar laughed.

A starving man doesn't look a gift horse in the mouth. The four of us repaired to the nearest McDonald's, after which I found a doorstep for my bed.

I got home at noon the next day. I roved in the ravine, trying to clear my head so I could put my conversation with Moonstar into perspective. The wildflowers of summer were replacing the wild flowers of spring. I saw yellow buttercups and early purple loosestrife and the occasional white bouquet of Queen Anne's lace. In protected pockets of the ravine, all manner of lilies greeted me—slim orange tiger lilies, buttery yellow lilies, startling red. Though I knew Tim Garrison considered them dangerous to the native species, I loved the criminal lilies that had escaped from gardens and greenhouses to go on the lam with me.

It was growing hot when, without thinking about where I was headed, I reached the part of the river crowned by my secret rock. I decided to take a swim.

I shivered as I plunged into the water. Though the river was still quite polluted, despite the best efforts of Tim Garrison and his fellow enthusiasts, here the gravel bed seemed to filter it, and the water ran clear and cold.

I lifted great dripping handfuls of it to my face, not losing myself so entirely that I let any of it run into my mouth or my eyes. For a little while, I forgot myself. I managed to dunk my whole body, then to jump up into the sun like some odd fish from whom the water splintered in glittering shards. I laughed out loud, then laughed again just to hear myself.

Since time had lost meaning, I have no idea how long I carried on in this foolish way, but when I was finished, I stretched out on the rough grass. Its prickliness reminded me of the time that Anne and I had developed an interest in exotic bath accessories. We found a seaweed gatherer in the Caribbean who regularly shipped us dried plants that we used to scrub ourselves. This cost thousands of dollars, especially since we had the things shipped directly to our friends as well. I don't know how long this fad lasted among us. I do know that the sharp grass of the valley against my belly felt just the same.

After an hour's idle rest, I decided to check the rock that served as my safe. I climbed up with no difficulty, negotiating the tricky swing of leg and foot with the ease of a much younger man. I slid the treasure box out of its hole. I lifted the lid.

At first, I thought the sun must have affected my eyes. Something was wrong. Something was missing—the ring I had taken off the hand!

Frantically, I poked through the other things in the box. Everything else was there, including my own ring.

Somebody was so close on my tail that they had found even this. I should have realized when I saw that photo in the library that despite all my joy at my free existence, I was neither free, nor safe, nor—and this was the worst—alone. To have someone watching me in the valley was to have what I had worked so hard to avoid—a jailer.

I felt a wave of dizziness. I nearly lost my balance. Forcing my fingers to be steady, I closed the lid of the box and put it back in its resting place in the rock. I no longer thought of it as a hiding place.

Already the coolness of the river against my body was a vague memory. I felt hot all over, and the rock burned against the soles of my bare feet. As carefully as I could, I swung around to get my footing for my climb down.

Just as I made it to the other side of the rock, I was stunned to clearly hear the soft neigh of a horse.

Frantically, I scrambled down from the rock. Even in the dryness of the hot sun, it was slippery, and I nearly lost my footing several times, scraping my ankles against sharp outcroppings.

The gravelly bed of the river cut into my feet as I ran, splashing and slipping toward the shore. Just as I got to the bank, my feet slid out from under me, and I flew up, then landed hard on both knees.

The pain nearly knocked me out, and I had to sit there in the water until I could get up enough strength to stand again. When I did, I watched a thin trickle of my blood mix with the river and slowly eddy away.

I managed to make my way up the bank, and limping along, I got to the place where I'd left my shoes. Without wasting the time to put them on, I carried them to the nearest patch of thick bush. There I hunkered—despite my discomfort—for nearly an hour until the birds resumed their song, indicating that no other human intruder remained near.

Was the police officer the only one tracking my movements? For her to destroy my site and steal the ring made no sense. Who else was following me? If they had found me in the secluded valley, that meant they might have seen me with Moonstar in the city—might even have overheard part of our conversation. I had thought that my connection with Moonstar was purely arbitrary, that she was just somebody Queenie was looking after in her way. But maybe this wasn't the case. Maybe Queenie had known something she hadn't told me. Maybe her sending me to Moonstar was more than an act of charity.

I needed to find out who was watching me—and who had stolen the ring. I needed to know why that picture of me and my hut was in Aliana Caterina's computer file.

And if Aliana wasn't going to help me find the answers to these questions, I would just have to go back downtown and find them for myself.

CHAPTER

EIGHT

BEFORE I COULD DO ANYTHING ELSE, I HAD TO PULL MY-self together, tend my wounds and get some decent sleep. That evening I cooked myself a stew of roots and greens and rabbit, flavored with "poor man's pepper," the dried seed pods of shepherd's purse I'd saved from the year before.

I noticed that my skin was beginning to itch. I used an infusion of the leaves of broadleaved plantain to soothe it and cleanse my knees. My feet, though the worse for wear, seemed okay.

I intended to make an early night of it, get a good rest, and get back up on the streets in the morning.

After supper I read, glancing up now and then toward the peaceful sky. The evening was warm. For the first time, insects bothered me as I sat by the river.

Out of nowhere came a memory. It was an afternoon in late spring, and our son and daughter were still young enough not to rebel when we took them on outings. We were in a large park, probably High Park in the city's west end. We were picnicking. I had spent the afternoon hiking in the wooded area of the park with my son. I often wondered whether Jeffrey took after his grandfa-ther, the diplomat. He was at all times calm, pleasant and controlled. He always graciously accepted anything I gave him and never asked for more. In fact, he never seemed to ask for anything. I should have questioned that, of course, but I never took the time. That afternoon, I had been showing him various mosses and ferns. He had been showing appropriate interest. At the end of our walk, he politely thanked me, as if our business for the day had been concluded.

My mother had cooked a huge Sunday dinner and taken it to the park in a complex array of bags, boxes and baskets, which Anne, my sister, and my brother Michael's wife were helping to unpack. Their lively laughter seemed to enliven Jeffrey, who became animated the instant he joined them at the picnic table. If I felt a stab of envy or jealousy, I ignored it.

"Let the women do the work. Come and play *bocce*," my father called to Jeffrey and me. Having grandchildren had finally motivated him to speak English.

My son ran off to play with his grandfather and his sister and cousins. I hung back watching them all. Anne and my mother were talking about some recipe that Anne had just tried for the first time. Anne's fairness was a startling contrast to the dark hair and skin of the rest of the family, but whenever she was with them, her natural liveliness seemed to take over. "I have to cook it right," I heard her joke. "I don't want to poison His Honor—not now when he's just at the start of his brilliant career on the bench!"

The affection in her voice was unmistakable. I was close enough to hug her. She blushed. My mother said something in Italian, and my sister laughed. I didn't quite catch it, but I laughed too and gave Anne another little squeeze.

For a while after that, Anne and I were nearly as close as we'd been in the old apartment. But soon my new duties began to claim more and more of me. Within a few years of that picnic, I was so caught up with my work in court, my pandering to Stow's clubmen, and my consuming dedication to materialism that it would be inconceivable to eat in a public park, let alone find the time to do so.

I had nobody to blame for my pride but myself. I made my own bed, as my mother always said. A bed of nails.

As I sat and watched the sun make its long, slow descent into the water, I made my own long, slow descent into thoughts of the past. During my time in the mental hospital, I refused to see any family but my brother, Michael. I asked him to tell Anne to begin divorce proceedings. I had never opened up to Anne about my progressively debilitating anxiety, which I thought I was hiding well. My final breakdown had been a shock to me. But it must have been an even more shameful shock to Anne. I had wanted to spare her any further humiliation, and I hoped she had begun a new life.

Yet I couldn't help but wonder, did any of them ever think about me? Would any of them—Ellen or Jeffrey or even, someday, one of their children—look back on the good I had done and be able to forget for a moment what my pride and anger had done to our family? I dared to hope so. Judge not lest you be judged.

I woke up in the middle of the night out of a startling dream. Brush fire. The whole valley was burning. The trees were nothing but black skeletons against the flame. Foxes, raccoons, squirrels were screaming as they ran to the river. They weren't making it. They were being burned alive on the bank. I ran, too, trying to save them. Then I was burning—my hands, my face.

I sat up with a start. My face *was* burning. Not with fire. Was it sunburn? No. It was something else. Not just burning. It was itching, too, and it was covered with pebble-like little bumps. In the pitch blackness, I ran my fingers over my cheeks. Even through the down of my beard, I could feel an odd sensation of itchy burning roughness. Sickeningly, I realized I couldn't tell whether it was my face that was lumpy or my fingers. It had to be both.

Whatever this was, there was nothing I could do about it in the middle of the night. When morning came, I could make more of the plantain infusion. For now it would be best to go back to sleep.

And I did. But all night long I tossed and turned. Sometimes I dreamed of *La Mano Nera*—the black hand. I dreamed I met with a Mafia don, who was terrifying, even though he looked exactly like Pete the Shears. He demanded that I rig a trial. I refused. The next day, a courier arrived at my chambers with a package. Yes. Yes, of course it was the hand.

It seemed that I had slept for hours, but then I'd wake up, realizing that I'd been asleep for only minutes. This went on hour after hour.

When light came, I knew I'd have to rouse myself and do something about my condition. My mouth was stuck together with dryness, and I was so thirsty that my throat ached.

For a while, I only dreamed I'd gotten up and found the two bottles of fresh water I kept for emergencies, but finally I forced myself to really wake up. When I tried to stand, my knees buckled from the pain, and the crude hut circled wildly around my head.

I tried to steady myself by grabbing onto the makeshift walls of the hut, but they threatened to fall away at my touch. I stretched out my arms in a desperate attempt to gain my balance. Like a tightrope walker, I carefully tiptoed out.

The brilliant sun assaulted my eyes, and a wave of nausea swayed through me. Stumbling toward the place where I stored my water, I grabbed for the bottles.

The first I spilled while trying to take off the cap. The second netted me only a few drops before it, too, went flying out of my trembling hands, landing on the ground and quickly seeping into the thirsty soil.

But by that time, I had nearly forgotten my thirst. I was shaking so badly, was so hot and so cold at the same time, that I alternately shivered and tore at my clothes. They came away from my legs in shreds. I was astonished to see that where my skin had been lacerated by the rocks and stones of the river, it was now a festering mass of pus-soaked welts.

I came to now and then. Above me, the light changed each time. At times, I was sure I had crawled back to my shelter and was safe in my bed, but then I would wake again, feel the earth beneath me and see the sky above. Often, I didn't really know whether I was asleep or awake. Struggling to decide which, I clearly heard the running hooves of a horse. Involuntarily, I strained to call out. My voice was trapped in my throat.

I no longer cared what would happen when the policewoman found me. I thought I was dying and it didn't matter whether I died indoors or out, a free man or a captive, just so long as this burning stopped.

No matter how hard I tried to shout, no words came.

So I was astonished when suddenly, there was a soft, cool hand on my face, a hand unafraid of the ugliness that I was sure now devoured my skin. It *was* the policewoman. She had found me somehow. I tried to let her know how grateful I was, but she kept telling me to be quiet, not to try to move, not to talk.

Casting a cooling shadow with her body, she knelt over me, her long hair completely loose, her compelling eyes searching my face for signs of—what? Life, maybe.

"It's okay, sir," she said softly. "We'll get you out of here."

She put her smooth hand at the back of my neck and carefully raised my head. She produced a canteen, and from it she let a little dribble of fresh water slide into my mouth. I passed out again.

The next thing I knew, I was wide awake and it was

pitch black outside. I thought I must have slept away the entire day, must have dreamed the policewoman. I forced myself to get up and managed to make my way to my hut and to sink down onto my bed. Parched, but grateful, I gave myself to sleep.

The roar of the rushing waters went on and on. The sky outside burst open with the violence of a summer storm. Now, all I had to do was open my mouth and cool water poured into it.

Fortunately, I was far too sick to realize that the welcome water was coming right through the roof of my hut, too dazed to understand that I was consumed with fever and in danger of death from exposure.

I felt nothing but soothing coolness, heard nothing but the calm fall of rain. There was no fear, no discomfort, and most mercifully of all, no memory. I lay in a gray-green twilight into which moved from somewhere, the beat of a steady, musical rhythm, a sound as regular as a clock or a drum. I didn't know then that it was the sound of my own breath.

How many hours this went on, I have no idea. I only know that after a while, the sound of the rain seemed to part like a curtain to reveal other sounds, which I was able to figure out were voices.

"This way. Move along. Watch your step." I heard somebody shout. I couldn't tell whether it was a man or a woman, but whoever it was sounded authoritative— used to giving orders and being obeyed. "Move quickly. Keep going . . ."

"There's the hut," someone else yelled. "But I don't see Ellis anywhere. Ellis?" this voice cried out. "Ellis, are you here?"

This was a familiar voice, the voice of a friend. It took me a while, but I finally recognized that it was Tim Garrison. It seemed like such a long time since I'd seen him that I was happy to think that he'd come to visit. I tried to get up, to go to greet him. But I couldn't move. I did manage to say his name.

The next thing I knew, he was staring at me, trying—without success—to hide the look of shock on his face.

"Ellis," he said. "Geez, Ellis . . ."

"Tim," I said, "I think I'm sick."

He reached down and touched my shoulder. I could feel the warmth of his hand through the rag of my shirt. "It's going to be okay, man. We're here to help."

The next few hours I can only remember in the most scattered way—fragments of voices, splashes of sun and water, a sudden lurching jolt that ended with the hard smack of the earth against my cheek.

Later they told me it had taken four police officers to carry me in a litter up the muddy walls of the ravine and at one point, two of them had slipped on the sleek surface of the slope, flipping the litter and dropping me.

I spent a week drifting in and out of consciousness in Pleasantview Memorial Hospital. It was the opinion of three doctors and a city health official that my condition was the result of polluted river water infecting my lacerated skin. Which was a grave disappointment to Tim Garrison, who had thought the water was cleaner and safer than that. Every day, Tim came to visit me and regale me with theories about the river. Too sick to respond, I just lay there and listened to him. Now that I think of it, he may not have really noticed the difference between these conversations and the ones we usually had. I didn't mind his idealistic notions about how the city could harbor nature, about how the river could be reborn. I didn't even mind it much when he included my own rehabilitation in his plans, though I saw that as just one more pie-in-the-sky concept, like ending world hunger or recycling human waste into environmentally sound fuel.

After another week, I woke up to find all the elements

of a new set of clothes spread out at the foot of my bed—slacks, a fine shirt in pale blue, socks, underwear, even a jacket.

I was staring at these items, wondering which social service agency was using them as bait to lure me into its clutches, when a nurse came into the room and handed me a further gift: a smart shaving kit with razor, mirror, and everything else I needed to make myself fit company for the decent.

"What's all this? Who's it from?"

"Don't know," she said with a smile, "but you've got an hour to use it. Up and out. Today's your last day."

Since I had no other clothes, I had no choice but to accept this mysterious gift. I had to wait my turn for a shower, one of my wardmates getting there first. But I would have risked being ejected forcibly from the hospital before I would give up the opportunity of taking a hot, pounding shower. I certainly had no idea where my next shower might be coming from!

Two weeks of decent food and enforced rest had a rather remarkable effect, for when I looked in the mirror and saw the face there, I hardly recognized myself.

It was not, I hasten to say, the face of Ellis Portal before his fall. That old face had been very unlined for the face of a man of fifty. It had, as I may have mentioned, a certain arrogance to it, the type of arrogance that admirers call commanding and detractors consider proud. That face was framed by black hair. This one was framed by steel. The curls that I had so cursed as a young man had relaxed. My clean gray hair was smooth.

But as I looked at myself, I almost liked what I saw. The jaw, no longer rounded due to excess nor gaunt due to hunger, was square and strong. The eyes, though no longer "searching" as they had once been called by Aliana, weren't desperate, either. I thought they looked clear. I thought they looked like a pair of eyes that could see clearly, too, and I wasn't thinking about glasses, though I needed to somehow find new ones. I hadn't been able to read anything the whole time I'd been inside—I mean, in the hospital.

"Well," the nurse said when she came to tell me that the doctor wanted one quick look at me before I left, "not bad, not bad at all. I didn't realize how cute you are!"

She was cute herself, a healthy-looking bright woman of about thirty or so. It had been such a long time since I'd flirted—or been flirted with—that I didn't know what to do or say. Maybe she was just flattering me to make me feel better. I smiled. She smiled and winked. And I amazed myself by blushing.

The doctor, also young and female, seemed as impressed by my improved appearance as I was myself. "Good," she said, holding my chin and looking into my eyes. "Good," this was my pulse. "Very good," my skin. "You know," she said, "you're in very strong shape for a man who lives on the street. There's no reason in the world why you can't last another twenty years at least, if you get yourself into a program."

I nodded. The last thing I intended to do was get into a "program." All I wanted was to get out of there. Since my unknown benefactor, the bestower of razor and clothes, hadn't showed up, I allowed myself to think that within minutes I would once again be a free man.

Not exactly. "There's a woman waiting for you in the lobby," the nurse announced.

Pleasantview Memorial, which dated from the Second World War, was northeast of the downtown core. Perhaps it had once been in the suburbs, but now traffic pulsed past it day and night. I toyed with the idea of throwing myself on Queenie's mercy, but I was reluctant to violate the privacy of her room (if she had one), and I certainly wasn't looking forward to negotiating the streets in the busy neighborhood around the hospital.

Nor was I looking forward to meeting whoever was waiting for me in the lobby. Under ordinary circumstances, I would have just bolted, but I was still weak, the old hospital was labyrinthine, and the nurse kept her hand on my arm all the way to the lobby.

Though the medical facilities had been updated, the lobby retained the elegance of the late forties: dark green polished marble floors, steel-framed chairs with black leather seats. The walls were a lighter marble—a rosy tan that gave a feeling of spaciousness and light to the crowded foyer with its busy comings and goings.

At the still center of this flustering cloud of people stood a woman with her back to me—a slender, dark-haired woman in a summer suit. "There she is," the nurse said, then disappeared, the way busy people do.

Before I could figure out who this woman was and what she had to do with me, she turned. Aliana.

"Ellis," she said, walking quickly toward me, her fashionable shoes clicking assertively on the marble floor. "You look wonderful, just wonderful." She held out her hand, and when I took it to shake, she squeezed my fingers. Simple as it was, the gesture shocked me. What was she doing here? Had someone dispatched her to take me to some desperate hostel?

"Aliana, it's, uh, it's very nice of you to come, and I suppose I have you to thank for the clothes, but I . . ."

"You're welcome for the clothes. It's the least I could do. If I'd been a little more sensitive, a little more courageous the last time we met . . ."

Her charitable attitude angered me, but only a little. "You don't owe me anything," I said, "and I would certainly prefer not to owe you anything either. If you'd be so kind as to give me your address, I'll reimburse you for the clothes and the shaving things . . ."

"Take it easy," she replied softly, pretty much ignoring what I'd said. "I have my car. Can you walk out or do you want a wheelchair?"

Ordinarily, I'd have just pushed past her and stomped out. Maybe I was weaker than I thought because suddenly I found myself telling her that though I could certainly walk to her car, I'd definitely appreciate a ride downtown.

She was a competent, assured driver, and she wove into and out of the traffic with ease. I liked the way she let the wheel slide beneath her strong hands when we rounded a corner, as if she could let things go a little because she had set them on the right course. Did she think she was going to set me on the same sort of course?

"Are you hungry?" she asked, as casually as if there were no mystery at all about her showing up at the hospital. I was, in fact, less hungry than I'd been in five years, having had decent meals for fourteen days running, but when I opened my mouth, the words that came out were, "Yes, as a matter of fact, I am."

"Good," she said, making another of those smooth turns, "because I've got lunch all ready."

Before I could ask what she meant, she pulled up into the driveway of an elegant townhouse, pushed a button somewhere that opened a garage door, slid the car down a steep incline, and pulled us into darkness.

I felt a rush of fear.

"This stupid thing!" I heard Aliana spit into the black. "It's supposed to turn on the light when it opens the door."

She fumbled with a remote. "There—finally," she said as the garage sprang into light. "I know I'm taking liberties here; I wouldn't blame you if you thought I was kidnapping you . . ."

"You aren't, are you?"

"No. No, of course not. I spoke to Tim Garrison the other day, and he told me you were about to be released from the hospital."

I felt a prick of fear here, too. How did she know Tim

Garrison? Was my life now so completely public that anybody could find out anything about me, including my friends and the status of my health on any given day?

While I was contemplating this, Aliana got out of the car and unlocked a door that led to the house. The remote must have been working just fine then, because in the same moment that I heard the house door click unlocked, I also heard the garage door slide closed and click shut. Any hope of an easy escape was gone, not that running up that steep incline would have been easy for me.

She gestured toward the stairs that led from the door. I followed her up.

"How do you know Tim Garrison?" I asked, trying to remain cool.

She turned at the head of the stairs and stepped into a spacious, sunlit kitchen. It took my eyes a moment to adjust, and I almost smashed right into her. "Oh, Ellis," she said, "I'm so sorry. Everything I do to help seems to scare you . . ."

"What?" I was suddenly dazed. By the feeling that she could read my mind. By the loveliness of her home that seemed to be filled with flowers and sun and her fresh perfume.

"You have no way of knowing what's going on here, and I apologize for that. Tim and I, despite our best intentions, have been careless!"

"Can I sit down?" I asked, feeling suddenly dizzy. Maybe I should have stayed in the hospital another day or two.

She led me down another small flight of stairs, and we were in her living room. Despite the intensity of the sun, it was here filtered through closed blinds that shaded the room and gave it a Mediterranean coolness. I sank into a deep sofa.

I may have slipped into a doze at this point, because Aliana seemed to disappear. The next thing I knew, there was an intensification of her perfume and I opened my eyes to find her standing beside me with a glass in her hand. "Here," she said softly, "drink this . . ."

I sat upright, instantly wide awake. "What is it?"

She laughed and took a long drink from the glass. "Iced coffee. If it's poison, it's because of the caffeine in it, not because of anything I added."

I drank it and asked for more.

"Ellis," she said when she came back with a fresh glass, "did you read the papers when you were in the hospital?"

"No. I need my glasses to read. I wasn't carrying much with me when I was rescued."

"I know." She hesitated, and I got the feeling that there was something she was trying to decide whether to tell me. "I was there, Ellis—I was covering the story."

"Am I such a spectacle?" I demanded to know. "Am I such a curio that even when my life is in danger, I have the media tagging along?"

"I don't tag along!" she insisted. She didn't raise her voice, but she was quaking with anger.

"I'm sorry, Aliana . . ."

She was bristling now, like a little porcupine. As I always do when I meet a porcupine, I stepped well back.

"You really have some nerve, Ellis Portal, you know that? Just what is it you're trying to prove, anyway? Is this some sort of martyr thing? Like here you are this poor brilliant man reduced to hunger and homelessness by the hand of fate?"

Was I furious? Was I enraged? Was I even mildly angry at this outburst? No. I had to try not to laugh. "Aliana, please. Don't be angry with me. You're right. You're a fine reporter. I'm grateful. I'm . . ."

"Forget it. I didn't mean to be so sensitive. I still feel guilty about how I treated you last time. I was shocked when I saw you the day you showed up at the office. I shouldn't be so blunt, but let's face it, I'm a reporter, I say what I have to say. You looked so much worse than the time I'd seen you in the mental hospital. Nonetheless, I recognized you at once, and I know enough about the street to know that that suit meant some kind of maximum effort on your part. Hard to get. Hard to get into. You were after something major, that was for sure.

"I knew it wasn't cash, though I could also see you didn't have any of that. You're not the sort of man to turn up after five years just to ask for a handout. No. You were after something bigger than that."

I kept my mouth shut. I really didn't want Aliana Caterina, for all her street smarts and her sensitivity, to learn just what a big thing a handout can be.

"So I had to make a quick judgment and ask myself what it was you were after, and of course, it had to be one of two things. Either you wanted me to put you in touch with somebody else or you wanted information—which of course is what you *did* want."

"Which is why you were so touchy about your sources . . ." I couldn't help but interrupt.

"I'm always touchy about my sources," she answered. She was smiling, thank goodness.

"Yes."

"Well in my business, giving information for free is as popular as giving advice for free is to a lawyer, no disrespect."

"But . . ."

"But then I thought about what it must have cost you to come up there like that. Judging by the look of you, you'd probably planned it for a while. It seemed cruel just to turn you away by pretending to give you an appointment that both you and I knew you'd never keep."

"So you fed me, and now you're going to feed me again?"

"Does that bother you?" she asked evenly.

"Yes," I said truthfully.

"I said it before, Ellis—you don't owe me anything. But I'm getting off track here. I was as surprised when you disappeared as I had been when you appeared. I figured you were convinced I thought you'd killed somebody . . ."

"You did think that," I said, "and now you've changed your mind. Why? No, wait—before you answer that, answer my first question. How do you know Garrison—and while you're at it, how did the two of you know I was in trouble?"

"I want to tell you about that," Aliana began, settling into one of the comfortable chairs in the shaded room. "I checked on some things, just as you asked. First I found out that photo of you by your hut was taken by one of the paper's stringers. I called him and got him to admit he had gained access to an apartment overlooking the valley and got the shot using a telephoto lens."

"The apartment overlooking the place where the river winds around a large rock?" I asked in alarm.

"I don't know the ravine that well; all I remember is that he mentioned railroad tracks."

"Then he saw me from the other side . . ."

"Other side of what?"

"Never mind. So the photo was taken by some paparazzo out to make a buck?"

She laughed. "You know, you're a changed man, but every once in a while, I see the arrogant Ellis Portal of old."

"Well the old arrogant Ellis is sitting here inside me waiting for any little opportunity to be obnoxious."

She went on. "Anyway, I had to ply Mitch—the stringer—with a lot of Press Box beer before I could get him to reveal that he knew you were down there because he monitors the police band. He heard a call to the ravine."

I was puzzled. "But that was before I got sick."

"Yes. I managed to pin this down exactly. Unlike the

cumbersome old clipping services, today the library updates its files by electronic transfer. A big library can subscribe to top-of-the-line features. If it has your name in its clippings data base, it can get electronic transfer of a photo of you directly from the database of the paper—before the newsprint version even hits the stands. That photo was published the morning after you came to see me.''

''Then it could have been taken only days before?''

''It was taken on the fifteenth of May. On that day, Mitch picked up a dispatch of police and medical personnel to the Don valley near Ecclestone and Swift . . .''

''Those are two streets off Eglinton—near my ravine.''

''So Mitch tells me.''

I calculated back. ''The fifteenth of May could have been the day I found the hand.''

''I know. But by the time Mitch got there, the action was over.''

''I don't know what this means.''

''I know one thing it means,'' Aliana said. ''The police have their eye on you. Or at least they have had since the fifteenth of May. They asked Tim Garrison for assistance. He's helped with ravine rescues before. I met Garrison when I got there to cover the story. Mitch had called me. He said that since I was so interested in photos of you, how would I like to convince the paper to buy another one, a shot of the rescue. But don't worry. I had him take it from far enough away that your rash didn't show in the picture.''

After lunch, she insisted that I nap on a couch in the sunporch at the rear of her compact little house. Lush plants covered every window, spilling flowers into the room and scenting it with subtle, exotic sweetness. ''I have to go back to the office,'' Aliana said, ''and it'll be late before I get home. I promised Tim I would look after you. When you're rested, we can go over some more of what I found out. My notes are at work. I'll bring them when I come home. There's plenty to drink in the fridge—and stuff to eat if you're hungry.''

As if her promise of information wasn't sufficient inducement for me to stay she added, ''I hope you'll still be here when I get back, but if you're not, I hope you'll call Tim Garrison and let him know I tried . . .''

I really intended to doze for only a few minutes, but it was pitch black when I woke to the sound of a key turning. I jumped up, my heart pounding, unable to remember where I was. Then from somewhere beyond me in the darkness, a light came on and I saw Aliana in silhouette, her slender form outlined in the doorway, her hand raised and resting on its frame. ''Ellis,'' she said softly, ''are you still here?''

''Yes.''

''Watch your eyes,'' she said, and I shaded them as she turned on another light. She looked tired.

''What time is it?''

''It's after eleven. Looks like you've had yourself a good nap.''

''Looks like you've had yourself a long day.''

She came out into the porch and sat down. ''Just a typical one,'' she said. She lifted her shining hair and massaged her neck. ''I guess you haven't eaten since lunch?''

''No.''

''We'll have a snack, then. We'll need it. We have a lot of business to get through. I brought some files back. We can go through it all while we eat. I'll call out for something. Chinese? Pizza? Thai?''

''Could we just have something simple?'' I asked. ''Like maybe a Coke and a cheese sandwich?''

She laughed. ''I'll make us up something, then,'' she said. ''I'll just be a minute.'' She left me sitting there wondering whether she was really as gracious as she seemed, or whether she was stalling somehow. Was I really a guest or was I a captive? I couldn't afford to be either. I'd eat a little, and if she hadn't shown me those files by the time she went to bed, I decided I'd get up while she was sleeping, find the files if they existed, read them, then head downtown toward Queenie.

When Aliana came back, she was wearing jeans and a tee-shirt. She looked like a teenager. She was balancing a plate of sandwiches and a plastic bottle of soda in one hand. In the other, she clutched a thin file folder that couldn't have held more than a few pieces of paper.

She pulled a little rattan table into the middle of the room and arranged a chair at either end. She put down the plate, the soda and the file, then she went to find drinking glasses.

I resisted the temptation to look into the file before she came back. Then I remembered that without my glasses I wouldn't be able to read it. When she came back the second time, she was carrying not only the drinking glasses but also a little package from a drugstore. She handed it to me. "Thought you might appreciate these," she said.

I opened the bag and inside I found a pair of reading glasses, the kind they have on a rack with little tags that tell you, "If you can read this tag, this is the right strength for you."

She got right down to business, attacking the file before the food. The first page was a scribbled mess of handwritten jottings, but Aliana didn't seem to have any trouble reading from them as she summarized her findings with the precision of a court reporter reading a transcript. "After I ran down the photo of you, I tried to get something on the rings. I'm sorry to say I came up a total blank. The pawnbrokers on Church Street were not helpful. One summed up their attitude by saying, 'I only talk to customers or cops. Show me your money, your badge or get out.'

"I was much luckier with the lawyers. Your old

friend, William Sterling, has a well-established law practice. He has an office on Parliament and caters to a local clientele. Does family law, some litigation, some immigration and quite a bit of human rights stuff—including same-sex spousal insurance benefits.

"Harpur Blane Stoughton-Melville . . ." Aliana continued, shooting a cautious glance my way. I nodded and she went on. "No professional credentials. Heavy commitment to volunteer charity work. Want a list of the charities?"

"No, thanks. What else?"

"I ran her name through the computer at work, and I found one small item that didn't have anything to do with her charity work. About six years ago, she was treated for some undisclosed condition. She was flown to the States, and on her return spent a few months in a private clinic. All of this information was squeezed into two sentences in a gossip column. I found no further mention of it. Face-lift, no doubt . . ."

I nodded again, then took a breath. "And Stow . . .?" I asked.

"I'm still working on that," Aliana answered. "He's going to Ottawa for his swearing-in probably in September. Becoming a judge means that between now and then, he's got to divest himself of his law practice. I suppose his law firm will go on as it has—it bills millions of dollars a year and is under the control of a CEO. I guess Stow will just step down from the board of the corporation. But his own practice is worth almost a million a year, and he has to give that up altogether. In order to take a job that pays about one hundred thousand a year!"

"But guarantees him a place in judicial history."

"Right up his alley, isn't it?" She put down her sheet of notes. "It doesn't sound like much, now that I read it to you—but it's a start."

"It's a great start, Aliana." Especially considering

that I was expecting nothing. "Anything else?"

"Yes. I thought maybe I should have a look at the missing person angle, too. Looking for a missing person—in any community—is like proving that something doesn't exist or proving somebody is innocent. You can prove existence and you can prove guilt, but proving an absence is almost an impossibility. Of course," she said, "I don't have to explain that to a judge, do I?"

An ex-judge, I wanted to remind her, but I didn't.

"So I had to ask myself what *can* I prove? Now there are hundreds of thousands of members of the black community in this city. As in any city, most are simply private citizens minding their own business. As you might expect, the only way you know whether they are present and accounted for is if somebody complains that they haven't been seen."

She lifted the second sheet from her file. It had four names on it. "These are the only reported missing adults from that community in the past eighteen months. One unfortunate man was an Alzheimer's patient who wandered away from home care and was found dead eleven days later. One woman showed up at the home of relatives and another was located at a shelter. The fourth man is a prominent businessman who escaped up north to his cottage."

"You wrote about him," I commented.

"Yes." She pulled a third sheet from the folder. "These," she said, "are missing adolescents . . ."

This, unfortunately was a much longer list and a much more difficult puzzle. "Kids run away all the time . . ."

"Right," Aliana answered. "Most of them end up back home on the same day. But lots don't. They could be on the street, they could be in another city. They could also be dead."

"I don't think I'm looking for a young man," I said, "but I'd still like to have a look at that list."

She gave it to me, reached for a sandwich with one

hand, poured herself a drink with the other. I felt as if she were studying my face as I read. I was distracted for a moment. Did she still think I was handsome? Once she had described me as handsome. But that had been years before. I forced myself to concentrate on the list.

There were dozens of names on it, and I couldn't always tell which were male and which were female. Out of the distant past came a memory about my sister Arletta. When we were at school, the others used to tease her all the time. "Are you a boy or are you a girl, Arletta? What kind of name is that?"

Gender didn't make any difference. All the kids on this list were in trouble, whether they were female or male. Beside each name was typed the last known address. Often the same address appeared over and over. It took me a minute to realize that these must be runaways from shelters and group homes. It took me another minute to see that two girls on that list had disappeared from the street address of the Second Chance home for single mothers.

"What is it, Ellis?" Aliana asked. I must have been right about her studying my face if she could see my puzzlement that quickly.

"Some of these young people have disappeared from a hostel called Second Chance," I explained. "I have a young friend who told me the same thing."

"Unfortunately," Aliana said, "it happens all the time. The population of every hostel is very transitory."

"But these girls were pregnant, or else they had recently given birth. It would seem unlikely that they'd just run off."

"Stranger things have happened." She paused. "Despite the good work they do, a hostel isn't exactly the sort of place that a girl who's used to her freedom would want to stay in any longer than necessary. Judges sometimes sentence girls to places like that, don't they?"

"They can," I answered, "but it's more likely that a

girl would be referred to a program as an alternative to sentencing.''

''You mean a lawyer might make a deal, or something like that?''

''Yes. I often had lawyers come before me on such matters. A girl might be charged with some relatively minor offense. She might be homeless and in trouble.''

''But you're not looking for a girl.''

A thought struck me. ''Aliana,'' I said, ''could you check one more thing for me?''

''I guess so. What?''

''Could you try to find something on an adult male pimp with the street name of Solomon? Maybe you could run the name through the computer, or even ask your photographer pal, Mitch. If he's so clever that he can get a picture of me from listening to police conversations, maybe he can find Solomon.''

''Is this Solomon black?''

''Yes. But whether he's alive is anybody's guess.''

CHAPTER

NINE

IT WAS WELL PAST MIDNIGHT WHEN WE FINISHED OUR discussion. I had little choice but to agree when Aliana suggested that I spend the night on her couch. I really had no further need for sleep, so I spent the long dark hours puzzling out our mystery. By morning, I was no further ahead.

As she left for work, Aliana mentioned again that I hadn't read the papers the whole time I was in the hospital. For a journalist to go without reading the paper every day held far more significance than it did for me, who hardly ever read one in the same month in which it had been printed.

But when she left—again trusting me alone in her house—I attacked a stack of newspapers that she left with me. I started from the bottom up—chronological order. About three weeks back, I came upon a small article about the possible murder of a prostitute on the Track. Always fuzzy on dates, I couldn't be sure, but I figured this girl had to have been killed about the same time as I had been prowling around looking for information.

When I realized this, a sickening suspicion hit. At the bottom of the page was a picture of the body. I held it closer to the new glasses Aliana had bought for me. The dead kid had her arm extended, the palm of her hand facing up as she lay on the pavement. There was a dark spot just visible between her index finger and her thumb. I couldn't see it clearly, but I knew I had seen it before. It was a spider tattoo. The dead hooker was Moonstar.

I considered calling Aliana at work and leaving a message, but that didn't feel right. I thought about writing her a note, but that didn't seem right, either. So I just left. I had to get to Queenie.

It was June, normally a pleasant month in Toronto, but the day was unseasonably hot. The streets were steaming, and I'd only gone a few blocks before I was steaming, too, though my personal hygiene on this morning had been impeccable because I'd used the supplies Aliana brought to the hospital. I had to leave most of them behind, but when I stuffed the last of the few things I could carry into my pocket, I discovered that she'd tucked a fifty-dollar bill in among the toiletries. I wasn't too proud to take it, though I knew I'd have to break it right away while I was still clean and decently dressed or it would be as good as worthless.

I had to plan what to do with the money. I bought a good supply of subway tokens for a start. Then I had breakfast in a restaurant that I used to frequent when I was on the bench.

I didn't know whether it was the ambiance, but I now felt the obligation to offer my formal condolences to Queenie. I had no idea what relation Moonstar had been to her, but it didn't really matter.

I had forgotten how good it felt to be dressed in clean, new clothes, to see something—even something as simple as an egg and a slice of toast—and to decide to have it and to have it without the least fuss or bother. I had forgotten what it felt like to be completely ordinary, to attract no attention whatsoever. In my other life, my old life, I had considered it a sign of failure not to be noticed, not to stand out. But on that day, as I sat like any other customer enjoying my breakfast, I felt myself disappear into the crowd, and I liked it.

But once I got back on the street, my new clothes were a bit of a detriment. Finding Queenie was harder than usual because none of our mutual acquaintances recognized me at first, and when they did realize it was me, I had to put up with a lot of ribbing. "Won the lottery, then, did you?" was the most common comment, and it did not come without the outstretched hand. By the time I found out where Queenie was, I had very little left of the fifty.

I found her sitting on a bench in the same park where'd I'd sat with Moonstar the night the girl was killed. I felt a stab of guilt when I saw that Queenie was sitting tall, like some sort of royalty. Instinctively I knew that this was the dignified posture of her grief. When I got closer, I was shocked to see just how devastated she looked. Her dark eyes were distant beneath the sweep of her finely arched brows, and they looked red from weeping. Her square jaw was set, and her shoulders, which I had never noticed before, were as gracefully curved as a girl's, but rigid now with self-control. It seemed to take a minute for me to register with her, and when she finally squinted up into the sun, she drew in her breath in surprise.

"Your Honor," she said. "What are you doing here? I heard you were real sick."

I took the liberty of sitting down beside her on the park bench. "I was," I said, "but I'm better now. I ran into a couple of friends who got me out of the hospital, put me up for a night and gave me clothes."

"Look good on you," she observed, but her eyes were soon staring off into the distance. I was never one for small talk, even in the days when Anne and I would go to a dinner party every night of the week. "Queenie," I said as gently as I could, "I'm sorry about Moonstar."

"Your Honor, you talked to her, didn't you?"

I wasn't prepared to lie, but on the other hand, I also

wasn't prepared for the woman's grief. "Yes, Queenie, I did talk to her. But I never meant to get her in any trouble. It's the last thing . . .''

"My poor girl—my poor little girl! She's been in trouble since the day she was born. It's my fault. I did what I could, but there was no way it could ever be enough.''

"I'm sure that everything you did for her was the best you could do,'' I said lamely, wanting to help but having no idea what I was really dealing with. "Was she your granddaughter?''

For the first time, Queenie met my eyes. I was stunned by the depth of her sorrow, and surprised when she slowly shook her head. "No, Moonstar was not my granddaughter. And Moonstar was not her name. That was just her street name, her hooker name. Her real name was Margaret Louise. I named her that because I wanted her to grow up to be like another Margaret Louise that I met once—a woman with education and manners—real nice manners.''

"You named her?''

"Of course I named her. She was my child. My only child. My daughter . . .''

I stared at her in amazement. I had always thought of her as older than myself. Her daughter hadn't been twenty years old.

As if she could read my mind, she smiled and said, "You know, Your Honor, you're kind of innocent, like. You've been on the skids for a while, but there's still a lot of things you just don't get. You always treat me like an old woman, and I let you because I figure, what's the harm? But you're way older than me. And dressed the way you are today, so elegant and all—well, it makes me think that maybe you're the one who should be thinking about grandchildren.''

"How old was Moonstar—Margaret?''

"She was seventeen, and she'd been working for a

while. I tried to talk her out of taking up the Life—but who was I to tell her a thing like that? I was a hooker myself when I was her age.'' She smiled her sad smile. ''And way past that age, too . . .''

''The police told you how Moonstar died?'' I asked carefully.

''Yes. And I told them about that hostel. Margaret didn't talk much to me anymore, but whenever she did, she talked about her time there. It was a . . . What do you call it when you can't stop thinking about a thing?''

''An obsession?''

Queenie's eyes filled with tears. I reached out to touch her arm, but she brushed my hand away. I had no right to touch her, and I knew better than to try, but I couldn't shake the thought that Moonstar's death was at least partly my fault.

She composed herself, drew in a deep breath and said, ''She was crazy. She thought her baby was stolen.''

''Why, Queenie? Why would she think a thing like that?''

''I don't know.'' Queenie glanced around the park. It was by no means empty. It never was. During the day, the park's clientele was nowhere near as disreputable as it was at night, but there were still a couple of drug deals going down in the shadows of the maples. There were also a few mothers fussing with small children as they visited with each other, used to the park and unafraid. I didn't know which Queenie was looking at—the dealers or the mothers.

''Margaret Louise didn't just pick that hostel on her own,'' she said. ''I convinced her to go there because I heard it was a high-class place. There was this cop, one of the Youth Bureau guys, who told me a friend of his could get Margaret in. Once she got there, she told them that she lived out in the suburbs with this mother and father who were always fighting and never paid attention to her and all that . . . She told lies about how she'd gone

to school and dropped out and all. But she picked that
up from other girls. There are plenty of kids on the street
that really do come from outside the city. But not Margaret. She came from here.''

Queenie's gesture took in the park—with its low-income regulars and higher-class daytime visitors—and
the street beyond, which seemed to be counting the
hours until dark. Her hands were the smooth, unlined
hands of a woman much younger than the woman whose
face she wore. Why had I never looked carefully at her
hands?

''Maybe she says she was told she could choose between going back home or going to the hostel, I don't
know. The real story is she could choose between going
to prison and going to that hostel. And I don't mean city
jail, either,'' Queenie said, ''I mean real jail. Margaret's
always been happy one minute, mad the next. She
stabbed another girl. They got into a fight over a rich
trick, and Margaret Louise went after both the girl and
the trick. It was lucky for her she missed stabbing the
trick, or we wouldn't have been able to make a deal
about jail.''

''A deal?''

''Yeah, that's how the Youth Bureau guys got into it.
The cops got Margaret right away. They waited for a
while to see if the other girl was going to die—it was
that bad. But she didn't die. All that time, Margaret was
in jail someplace here in the city. I never been in jail,
myself, never—only to visit. Then one day the Youth
Bureau cop told me a lawyer wanted to see me.

''I had to steal some money to buy a dress at the thrift
shop.'' She stared down at the skirt she wore. It was
light denim patched with darker pieces. Under it she
wore more denim. Jeans. And over it all, her long shawl.
It made me sweat just to look at her. ''I probably still
looked pretty bad even in the new dress, but the lawyer
the cop sent me to, he was decent. He had a quiet way.

He listened when I talked. He acted like somebody who maybe had troubles of his own and knew what it's like.''

A thought struck her and she paused. "He knows you, this lawyer . . ."

"What? How does he know me?"

"From the old days, I guess. He come down here to see me the second time, so I didn't have to go to his office. And that day, you were up in the city. He saw you on the street here and asked me if I knew your name. I didn't want to say nothing. 'Just some bum who lives in the Don valley,' I told him, and he said, 'I used to know that man well.' "

"He probably meant he had been in my court when I was a judge," I explained. "What was his name?"

She gave the matter some thought. "This stuff I'm telling you, it happened a couple years ago. I don't remember the man's name."

It was a lie, but I was sure she had her reasons.

"What sort of deal?"

"It was simple, really," Queenie said. "Margaret Louise would get out of jail—no charges filed—if she would go to the hostel and stay there until her baby was born. I asked them if she had to give up the baby, and they said no, that wasn't part of the deal. Of course, Margaret always said that it *was* part of the deal and they were lying—she was so sure the hostel was crooked or something."

"She still thought that on the night *I* talked to her."

"I know. So crazy . . ."

Queenie stopped. Her voice was choked, and her eyes filled again. I felt the same overwhelming sense of uselessness I had come to feel when I sent some promising young man or woman to detention for shoplifting a few dollars' worth of toiletries from a drug store or punching each other out in a fight, starting them on the long slide down into a life of crime. In all my years of living intimately with the law, and in my most recent years of living outside of it, I had never been able to figure out an answer to the question of what to do with promising young people who would most surely come to naught. That was one of the things that had burned me out.

"Queenie," I said as gently as I could. "Why do you think Margaret Louise was murdered?"

"They say she was beat to death. It happens to a lot of girls. Could have been a trick who got mad or somebody trying to steal her take. Could have been a dealer. Or it could have been that she shot her mouth off one time too many."

"Did you send me down to talk to her because you thought she was in some kind of danger?"

"Your Honor, I told Margaret about you once because she told me that sometimes she would have lawyers—and even once a judge—as tricks and that she wanted to tell them about that hostel, but it never felt right. That sounded dangerous to me. So I told her that I knew you a long time, that I didn't know anything about what happened to you but that I got a good feeling from talking to you."

"Maybe it was my talking to her that brought this about, Queenie."

She shook her head. "I keep asking myself this question, 'Who in the world would care what a crazy little hooker was saying about Second Chance hostel?' "

"I can't imagine."

"But you can find out." She reached out and took hold of my arm. There was desperation in her touch. I didn't shake her off as she had shaken me off.

"You could go there," she said, "especially the way you look now. You could go to that hostel and get inside. You could find out what happens to the girls and their babies. If you did that, then Margaret Louise would get what she wanted, even if she didn't live . . ."

"Queenie, you don't know what you're asking. I'm a street person, just like you. I can't . . ."

"You have friends who can help. You said so."

Her plea hung in the thick hot air. During the day, people worked in offices on the streets neighboring the park, which made it less dangerous than at night. Along the park's edges, the dispossessed of the city mixed with business people on lunch break, even an executive or two. Both the rich and the poor flattered themselves into thinking that Toronto was a place where everybody got along with everybody. And yet, the walls between the rich and poor were impenetrable. Queenie, like everybody else in this neighborhood, dreamed of winning the lottery. If she won, she would have money, but she'd never be rich, just as I, who lived on leaves and leavings, would never truly be poor. I thought I'd lost everything. But I hadn't lost my education, my intelligence nor the orderly progression of my traditional upbringing. I hadn't lost all my friends, either.

"All right," I said, "I'll see what I can do."

Queenie nodded, then turned her eyes back toward the park and the street.

As I followed her gaze, I saw two police officers walking along the sidewalk. With a start, I realized that one of them looked like the female cop from the valley. My impulse was to run, to escape, but I forced myself to sit still. To move would surely draw attention, and from a distance, dressed as I was, it was extremely unlikely that I would be connected with the bum she may or may not have recently rescued from the wilds!

Whatever she was up to, the cop didn't hold Queenie's attention. Queenie's mind was elsewhere.

"Did anybody tell you I was lookin' for you a while back?" she asked.

"Yes. I would have come back up to see you sooner, but I got sick."

"I got something for you." She pulled aside her shawl and lifted her skirt to reach into the pocket of her jeans. "I been carrying it around so long it's probably useless."

Finally finding what she was digging for, she withdrew a wrinkled, soiled envelope. I was touched to see that whatever it had been through, it was still tightly sealed. As she handed it to me, I saw that my name was written on the front in a hand that was vaguely familiar.

"A woman brought it," she said. "Good-looking woman—young . . ."

My first thought was that Aliana had come looking for me. I would have asked Queenie about this, but there wasn't time. Suddenly, without either of us realizing how close they were, the two cops were nearly upon us.

"Thanks, Queenie," I said, stuffing the envelope into my own pocket. "I've got to get moving. I'll do as you ask. I'll go over to Second Chance and see whether I can find out anything. But I have to remind you I'm not a detective. You can't get your hopes up."

"They never been up, Your Honor."

Despite the heat, I felt strong enough to get across town to the hostel. Of course, it helped to be dressed inconspicuously, have enough money to get a cool drink if I needed it, and be able to travel on public transit instead of walking.

As I approached, I saw that the police officer who had chased me away the first time was still outside. Then it had been night. Now it was the middle of the day. It wasn't impossible that the guy had changed shifts— most cops on the force worked all three. It seemed very unlikely that this man's sole duty was to stand outside a hostel and watch it. What for?

Though in a quiet neighborhood, the street on which the hostel sat was still relatively busy—much busier now than it had been at night. This gave me an advantage because it was easy for me to mix in with people on the sidewalk, walk past the cop, and slip around the back of the building.

I was a little more careful in my choice of hiding place this time. At the back was a crowded parking lot. Judging by the size of the lot, it served more than just the hostel. That meant that it was unlikely that people using the lot would be familiar with each other. I could probably stay out there for some time before arousing suspicion.

From the rear, I had a good view of the place. I could see a patio and a playground, separated from the parking lot by a row of shrubs and a sturdy chain fence. I positioned myself behind the bushes, close enough to the fence to hear snatches of conversation.

I could see women with babies, social workers, a pregnant girl. I listened intently as they talked, and at first, it was interesting just because I was eavesdropping. But as with all eavesdropping, the mundane soon overwhelmed the novelty.

I don't know how long I had been standing there before something interesting happened. Suddenly, there was a voice of an entirely different quality wafting past the trees and through the fence. It was not the youthful voices of the mothers nor the officiously soothing voices of the social workers. No, this was a voice of refinement, culture, and unless I missed my guess, wealth.

"Good afternoon, dear," I heard the voice say. "It's good of you to meet me this afternoon. How are you feeling?"

Making sure that no one was watching, I moved slightly away from the shrubs to see who was talking. The voice belonged to a middle-aged woman with red hair, perfectly coiffed, whose back was turned. The woman wore a white linen suit, and there was discreet gold everywhere—on her fingers, her wrist, her ears, the clasp of her purse, the tops of her shoes. She was seated at the nearest patio table across from a young woman

who was also a redhead and also, I thought, extremely
well-dressed for such a place. I thought I must be hallucinating with the heat and the strain. It was like looking at both the young and the middle-aged Harpur at the
same time.

In my stunned state, I must have made some sort of
sound, for suddenly, the older woman turned. I jumped
back behind the bushes. She couldn't see me, though her
face was now turned almost fully toward me. I was suddenly ashamed of myself, of my imagination. The only
thing even vaguely similar between this woman and Harpur was the hair color. I noticed that the movements of
this woman were nervous, lacked the easy grace of the
truly well-bred. She sat a little too slumped. Her voice
was a little too loud. Her gold was not gold. She looked
like someone who spent a lot of time among the rich
and tried hard to resemble them.

I sank further into the shadows, afraid I'd blown my
cover. But the woman turned back and continued her
conversation with the girl. "Have you given some
thought to the matter we discussed the other day?"

The girl shrugged in the manner of young women
these days—"I guess so," she said.

"I needn't remind you that if you stay here and complete the program, both you and your child will benefit
in ways that wouldn't be possible otherwise."

The girl smiled, but I could sense that she really didn't
care about what the woman was saying. She certainly
didn't look like a girl who had no alternatives. I wondered where her parents were and what they had done
to lose her to the workers and volunteers of Second
Chance hostel. Then I remembered what I had done to
my own children when they were adolescents—given
them ski vacations and new cars instead of attention,
instead of the open-handed love my parents had given
me.

"I have a special piece of good news for you," the

woman was saying. "Our president would like to meet you—he'd like to take you out to lunch."

"President?" the girl asked, as if she couldn't imagine what the woman meant.

The woman laughed gently. ". . . the president of the Board of Directors of this hostel. He's the person whose kindness has provided the program here—the residence, the resource center, the . . ."

My boredom at this list of benefits to the needy was about equal to the boredom of the girl, who seemed to have become lost in her own thoughts. My attention wandered from the pair, and I looked around, studying the patio and the adjacent playground.

There could be no doubt that Second Chance hostel was well-endowed. All the equipment on the playground looked brand-new. The few children climbing on it were well dressed, not just in the sort of serviceable institutional clothes one might expect, but in Oshkosh and Baby Gap. There was nothing suspicious about the clothes themselves. They could be donations from anybody. I remembered how people had stood before my bench dressed in clothes that charitable workers had brought to the courthouse so that the indigent could put on their best appearance when they faced me and my brethren in the law.

The patio itself was well designed, too, the furniture attractive, modern and clean. I tried to imagine Moonstar seated at one of the tables, but it was hard. She must have felt horribly out of place. Was that why she had concocted the story about her parents in the suburbs? What else had she made up?

Then my eye caught something at the farthest edge of the patio behind a set of glass doors that apparently led to a recreation room. The doors were lightly frosted, but I could make out somebody standing behind them, somebody who, like me, appeared to be observing.

His stance was somehow familiar. I blinked to focus

my eyes. He was tall, gaunt, not in a business suit, I realized, but in field clothes. Even though I'd not looked him in the eye, I knew the man. He was the birdwatcher I'd seen the day I found the hand. Try as I might, I couldn't make out his face, but I had the uncanny feeling that he could see as much of me as I could see of him and that he was equally shocked.

A wave of weakness overtook me. The exertion of the morning, both physical and mental, was taking its toll. Not only was I confused as to what was going on at Second Chance, I was dizzy from the heat and again hungry. In the valley I could go days without much food, but now regular meals had spoiled my endurance.

I pulled myself together long enough to escape to the subway.

A single bus token brought me to Aliana's office. Like a bad penny, I was turning up again.

She seemed happy to greet me. She looked fresh but harried, and I had to assume that despite her willingness to sit down with me, she must be extremely busy.

"Are you okay?" she asked.

"The heat's a bit intense."

"And you've been running around in it? How could you be so foolish?"

"Are you scolding me?" I asked with a smile.

"I wouldn't hesitate to do so if I thought it would be effective," she said sweetly. "Where have you been? I called my place to make sure you were all right and all I got was my machine."

"Aliana," I said, "I left in a hurry because I found out something very disturbing."

She leaned across her desk, sending the lemony scent of her perfume into the air. "What is it, Ellis? What's happened?"

I told her about Moonstar's death. I told her about seeing the article and the picture. I told her about going in search of Queenie. I told her about the conversation

I'd had with Queenie and about how guilty I felt. I told
her about going to the hostel and seeing the red-haired
woman, the girl and the birdwatcher. It seemed to me
that I talked and talked and that Aliana listened and listened.

When I finished, she hesitated, the same sort of hesitation I always had at the end of the testimony of a
witness. I wanted to make sure that they were done. I
wanted to make sure, also, that my own comments were
framed by impressive silence.

So she was silent. Then she said, ''Ellis, I think you
overdid it a little today. If I were you, I'd forget about
the birdwatcher.''

''Maybe you're right.''

''I checked the Solomon angle.''

''Any luck?''

''No. But while I was at it, I found out something
else. It bothers me that the cops seem to be all over you.
I mean, what for? You haven't breached your order
again—you haven't gone near Harpur or Stow?''

''Of course not. So you found out something about
the police?''

''Yes. But I want you to be feeling better before we
deal with it. I'm finished for today. Let's go get some
supper.''

A haze hung over the city, and the temperature
seemed to have risen just in the hour I'd been inside,
even though the day was waning. Mugginess caressed
us like the unwelcome hug of a distant relative.

Without deciding exactly where we were going, we
wandered toward the harbor, across from Aliana's office.
It was busy. Two decades of development had turned
abandoned warehouses into trendy boutiques. A flotilla
of touristy cruise boats—from Chinese junks to paddle-
wheel steamers—were doing a booming business ferrying people among the city, the harbor islands, the harbor airport and the lake beyond. The boats were having

a hard time staying out of each other's way.

"It's a madhouse down here," Aliana said with a laugh. "I was thinking of a quiet walk, but I guess we picked the wrong place."

"I guess so," I said, narrowly missing a woman who was carrying a large shopping bag. "Let's just walk along the water. At least it will be cool."

She nodded in agreement, and we made our way through the crowd and toward the walkway skirting the inner harbor that lay between the harbor islands and the downtown streets. Even here the air seemed thick, and we walked in silence for a while, just trying to catch our breath.

Within minutes, we were near the public ferries that commute to the islands. Almost as if we were reading each other's mind, Aliana and I stood in the line that led to the toll booth.

When we got to the booth, I was standing in front of Aliana. Without even thinking, I reached into my pocket for the money. I found enough for two, handed it to the attendant, took the tokens he held out to me, and dropped first mine, then Aliana's into the turnstile beyond the booth. I turned to make sure she was behind me. As I did, I caught a look on her face that I found startling, but hard to figure out. Did she think it arrogant of me to pay for her using her own money? Did she pity me? Or was she surprised that years of living off street leavings hadn't knocked the gentleman out of me?

I didn't know what she was thinking, and I had no right to ask. But I couldn't fault her. I, like most beggars, had bit the hand that fed me more than once, had shown contempt instead of gratitude and arrogance instead of humility. But not with Aliana. Despite her sharpness as a reporter, she had a soft heart, and she softened me. I could little afford to be softened, in fact I could afford it far less than I could afford the price of two ferry tokens. Forewarned is forearmed. It was time to tear away.

But the evening was so hot, the harbor was so cool, the fare was already paid. And I needed to know what she'd found out.

We disembarked and after a short walk, found ourselves on the grassy beach that faces out over the endless waters of Lake Ontario.

"Do you realize," I said, "that the southern boundary of the City of Toronto is the northern boundary of the United States of America?"

"Out there in the middle of the lake? I never thought of it that way. I guess you're right."

We walked past the grass and onto the sand lapped by the waves.

"Finally," she said, "finally we can talk away from all those people."

"Yes."

"But we forgot to get something to eat. And you've been sick. You shouldn't be careless . . ."

"Look, Aliana, I'm fine. Let's just forget about my condition, shall we? Let's just talk about what we came here to talk about, okay?"

The words sounded far harsher than I'd meant them to be, and she drew back visibly from the sting of my tone.

"Maybe you are okay. You're starting to sound like your old self."

"I'm sorry. I just feel that I've presumed upon your kindness long enough."

But she didn't go on. We just sat there in a ridiculous, silent funk. It occurred to me that in the years in which I'd been an outcast, I had had fistfights, shouting matches, even knock-down, drag-out battles with people, but this was the first time I'd had a cat's-tongue, cold-shoulder argument with another person since I'd lived among the lichens and the bats. The realization made me laugh.

"I really don't know why you laugh at me, Ellis,"

Aliana said, clearly still angry. "I know you're arrogant and touchy, but why you have to be dismissive as well really mystifies me. If you're so proud that you can't accept simple gestures of friendship, then we can forget about being friends."

I suppressed the urge to tweak her nose and ask her why it was out of joint. "Do you want to tell me what you've found out?" I tried to sound gentle—even contrite.

She dove right in. "I tried to find out about Solomon, as I said, and got nowhere. I thought some more about the police. I had to narrow things down, so I took the youth angle—because of Second Chance. My usual contact on youth issues is a guy named Matt West. He's quite a cop, this guy. He's done a lot of work with kids on the street—Youth Bureau, School Squad, Gang Unit—the works. If there's one person on the Force who'd know what's going on with the kids, it's Matt.

"I've never had the least trouble getting in touch with Matt before," she went on. "But this time, I ran into a great deal of difficulty. I called his desk and got a taped message saying he was away or on the phone. The next time I called I got through to his partner. She said she'd give Matt a message. A couple hours went by. No return call."

"Maybe he was just out for the day."

"I thought that, too. But I don't give up that easily. I called another contact—in personnel. She's limited in what she can tell me, of course, but what she did tell me was that Matt's on sick leave—has been for about a month."

"Discrepancy."

"Exactly. Why were his fellow officers so evasive? I decided to do a little computer work. Crime reporters subscribe to a number of information services, and one of them is a sort of on-line police blotter. I knew the Youth Bureau contributed to this because I'd read Matt's stuff there before. I dialed up the service. Matt's reports were all there, neat and complete, month after month. Until about three months ago; then the reports disappear. They're just not there. I know the Chief File Clerk at Police Headquarters. I gave her a call. She clicked a few keys on her computer and came to the same conclusion as me. Three months of reports not there. When I asked her why that might be the case, she said they'd had some down time on the computer lately and that some things just weren't caught up yet.

"Well, I checked that, too. I've been a reporter for more than fifteen years, and you can imagine the contacts I've got by now."

"And the favors owed," I added.

"I asked a friend of mine who has access to one of the other squad's records to check the computer for his squad. The last entered record was for yesterday."

"So you think . . ."

"I think Matt's reports are really missing."

"But what does this have to do with our case?"

"As I see it, there are three possibilities. First, the reports may have been lost somewhere in the computer, just as the clerk suggested, but I doubt it. Or Matt may have gone undercover. Or he might be missing . . ."

I let this sink in.

"Yes," Aliana repeated. "I think Matt West is missing somehow. He could be working on a case. He could be deep undercover . . ."

"But if he were missing, surely the Force would know."

"Even if they knew," Aliana answered, "they wouldn't tell me. But more to the point, they might *not* know. There have been times when Matt has been so deep that he hasn't been in contact with his superiors for months . . ."

"But what sort of a case could he be on that would require that level of cover?" I asked. I thought about the police officer that Queenie had told me had helped get Moonstar to Second Chance. This Matt West was a youth worker. He could have been out there asking the same questions I'd been asking Moonstar. Had he been killed? And if he had, was his killer the one who got the girl?

"That isn't all, Ellis," Aliana said softly. "That isn't even the most interesting part. I do most of my research now by phone and computer. I can work with somebody for years and never set eyes on them."

"You mean you never met Matt West in person?"

"Right."

"And . . ."

"And so I called back my friend in personnel. You can't ask what race an employee is, but you *can* ask for a physical description. Matt West is black."

CHAPTER

TEN

WE WALKED SLOWLY ALONG THE EDGE OF THE WATER AS we talked.

"If you never saw Matt West, you don't know what kind of jewelry he wore," I said.

"No."

"And I never got a chance to ask Moonstar if Solomon wore any gold rings."

Aliana stooped down toward the sand, picked up a flat white stone and turned it over and over in her hand. "What should we do next?"

"We?"

"Yes. We."

"I don't know what the next step should be. Up until this morning, I just planned on going home and forgetting about the ring, since it's gone anyway. I figured I'd stay in my ravine until I got the strength to move on. Now that Moonstar is dead and an officer from the same police unit that recommended her to Second Chance is missing, everything has changed. It's dangerous to go back, but I left things down there I need." One of them was my solitude, but I didn't mention that.

"You could stay with me a little longer . . ."

Her offer seemed sincere, but I didn't know what she was thinking. I changed the subject.

"What would be your next move on this, Aliana?"

"I could see what more I could find out about Matt's

disappearance. It doesn't take a genius to figure out that I'm not going to get anything more from the police, but maybe I can think of another way to come at it. I also need to get more on Stoughton-Melville and on William Sterling . . .''

She picked up a handful of sand, letting it run through her fingers. "If Queenie is a friend of yours, presumably you're going to keep inquiring until you've found out who killed her daughter instead of going back to that miserable hut."

"I've got to go back for a bit."

"Look, Ellis, either you're in this or you're not. Which is it?"

Now it was I who lifted the warm sand and held it in my hand as if it couldn't escape.

"I'm in," I said. "Just give me a little time to get organized. Then I'll go back to the hostel. And I'll talk to Queenie again. You can keep looking for whatever you can find on West. Try his partner, too. And maybe you could look into Second Chance from a couple of different perspectives. Try to find out how it's funded. See if you can find out who's on the Board. There are plenty of angles—we'll check them all out."

"We?"

"Yes. We."

We found a place on the island that served supper. The sun set as the full moon rose. It was so peaceful to be walking along the shore in the dark with the breeze off the water cooling the astonishing heat, blowing away the heavy air that had hung about us all day. And it was peaceful to walk in silence with another person.

But still, I'd spent an awful lot of time away from the valley. I had to get back, though it would be crazy for me to try to do so in the dark.

So we went back to Aliana's, and when we got there, we had a visitor: Tim Garrison. Since they'd met the night I was rescued, he and Aliana seemed to have joined forces in keeping an eye on me. He was full of news of the deal the consortium had proposed. They were prepared to buy the valley, then turn it over to a well-known nature conservancy in order to "save" it.

"The deal even includes the lodge at the headwaters—the one the Ministry of Natural Resources used as an experimental fish hatchery before they closed it during the last round of budget cuts. It's a beautiful building—a real woodland retreat."

I wanted to talk about other things. "Tim, the day that I was rescued, how did you find out I was sick?" I had asked him all this at the hospital, but I wanted to hear it again.

"Well," he answered, "there was a message on my machine. It was from a man who didn't give his name. He said that one of the people who live in the valley wasn't doing so well and he thought somebody should come down and check him out. He said he was a bird-watcher. I was on my way down to check on you when I ran into the rescue team at the top of the ravine. The police asked me to help out. Right away I asked, 'Is it Ellis?' One of the officers said yes. Then she asked me if I knew the fastest way to get down to your camp."

Aliana caught my eye. I knew we were both thinking the same thing. "Tim," I said carefully, "is that *exactly* what the caller said?"

"Huh?"

"The man said he was a *birdwatcher*?"

"I'm sure he did, because I remember asking him whether he belonged to the Toronto Friends of Ornithology."

I hadn't imagined the birdwatcher at all. Knowing he had shown up at Second Chance and also in the valley made it even more dangerous for me to return to my ravine. It also made it more necessary.

I left Aliana's at dawn. Standing at a twenty-four-hour

transit stop, I reached into my pocket for a token and
found the letter Queenie had given me. I'd forgotten all
about it. I was pretty sure I recognized the handwriting.
If it was from whom I thought, I didn't want to read it
in public. I'd have plenty of time when I got home—
assuming there was any home left.

The final bus dropped me on a street near the grassy
park at the northeast corner of the ravine. By the middle
of June, the early morning sky was bright. The full moon
that had risen over the lake when I'd walked with Aliana
was now setting. Despite the unusual heat, there was an
early freshness to the air that I realized I had missed
downtown.

There was another thing that I'd missed: birdsong.
The air was full of their sweet morning hopefulness. I
thought of my father, who on a June morning like this
might get out of bed and go into his garden and sing
toward the trees, soliciting—and sometimes getting—a
response from the birds. How did I know he was doing
this? Because I was watching him from my childhood
bedroom window and wishing I, too, could sing to the
birds, but not letting myself because of my determination to be different from him.

In just two weeks, the vegetation around my place had
grown tall. As I neared, I could see that the path I'd
made from the river to my hut was no longer visible. I
felt a surge of relief. Nobody had walked there in a
while.

I pressed on. The shoes Aliana had provided were
good ones with thick soles. It was easy to walk through
the summer grass, which, though high, was not yet
tough.

The closer I got to my hut, the better I felt. I was
stronger than I had been in years. As soon as the op-
pressive heat wore off, I would take a good long hike
in my ravine. And then I would sleep under the bare
stars. Then and only then would I feel clear enough to

go over all I had learned about Moonstar and try to figure out if it was connected to my finding the severed hand—the hand of Solomon? Of Matt West? Or the hand of someone else altogether?

Lost in thought, I was startled to hear the sound of someone moving around in or near my shack. I couldn't see my hut when the sound hit my ear, but I knew it was around the next bend in the river. Though tempted to run and flush the intruder, I instead proceeded slowly.

Anger filled me, more anger than I'd felt in a while. I could clearly hear the sounds as I approached. Someone was rifling my belongings! I could hear them pick something up, throw it down, pick up something else.

Within seconds, I could see the hut. But that's all I saw. I didn't see any damage to it. It stood exactly as I left it, except that two of my ragged blankets were piled beside the opening. I must have been wrapped in them the day I'd been rescued.

But I could still hear the sound. Someone must be behind the hut. Why? There was nothing stored there.

Suddenly, to my amazement, one of my plastic water jugs came rolling out toward me.

Whoever was raiding my site had neither a clear idea of what to steal nor a very effective method for scaring me off.

Silently, I made my way to the back of the hut. Another water jug came rolling out, hitting my foot and spinning erratically away. When I got all the way around the back I saw a pair of bright eyes staring out from a small masked face. A baby raccoon!

"Hi, little fellow," I said to him in relief. Usually I didn't make it a habit of talking to animals.

The raccoon did precisely what I thought he would do, which was to take off as fast as his short legs could carry his fat little body.

Though well aware that I could no longer be sure I was alone in the ravine, I felt a surge of the old happi-

ness I'd felt in being at peace in the valley. This was
still the only home I had. I surveyed the scene. The baby
raccoon hadn't been the only visitor. There were claw
marks and teeth marks everywhere. I entered my hut
carefully, letting my eyes adjust to the dimness. There
might be a larger animal inside.

In fact, I did hear something scurry as I moved further
in—something small, a ferret, a vole—nothing that concerned me.

A single board of the roof had come loose, allowing
a ray of sun to fall on my tattered bed. The scraps of
blanket covering it looked twisted, whipped up. Partly,
I was sure, this was because animals had begun to build
some sort of home for themselves before changing their
mind.

The thought crossed my mind that perhaps whoever
it was that was pursuing me had come back in my absence and had dug around—even in my bed—looking
for whatever they seemed so convinced I had.

But I found no mark of humans—no footprint, no
evidence that a human hand had moved anything. My
own fevered motion when I had been sick had tousled
the bed. I moved to straighten it, but I stopped before I
touched anything. I didn't know what in the water had
made me sick. It could easily have been bacteria. Maybe
the blankets were full of infection. The rough rags dis-
gusted me. In such a short time, I had gotten used to the
smooth sheets of the hospital, Aliana's scented towels.

I pulled every piece of cloth out of the hut, and using
matches I'd saved from the restaurant where I'd had
breakfast the day before, I set fire to the whole pile. The
only thing I spared was my judge's robe, but I threw the
bag I'd stored it in into the flames. I walked a little
distance away and waited until the fire burned to embers.
Then I snuffed it out completely. With the heat and dryness, I didn't want to take any chances.

When that was done, I decided the time had come to

read my daughter's letter. I had figured out that Ellen was the young woman who had been asking Queenie about me.

My fingers trembled as I turned the letter over and prepared to unseal it. Of all the dangers the valley now presented, none was greater than the danger of reading this. If it contained bad news, I would be filled with sorrow and guilt. If it contained good news, I would be filled with longing and regret.

The paper was creamy and thick, and the flap of the envelope was still stuck fast. My daughter had inherited a taste for quality. When my daughter was young, nothing had stood between me and my love for her. She was the blood of my blood. I had loved her even when I had, in my rush toward success, seemed to forget she and her brother existed.

I unstuck the envelope carefully, not wanting to tear anything. I slid a clean, folded sheet of paper from the rumpled envelope. Something pristine out of something ruined. Yes. Oh, yes, exactly. The handwriting of my daughter was similar to my own, I now realized, because it was I who had taught her how to write.

At first, I just held the piece of paper, not certain whether to unfold it.

If I didn't read it, I might regret it for the rest of my days. But if I read it, no matter what it said, everything would change. I understood that quite clearly. I had been completely separate from my family for five years. Not a word, a document, a message had passed between us during that time. Now, just because I held this letter in my hand, I was to be connected to all of them again. To Anne. To my son. To my brother and sister and even my dead parents. Each of them was all of them. That is what a family is.

Dear Daddy,
    Over the past five years, I've wanted to write to you many times, but I never knew how to find you

until I heard about your friend Queenie from one of the Faculty of Law at the university a few months ago. I finally decided to contact her. A lot of things have happened that you need to know about. Some were happy and some tragic. I don't know how you're feeling right now, so all I'm going to tell you is something wonderful.

I got married three years after you left, right after I finished law school. I worked for a year or so, then I got pregnant. Two and a half months ago, I gave birth to your first grandson!

Of course I named him after you and Grandpa. His name is Angelo. That's right, Angelo. He's pudgy and beautiful with black curly hair—and he really looks like our family.

Of all the things I've wanted you to know over the past five years, Daddy, this is what I wanted you to know the most.

Last month, Mom, Jeff and I saw your picture in the paper. Daddy, it broke my heart. I want you to know that you can come and live with me any time you want. There's nothing to be ashamed of. A lot of lawyers I know are burning out, too. About the only ones who *aren't* burning out are the ones who couldn't find a job in the first place!

I want you to see my baby. And I want to see my father. You can call me at 555-1234.

Think about it.

And say a prayer for little Angelo.

> Love,
> Ellen

I felt I should pray that he didn't turn out like me. I did pray that. Then I prayed for Ellen. All of which was quite remarkable considering that I no longer believed in God. I folded the letter, put it back in its envelope. I didn't know what to do with it, what to think about it.

I felt the threat of tears and I blinked hard to keep them back, but when I closed my eyes, images of my daughter danced behind them.

I remembered the day *she* was born. She was our first child, and I was twenty-seven, a year younger than she was now. Not only was she a mother, but also a lawyer! I wondered about her brother. What had he become? He had had no plans, even when he entered the university.

My children! I remembered how they looked the day I was sworn in as a judge. They weren't small. Ellen was thirteen and Jeffrey eleven. The five of them—my mother and father were present, too—stood in a stalwart row, like soldiers—so proud. I glanced at them before I took the simple oath that was powerful enough to bind me for the rest of my life in the law:

"I solemnly swear that I will faithfully, impartially and to the best of my skill and knowledge execute the duties of Provincial Court Judge. So help me God."

When I finished the oath, my eye sought the face of my father. For the first time in my life, I saw that I had succeeded in doing something that was good enough for him.

I found it so hard to believe how the time had passed. Ellen was the child I had taken down into the valley to find butterflies and beetles. This was the child I had balanced on my shoulders as I waded in the river—risking then, even more than now—getting sick from the water. Which was why I made sure no drop of it ever touched her. This was the child I took with me to court when I was a lawyer, letting her sit on the bench when I was sure that nobody would see us.

And now she was a mother. And I a grandfather. I was pondering that when I suddenly heard the unmistakable sound of a canoe paddle cutting the stillness of the river. I dropped the letter into the plastic bag where I had put my robe and moved closer to the bank. At first

I saw nothing, heard nothing further. Then the sound came again.

This was no idle pleasure-seeker. The remoteness of the ravine, the possible pollution of the water, and the uncertain navigability of the river made canoeing hazardous for all but the most skilled. And anybody skilled enough to canoe here wouldn't have wasted his talent and time. They'd have gone up north.

The soft grass at the river's edge was approaching its full height. It was easy to slip behind a tall stand and observe the canoe as it came toward me.

I was not surprised to see that the canoeist was the birdwatcher. I hadn't decided what he wanted or what I should do about him, but I'd been expecting him. He had neglected to hang his binoculars around his neck, but he hadn't forgotten his hat, which was pulled low over his brow as if in a deliberate effort to make it impossible to see his face. I could however see his gloved hands and noticed the ease with which he paddled. He was a strong man despite his lean frame.

He was studying the river bank, looking for a place to land.

My site, including the hut, was not visible from the river. But still, a person landing here would have only a short walk to get to my compound.

I watched him. He watched the shore. I thought he sensed my presence, knew that I had been away from my place, sensed that I had returned. There was no way I could know this, of course, but I am used to watching animals, including man. Instinct told *me* that instinct was speaking to *him*. His motions, his attitude again seemed familiar, like those of a man who had just understood that the time for whatever he was contemplating was not yet right. As he passed the place where the beaten path to my compound had met the river before it became overgrown, he executed a neat turn with his paddle, stalled the canoe for only a moment, then headed back upstream.

That was when I made up my mind to confront him. I parted the river grasses. I leaned over the water. I shouted with all my might, "Get the hell away from my place! Leave me alone!"

The silence of the ravine seemed to magnify the sound of my voice. In the middle of the river, the startled canoeist lost control of his craft. For a moment he swung wildly. Then, with a few skilled strokes, he righted the canoe and paddled away as fast as he could until his efforts carried him beyond the river's nearest wide bend and out of sight.

As he sped off, I thought I heard him shout back at me, but then I realized that what I'd heard was only thunder.

Far in the distance, I could hear the faint rumble of another peal, though the sky was a clear cloudless blue, softened by the haze of heat that hung over the day.

I spent the rest of the day cleaning up the compound, boiling water for drinking, gathering food for supper. After supper, I thought I might read the letter again. I reached into the plastic storage bag, and my fingers touched my judicial gown. I had always loved the feel of it. It seemed heavy, hefty with the weight of itself and its meaning. It was made of very high-quality silk. It wasn't smooth to the touch; it was rough, as if to remind its wearer that it was, in fact, a uniform, like the uniform of a soldier or a nurse.

And it seemed very black in the bright light of the summer evening. The black of solemnity, of dignity, of the shadows from which come the answers to the most profound questions of life.

For a little while, I just looked at it, just held it, the rich fabric feeling foreign to my fingers.

All that had been mine, and was mine, and would be mine . . .

Despite the danger challenging me, despite the heat, despite the distant thunder and the impending sunset, I gave in to the desire to dress in my old robes. Like a child craves dressing in a grown-up costume.

Carefully—with as much care as I had exercised in the old days—I placed the robe over my shoulders, drew my arms through, smoothed the fabric over my chest.

As if out of a dream I seemed to hear the old words. "All rise."

I stood tall, the heavy black cloth falling past my knees, the weight of it on my shoulders an old familiar burden. I looked about me, as I used to do then, surveying my court.

I saw not the concerned, pinched faces of the jurors. I saw the sumac trees, their forked trunks as thick as the twisted tales of a witness. I saw not the prisoner in his glass-enclosed dock. I saw the clouds turning pink with the setting sun. I saw no bailiff, no recorder, no guard. I saw the summer grasses lush in their silent green. And I saw no criminals, no criminals at all.

"All rise," I whispered to the hushed valley.

And a rush of nighthawks swirled up from the brush and wheeled into the failing sky.

CHAPTER

ELEVEN

FOR THE NEXT COUPLE OF DAYS, I TRIED TO GET BACK into the swing of things. Without a decent garden, it was going to be hard going. Planting a new one was out of the question. I had nothing to plant. And the earth was dry from the intense heat that always seemed ready to break but never actually did.

All day I heard the distant rumble of thunder, but the sky stayed a cloudless blue. At night, flashes of lightning illuminated my hut, making bizarre patterns as I watched it between the slats of the walls.

But there was no rain. And all I could think of was my drinking days. Dry heave.

Worse than the weather was the sense of unease I now felt steadily. My ravine had been violated. Yet where else could I go? To stay with Aliana would have been uncomfortable. To go to my daughter impossible. There was also the anxiety of knowing that I was no longer at liberty to dismiss my involvement with the mystery that had turned my summer upside down. I gave myself two full days to put my home to rights and clear my head. In the meantime, I hoped Aliana would come up with something that would help us know what to do next.

I worked, despite the heat, as quickly as possible to clean up my hut and organize my few belongings. I went through my books, burning any that had been chewed or stained by animals and insects. I also remade my bed, going up to the free store near the welfare office to get new blankets. With the hot weather, it was a cinch to get blankets. They couldn't get rid of them fast enough, and I got several excellent ones—with a couple of sheets and towels thrown in.

I also made a trip to the rock in the river, where I intended to deposit my daughter's letter among my other treasures. The thought that she had written had given me a little jolt of something I hadn't felt in a long time—hope.

Before I put the letter away, I re-read it. Suddenly something I'd failed to notice the first time leapt out at me. A lawyer from the Faculty of Law knew about Queenie, knew where she lived, had told Ellen only months before. How many lawyers was Queenie likely to know? Not many. She'd had to buy a new dress to talk to one about Moonstar and Second Chance. And whoever that lawyer was, he had been recommended by a police officer from the Youth Bureau—an elite unit with fewer than a dozen members. Moonstar would have known Matt West. She was dead, and Matt was missing. Who was the lawyer that linked them?

I opened my safety box and lifted my ring. "*Impegno l'onore.*" "I pledge on my honor." The words sent a shiver through me that made me tremble even in the overpowering heat. I slipped the ring on my finger.

When I finally found Queenie again, the city's heat was unbearable. I was determined to pry names out of her, but I knew she wouldn't respond to any sort of pressure. "Hot enough for you, Queenie?" I joked, as we stepped into the shadows of an alleyway between the community center and a chicken take-out, sharing a soda Queenie had lifted from a hot-dog cart.

For the first time, she asked me back to her room.

"I've got a surprise for you, Your Honor," she said, her rare laugh deep and appealing.

And she did have a surprise. Air conditioning! "How did you get it?"

She ushered me to the room's only chair and sat down on the bed. "This here's a government-assisted building," she answered, "and last year—when it wasn't even hot in the summer—somebody put in a claim saying that we were being discriminated against because we couldn't afford air conditioning. They said the poor have just as much right to be cool as the rich. So the government put it in."

"It certainly comes in handy," I remarked, sure the comment sounded awkward and insincere, though I was grateful to be cool.

Queenie studied my face. "You're looking real pale today. And it's so hot. I know you don't want no friends—the way you live rough and all—but I don't like to see you sweating out there in the sun . . ."

"It's kind of you to have me in your place, Queenie," I said sincerely. Her room was very homelike. She had only a few belongings, but they were carefully displayed on the shelves the "government" had provided. I saw a wreath of sweet grass, a little clay pipe, a mug with a World Series Blue Jays insignia. I also saw the silver, turquoise and coral necklace that Moonstar had worn.

"Queenie, I want to talk to you about some of the things we've talked about before . . ."

"You mean about my girl?"

"Yes."

"We don't need to talk. I only need you to find out what they done to her at that hostel—in honor of her memory because it's what she always wanted."

"I need you to help me do that—to answer just a few questions."

"Sure," she said, but she sounded wary. Her guard was up.

"Okay, then. First I'm going to ask you about the

police officer that helped Moonstar, the officer from the Youth Bureau. What did he look like?''

"What do you mean?''

"Describe him—tall, short, white, black?''

"I can't remember.''

"Come on, Queenie. You and I are friends.''

"You're not acting like a friend. You're acting like a judge.''

"I'm sorry. I'm just trying to figure out a few things here. I feel responsible for what happened to your girl. And I want to keep it from happening to somebody else.''

"He was tall. Good looking. Black.''

I carefully guarded myself from showing any reaction.

"And the lawyer?''

"What lawyer?''

"The one you told me about—the one you said knew me. The one who sent my daughter to you because he knew where you lived. Can you remember what he looked like?''

"A guy in a suit.''

"Fat, thin?''

"He was, I guess you'd say, scrawny.''

"Okay. And how old was he?''

Queenie gave this a little thought. Finally she answered, "About your age, I'd say.''

"Was he dark, light?''

"He was kind of English-looking or something. He looked like he used to have brown hair, but now it's mostly gray.'' She hesitated and I thought she was going to give me a better description. Instead, she threw me a curve.

"That letter I gave you the other day, you say you read it?''

"Yes.''

"You gonna do something about it?''

"Maybe.''

"I knew that letter was from your kid," she said softly. It struck me again that years of rough living had not destroyed the grace of Queenie's inner life, her wisdom, her kindness.

"How could you know that?"

"I got evidence, Your Honor."

I had to smile in spite of myself. "Like what?"

"The evidence is that she looks just like you. Spitting image. Same serious face like you're always thinking about something real important. I knew she was your kid, even if she didn't say. And she ain't looking for money, is she?"

"Queenie, how could anybody in the world be looking to me for money?"

"Hey, listen, you wouldn't believe it. Lots of people think that street people are really rich—especially relatives. I had this friend once, real down-and-outer name of Barnes. Barndoor Barnes we always called him, except I don't know why. But anyhow, he died and we had to bury him, me and a couple other people. We decided to be decent about it and put a notice in the paper. The government was paying for the whole thing, anyway . . . Well, we done it. We spelled out the notice with his name and all—his real name, which we got from the hostel where he lived. Before the guy is even in the ground, he's got long-lost relatives showin' up from all over this country and a couple other countries besides. Everybody wantin' to know whether he left a will. A will! Old Barndoor didn't even leave a pair of socks!"

We both laughed at that, tragic though it was. "No, Queenie, my girl wasn't asking for money."

"Well, listen," she said, trying to sound angry, but not fooling me. "If you're not going to do something about that letter, then you better stop wasting my time. I ain't one of them answering services, you know. I'm not here to take messages nobody does nothing about."

"Messages?"

"Yeah. Your kid isn't the only one looking for you. I was having lunch at the shelter and this really good-looking babe comes up to me asking for you. Says she's a reporter—Anna or something . . ."

"Aliana?"

"Yeah."

"What did she say?"

"She just said to call her. So why don't you? And call your kid, too. I can't be the only woman you ever talk to, then, can I?" She winked at me.

I could have leaned across her little room and given her a kiss on the cheek. Maybe someday I'd risk it. "Thanks, Queenie, thanks for being the best friend I've got."

"You're welcome."

She hadn't sidetracked me even if she thought she had. "What was the lawyer's name, Queenie?"

She got up and went to the window. Her back was to me as she spoke. "I thought I told you I forgot his name."

I went to the window and stood behind her, keeping a respectable distance. "I forgot to thank you, Queenie. I forgot to thank you for being kind enough to pass along a letter from my daughter at a time when you are grieving the loss of your own."

She remained silent for a moment. Then she said, "Lawyers got a lot of power. You think a lawyer did something to those girls at Second Chance?"

"I don't know."

She turned and I stepped back. I had to reach out to keep from falling. To steady me, Queenie caught my hand. Before she released it, she stared at my ring.

"They had rings like that—both of them."

"Who?"

"The lawyer and the cop. They both wore gold rings just like yours."

•   •   •

When I recovered my composure, I told Queenie I needed to talk to Aliana right away. She showed me the pay phone at the end of her hall and lent me a quarter to make the call.

"I've got something big," Aliana said as soon as she heard my voice. "Harpur and Stow are on the board of Second Chance. Stow is President—Ellis, are you still there?"

"Yes. I'm just stunned, that's all. And I've got something big, too. I'm on my way. Stay at your office."

I had to borrow a token from Queenie—and also promise her I'd be back soon. On the subway on the way to Aliana, I meant to think about the mystery. About all the mysteries that rolled into the big mystery: how had the wearers of the ring come together in this twisted knot?

When I got off at the stop for *Toronto Daily World,* the weather was like a hot towel draped over my shoulders, my head, my neck. I couldn't think. I couldn't breathe. Before I talked to Aliana, I needed to get some air.

I made my way down to the harbor. Despite the heat, there were still quite a number of people around. I stole a hot dog while a vendor was giving directions to tourists.

A haze hung over the water, as if the air was too thick even to be sliced by boats.

I stood at a railing and stared out over the harbor toward the islands. I thought about what Aliana said about Stow and Harpur.

If only I could be cured of my obsession with Harpur, but some sickness is incurable. My thoughts turned to her, and even the strange heavy heat seemed to disappear.

•   •   •

The first few months after Gleason's death, the four of us on the "team" made a conscious effort to see each other socially. I was even able to reciprocate in a modest fashion, having given up the attic in my parents' house in favor of the apartment overlooking the ravine.

Even in those early days, my practice was already flourishing. And despite myself, I was enjoying it. I had been afraid my ambitions would make me uninterested in the problems of the people I had been hired to serve, but in fact I was able to forget myself in their woes, and I felt a real sense of power whenever I was able to help them with the relatively uncomplicated legal matters that are the backbone of the practice of a "community" lawyer. I wrote their wills. I helped them bring their relatives "over." I assisted them in buying houses. One thing I didn't do for them was divorces. In our community then, there weren't any.

So, for the first time in my life, I had money. I had enough money to invite my three friends over for dinner.

When I look back on it, now, I marvel at how very well behaved they were. They must have pitied me for how hard I was trying to impress them. But Harpur commented on the excellence of the roast, and Stow graciously uncorked the wine, and William in his quiet, thoughtful way studied my small art collection, which consisted of two paintings and three pieces of modern sculpture—all of which had been purchased directly from the artists down in Gerrard Village—as intently as if he were a student at the Louvre.

We didn't mention the absent fifth member of our little circle. Nor did we say anything about our promises to him or to each other. We did, however, wear our rings. That I remember.

A few weeks after this little soiree, I got a phone call from Harpur.

She had seldom called me and never at my office, and to my embarrassment, I didn't recognize her voice.

When she finished gently teasing me for that gaffe, she told me that she "and the boys," as she put it, had so enjoyed their dinner at my place that they were inviting me to a picnic that evening. I didn't have to bring anything but myself, she said. Could I possibly come?

In those days, my office was the smallest in the firm for which I worked, and the closest to the waiting room. Though the senior lawyers would, of course, see people only by appointment, there were a fairly large number of our clients who were walk-ins. It was my job to handle any new client who came in without an appointment.

I glanced out my door. To my joy, I saw but a lone man sitting in the waiting room. I told Harpur I would be free.

It never occurred to me to question the spontaneity of the invitation. We were still young and we had always been spontaneous. I finished with the client, straightened up my desk, went out to the street—at a time when you could still park on the street—and got my car.

I remember even now how beautiful the weather was that evening. It was full summer, but not hot, just gloriously warm. Throughout the city, the trees were thick with dark green leaves. The flowers of our northern summer—impatiens, begonias, geraniums and portulaca—poured out of their containers, burst the careful bounds of their beds. Cardinals and jays—there were still many of them in the city then—cried out. The sun, still high in the blue sky at seven, blessed everything with a clear topaz light.

I was in love with the city, with my prospects, and with myself.

And with my friends.

It took me about half an hour to drive from my office to the park where I'd been told they'd be, a park, in fact, at the fork of the two major branches of the Don. It was nearing eight when I finally found them. Though Harpur had given me general directions to their whereabouts in the park, I had neglected to ask her to be specific enough, and I had to wander around a bit before I saw them sitting together at a picnic table under a towering maple.

The minute I saw them I realized I had forgotten something important—to take the time to change my clothes. They were all in shorts—Harpur's being a fine khaki pair set off by a dark green blouse that made her hair look like flame.

I, of course, was in a business suit.

"Here he is—at last!" she said when she saw me, waving her hand and gesturing for me to hurry toward them.

It was hard to walk on the thick summer grass in my business shoes, and, never one for staying on my feet if there is an opportunity to fall, I slid, almost losing my balance.

This the three of them seemed to find funny. And when I heard them laugh, I realized that they had been drinking while waiting for me.

"Here you are, dear," Harpur said gaily, spreading a linen napkin on the rough wood of the park picnic table. "We've saved all these lovely things for you."

I felt a twinge of disappointment to think they'd eaten without me, but what could I expect? They must have been waiting for over an hour.

The delicacies that Harpur put before me were impressive. There was caviar, which until then I had tasted only once. And there was avocado and imported cheese and a variety of breads. There were exotic fruits—things I didn't even know the names of. And there were real glasses for some very fine wine, a couple of bottles of which seemed already to have been drunk. Years later, when expensive picnics purchased in elegant baskets had become a fad, I sometimes thought about that strange picnic and how exotic it had been. And how humiliating.

For, whether it was from drunkenness or from something else, Harpur, Stow and William—who was easily led by the other two—seemed to find everything I did uproariously funny. When I tried to straddle the seat of the picnic table in my suit, they thought that was funny. When I lifted my wine glass to toast them, they giggled. When I thanked them for the meal, they laughed and said, "Oh, dear, dear, Ellis, this is nothing, *nothing*! Not a dinner—it's a snack!"

Naturally a person can take only so much of this before he starts doing stupid things. Starts dropping caviar—which leaves a very startling stain on anything white, such as a shirtfront. Starts knocking over wine glasses. Even starts choking on crusty bread.

Oh, I was hilarious. A regular laughingstock.

But of course, they, in their unfailing politeness made a big joke of it all. "Our Ellis," they mocked. "Our dear, clumsy friend . . ."

My unease grew by the minute. Were they humiliating me on purpose? Or was I overreacting, seeing insult where none was intended? Whatever was going on, I was suddenly more than ever a complete outsider. I wanted them to stop laughing at me, but if they did, I was sure, they would stop noticing me at all.

When I had finally managed to finish eating, Harpur threw everything back into the picnic basket with an abandon that before that night had always seemed very attractive. I realized that some maid was going to clean up that mess, some servant who was not invisible—as they always seemed—but a real person, like one of the people who would be sitting in my waiting room the next day, having worked years for women like Harpur just for the privilege of bringing over a sister or a daughter or even a mother who would end up working in the same way.

"Cheer up, Ellis," Stow said graciously. "We've been rude, but you must understand that it's all in the way of friendship."

Some friends, I thought, but of course I buried that thought along with my feelings of hurt, shame and resentment. I'd known these people for years and they'd never offended me before. What had changed?

The beauty of the evening wiped away some of my negative feelings as the four of us strolled through the lovely park. At its center was a public stable that housed horses belonging to one of the mounted police units. This building was possessed of a certain rustic charm, with white clapboard sides and a red barn-like roof. In a fenced paddock in front of the stable, a sturdy but pretty bay mare ran at her leisure, free of saddle and rein, as if celebrating her youth and strength.

Beyond the stable was a riding school, idle now that the day had drawn to a close. It, too, had its own little stable. But unlike the police stable, this one was luxurious, not rustic in the sense of barn, but rustic in the sense of country estate.

Without a word, Harpur led us toward this building, and we all followed. I thought we were just going to peek in, in an idle sort of way. But the nearer we got to the stable door, from which issued the sweet smell of hay and the soft whinnying of happy horses, the more determined became Harpur's step.

When we were on the path that led directly to the padlocked door, Harpur, her voice still a little slurred from the wine, said, "I want to check on my little horse."

"Come on, Harpur," Stow said gently, "you don't have a horse here."

"Oh, but I do," she insisted. And to the evident surprise of Stow, she took a key from her pocket and unfastened the padlock, swinging open the stable door and gesturing with her hand for us to precede her in, which we did.

Soft light from late evening sun filtered through the warm stable, catching on clean straw that seemed to be everywhere and turning it into gold as pure as the gold spun by Rumpelstiltskin in exchange for a first-born child.

"I *do* have a horse here," Harpur said. "Come along and I'll show you. It's my own dear horse from when I was little . . ."

I thought she must be much drunker than she seemed. She wasn't making any sense at all. But we followed her past the stalls of the riding-school horses.

They stared at us, wary and sad, the way, years later, I would see people stare from the bars of prisons and prisoners' docks.

But the stable was very well kept. There were brasses and decorative blankets on the walls, which were weathered barnboard. Beside each stall was a carriage-house lamp, softly illuminating the shadows that were gathering now that sunset was near. By the light of these lamps, I could see that each stall bore a little brass plaque engraved with a horse's name.

Harpur led us—Stow hovering at her side and William and I following behind—to the very last stall.

There, wearing a dark green blanket and having the face of tired, old patience, we found a mare with a gray muzzle. I have never held with those who believe that a person can read the face of an animal the way he can read the face of a fellow human, but it *did* seem to me that this horse knew Harpur and that she was overjoyed to see her. She moved as close to the front of her stall as she could, stretched her old neck, and thrust her wizened muzzle into Harpur's pale, outstretched hand.

"Old girl, old sweetheart," Harpur crooned, in a display of tenderness that made me more in love with her than ever, though such a thing seemed impossible. "You still love me, don't you?" she asked, and I jumped, though of course she was talking to the horse.

"You see, I *do* have a horse here," Harpur said to Stow, as if challenging him. "She's my old mare that

I've had since I was a girl. Used to have. My father donated her to the riding school so that the little girls who are afraid to ride can start out on her. And I can come to see her whenever I like, though, I must admit, I seldom come anymore . . .''

As if she didn't want to lose even a moment of Harpur's attention, the old horse nudged her shoulder, and Harpur once more lifted her lovely fingers to caress the old face.

As she did so, the carriage-lamp cast its light on the gleam of gold—the ring, the ring of the promises.

The light fell also on the brass plaque that bore the old horse's name.

With natural curiosity, I leaned closer to read the plaque.

I thought my eyes must be playing a trick on me. But the light was clear enough for me to read the plaque, clear enough for me to make out the horse's name.

It was Jay-lo.

Little Harpur years before had named her horse after the boy who had worked on his hands and knees in the front yard of her father's house.

I gasped, then tried immediately to hide my shock.

But Harpur heard me. And when she did, she looked up, caught my eye, winked and laughed.

Over the years I'd kept this memory intact, forced myself to remember the careless, hurtful joking of these people, trying to figure out how they could get to me so. Eventually I came to understand they had only been teasing. And like the perfect tease she was, the more Harpur saw results, the more she kept it up and the more complex and exquisite her ploys.

It was my own sense of myself, my fear of inadequacy combined with my puffed-up ambition, that made me such a tempting target. I felt I was beyond all that now, considering what I'd been through.

So why did the news that Harpur and Stow were on the board of Second Chance make me feel suddenly less like an ex-judge trying to solve a mystery and more like an ex-con getting closer and closer to going back to jail?

CHAPTER
TWELVE

"ONE PHONE CALL, THAT'S ALL IT TOOK!" ALIANA WAS SO eager to tell me her news that I couldn't get a word in.

"I have a contact I use whenever I need information about social service agencies," she began. "Her name is Kate Martin, and she runs a large community center near Parliament Street."

"I know Kate. She's personally escorted me out of her community center a number of times."

Aliana made a wry face. "I chatted with Kate for a while, then I casually mentioned Second Chance. Before I said anything else, she said, 'I guess they'll be looking for a new president. Now that Stoughton-Melville is becoming a judge, he'll have to give up all his boards.' I couldn't believe what I was hearing! I went up to the reference library and checked out the Second Chance annual report. It's true. Stow is the president—and his wife, Harpur, is the vice-president."

"So Second Chance is a registered charity?"

"Legally," Aliana said. "But it does offer certain programs on a fee-for-service basis."

"You mean some clients have to pay for programs? Isn't that unusual?"

"Not as unusual as it used to be. With cutbacks in government funding, new methods of fundraising are picking up some of the slack these days. And there's not a large surplus. For the past five years, Second Chance has just about broken even.''

''But how would they make money? What would the surplus come from?''

''Ostensibly from fees . . .''

''You don't sound a hundred percent convinced.''

''John Stoughton-Melville's record is impeccable,'' Aliana said. ''Otherwise he'd never have been appointed to the Supreme Court. But he is enormously wealthy—not only through thirty years of building up his law firm, but also through inheritance. Why would he need to skim funds from a halfway house for single mothers? But even if the hostel is financially on the level, it could still be a front for something else.''

''But what? Not money-laundering—there's no large flow-through of cash.''

''No. Whatever it is, Ellis, until we find out, we're not going to know how Moonstar is connected.''

A thought struck me. ''Aliana, on those annual reports, was there a lawyer listed as representing the corporation?''

''Only Stow's firm—why?''

Now it was my turn. ''I talked to Queenie today. I tried to get her to name the lawyer who got Moonstar into Second Chance. She was evasive, as I expected.''

''So you didn't get the name?''

''No. But she told me something just as important. She said both the lawyer and the Youth Bureau officer were wearing identical gold rings.''

''So?''

''Aliana, I was wearing my own ring. Queenie saw it. She said their rings were like mine.'' She drew a sharp breath. ''There's something else. The last time I saw Queenie, she had a letter from my daughter, Ellen. Ellen saw that picture that Mitch the stringer took. She talked to a lawyer at the Faculty of Law who told her that I could be reached through Queenie. He even knew where

Queenie lives, which is more than I knew myself until today.''

"What are you getting at?''

"I don't know much anymore about William Sterling . . .''

"The fourth lawyer with the ring . . .''

"Yes.''

"He never came before me in court; with a practice like his, he would only have handled criminal cases in the most exceptional circumstances. And he was shy, never much of a socializer. Our paths have only crossed four or five times over the years. But the last time I talked to him about seven years ago, he was teaching part-time at the Law Faculty . . .''

She thought about that for a moment. "So you think he's the lawyer who talked to Queenie—which also means he'd most likely know everybody in the Youth Bureau, including Matt West.''

"Yes. The Youth Bureau officer was black. That much Queenie was willing to offer.''

"But why,'' Aliana asked, "would Matt West be wearing the fifth ring?''

"Maybe the answer is obvious,'' I said.

"Yeah.''

"It's possible,'' I reminded her, "that Moonstar was killed because of something she knew was going on at Second Chance—something Matt and William might have known about, too.''

"And Stow?''

"I don't know. People would assume he knew everything about all his companies, but it's a big assumption. A man who's running one of the largest law firms in the country might figure he'd be forgiven if he didn't seem to be paying enough attention to what had to be his smallest operation.''

"Yes. But William Sterling would have known something about Second Chance if he sent Moonstar there.''

Aliana paused. "Do you realize that he's the key to this whole thing? He's the only one who's connected to everybody else."

"We have to find him."

"How?"

"One way is to get back to Kate Martin. That first evening at your place, didn't you mention that his practice is on Parliament Street?"

"Yes."

"Near the community center—Kate might know Sterling. If she knows the local community, she might also know whether William handled same-sex spousal benefit cases out of more than purely professional interest."

"Okay. I'll call her back. What about you? What will you do?"

There were two things. The first concerned my suspicions about the so-called birdwatcher, but I wanted to check that out before I said anything to anybody. "Aliana, I've got to talk to Stow. If he is somehow involved in the deaths of innocent young women . . ."

"Ellis, we don't know that. You can't risk going to jail on mere speculation." She knew about the conditions of the restraining order. Though I hadn't gotten far enough in her article to read about it, Aliana was too good a journalist to miss the irony. I who had once been friends with Stow was now prevented by the conditions of my release from jail from even being in his presence. She insisted, "You just find out what you can about William. Leave Stow to me. I'll think of something."

I rose and walked toward the door.

"Where are you going?"

"Home. I need to figure this out. It's cooler by the river—and it's still the only place where I can stay calm."

She wasn't convinced. "You can't hide out there forever, Ellis. It's dangerous. And you're wasting . . ."

"What?"

"Your life. You want a ride?"

"No thanks, Aliana. And I don't want advice, either."

I walked along the river for hours, coming no closer to figuring out how I could confront Stow without his having me arrested for breaching the order by harassing him. As I walked, a stiff breeze arose, and by the time I got to my ravine, the hazy sun of the previous days was gone, the sky was overcast, and the air was cool.

As I got close to home, I once again heard the rustle of an intruder. This time, I was ready. Though now I was fairly certain who it was, I wanted to catch him unaware, to gain my sole advantage: surprise. I felt vindictive, too. He had caused me a great deal of inconvenience.

My years in the valley had made me a silent stalker. I was close enough to my hut to see it and to see the back of the intruder's head. Though I was within a few feet of him, he didn't hear me when I retrieved my judge's robe from a nearby hiding place and put it on. *This,* I thought, *will serve him right.*

Dressed in my fine black silk, which had been fitted to a much fuller body than the one I now had, I figured I would look like some avenging monk.

It was one of those moments in which time slows. The other birds, the real ones, were momentarily silent. The wind was increasing, blowing dark clouds across the sky, giving the day a feeling of impending trouble. And I, like some gigantic misshapen creature of the leaden air, was suspended in mock flight over my prey.

His face, turned toward me, was frozen in shock and fear. In that still immobility, I saw two things: that I was acting foolish and that I was right about who the birder was—William.

Absurdly flapping my silk wings before I could stop myself, I scared the wits out of him.

He tried to run without first standing, which resulted in his scrambling along the dry ground like an animal. He wasn't able to get very far this way, and he soon fell, spreadeagled in front of me, his gloved hand hitting against a rock.

When I tried to move close, his escape attempts intensified. He managed to get to the hut and propped himself against its shaky wall.

His wrist was bleeding, and a smear of red marred the perfection of his shirt, one of those expensive khaki ones with a lot of pockets.

As he had always been, he was wiry and muscled. No doubt his canoeing and climbing in the valley kept him fit. He wore leather sports gloves, and he didn't take them off as he reached into one of the pockets of his shirt, pulled out a white linen handkerchief and wiped the sweat from his face. Then he took a swipe at the blood on his arm. There was a self-confidence when he spoke that belied his fear.

"Despite appearances," he said, "I am not a nature aficionado who has overstepped his bounds . . ."

"I know who you are, William. What I want to know is why you're hounding me."

He didn't answer. He just kept wiping his wrist until every trace of blood was gone.

"What's going on, William? What are you after?"

Silence. I felt like shaking him, but I waited until he spoke, halting, verging on incoherence. "I didn't tear your other place up," he said. "You really must understand that, because I've worried about it since I first came here a month ago. I know how particular a man you are. Even though we haven't been friends in a long time, I haven't forgotten about you."

"Obviously. Tell me, if it wasn't you who tore up my other place, who did?"

"Vandals. Mountain bikers. Some mountain bikers are nature lovers, but others are totally destructive. They harass me down here all the time because I'm a nature lover. They were following me and when they saw your place, they thought it would be great fun to tear it up. I felt horrid about it. Not only did I lead them right to it, but it seems to have quite satisfied their need for violence. That particular group of boys hasn't bothered me since.''

''Why were you here? Why are you here now? I *demand* to know!''

He pulled himself into a more upright position against the tottering wall of the hut. ''Oh, my dear, Ellis,'' he mocked. ''All these years and still such passion, still such a will to command!'' The tone of amused condescension. The tone of jovial disregard. The tone of Harpur. The tone of Stow. Gone as quickly as it had come.

''I'm sorry,'' he said, brokenly. ''I have no right to joke with you. I have come for help, Ellis. I have come because my life is shattered.''

It was embarrassing. The man seemed about to cry. I really couldn't take that on top of everything else. ''You're making quite an assumption thinking that I have the resources to help anybody. *What do you want?*''

''You owe me a favor. And I've come to collect.''

I stood still, but everything was making a circle around me. The black clouds. The screaming birds. The whipped leaves and blown grass. Time. Space. My own life. Everything was making a circle around me, and I was standing in the middle of it trying to figure out what to do.

''May I please have a drink of water?''

I couldn't even offer William a cup. I seldom used one and I had quite forgotten what I'd done with the one I had. He took off his gloves. Gamely, he cupped his hands—hands I now saw were as calloused as my own. William the sculler. William the canoeist. Carefully I poured water into them, into the cupped hands of my guest, my old friend, the wearer of one of the rings. *Impegno*.

"It looks like rain," he said absurdly, in the same tone in which I had heard conversations conducted in jail, in court, in places where people are avoiding talking about the thing they really must talk about.

"Looks like bad rain," I answered. "Maybe we should go inside."

Again, there was an absurdity to the invitation. In his fashionable field outfit, he didn't seem the type of man who'd be comfortable in a shack made of packing-crate slats.

But he accepted the invitation, and as I motioned for him to precede me, showing him, as I had always wanted to show him, that my manners were above reproach, he nodded, bowed his head in order not to bang it on the top of the crate, and slouched in.

I gestured toward the bed, grateful when he sat down without evident distaste.

For a long moment of awkward silence, we just sat there, as far away from each other as possible. He must have been curious, but he kept his eyes downcast.

"I've come, Ellis, because I have no one else to turn to . . ." His voice broke, and I felt a jolt of compassion that quite shook me. Moonstar had sought my help. And Queenie. Now him.

"Perhaps if we go slowly, William, you'll be able to tell me one step at a time what this is all about." It was as if someone else was speaking: Ellis Portal who had served the waiting-room clients so long ago. Ellis Portal not only before the fall. Before the rise. I reached out and touched his hand. To my surprise, he covered my fingers with his own. And he began to talk.

"I always wondered why you never bothered with me after you got married, Ellis. I knew that Stow and Harpur liked to tease you and make you angry, but it was all in fun really. I thought maybe it was because you knew about Gleason and me, and that it bothered you some-how.''

''No . . .''

''Ellis, I've been a decent, law-abiding man and a good lawyer. True I've lived what some still consider an unconventional life. Gleason was the first man I ever loved, but I had other partners before him, and I have had some since. But I never loved anyone else until Matt West.''

He waited for my reaction and when it wasn't one of surprise, he said, ''So you know about Matt and me?''

''Yes.''

He accepted this news without comment and went on. ''All these years I have prided myself on my discretion. I've never, ever had any sort of threats or trouble. Not until now. Not until Matt . . . What I mean is, something has happened to Matt. And I can't get help without letting his co-workers know more about him than he'd want them to know . . .''

''William, surely . . .''

''No, listen, I'm telling this all backward. I've got to tell you how it started. As time went by and attitudes changed, I became more comfortable with myself and the facts of my sexuality. Except for my part-time teaching at the Law Faculty, I've dealt with gay clients almost exclusively, except for one set of people . . .''

''Who?''

As if he hadn't heard me, he kept talking. ''My life has been good, I'm not complaining, but when the AIDS thing struck, I had to look at my sexual life and decide what to do. I was past forty, and I was busy with work and my bird studies. I decided to opt out of the scene. I mean, I decided to stay celibate.''

He smiled wryly. ''That lasted about a month—then I met Matt.''

''Is this about AIDS, William?''

''No, quite the opposite. It's about luck and love.

When I met Matt, I was working on the case of a young man who'd been bashed and had fought back. Matt had to bring my client in on assault charges, and I could see that he was upset at having to do so. I thought that was quite unusual in a police officer.''

Again he looked up, as if to see whether I'd also figured out that Matt was on the police force. I nodded and he resumed.

"This was almost fifteen years ago. Matt was still in his twenties then. He was tall and slim, but not slim like me. He had the physique of a lion. He was the most beautiful man I'd ever seen . . .

"Well, I was with him for hours that first night, trying to put together charges that wouldn't destroy my client's fragile self-esteem but also wouldn't result in a public outcry because of appearing lenient. It took a long time. I'm not, as you probably know, a criminal lawyer. And in the course of those hours, I fell in love—for only the second time in forty years . . ."

"And Matt, how did he react?"

"Well," William said with a grimace, "it was interesting . . . You see, Matt hadn't come out. He'd been married. In fact, he'd had a child. But the marriage had broken up immediately after the birth of his son. He was a virgin, if you know what I mean. He knew what he wanted, but he was a policeman. Policemen don't take homosexuality lightly. Even now."

"No."

"So it was slow and it was careful . . ."

He stopped; he needed to gather himself. "With Matt, a life was possible. A real life. We had a place. We had friends. We had to be careful around some of his fellow officers, just as we were careful around other professional associates, but Matt wasn't the only gay cop in the city and I am certainly not the only gay lawyer."

A sudden noise startled us both. Thunder—surprisingly close. The sky had turned woolly gray and whipped up. It was hours until sunset, but the gloom was like four o'clock on a December afternoon.

Almost as if talking to himself, William spoke again. "We had a life. Matt was doing well, moving up. He was getting more and more complicated work. For years I was happy about that—as happy as he was. But then things started to become frightening."

"How?"

"He started to go undercover more and more," William answered. "I could see why they needed him so much, of course. He could do anything they asked. Matt was so intelligent, so . . ."

It was impossible at first to tell the sound of his weeping from the sound of the wind in the valley grass. I turned toward the door. I stepped outside. Gusts shook the tall reeds by the river. When the sound of weeping stopped, replaced by the sound of even, smooth breathing, I stepped back inside.

"Matt was gone for longer and longer periods of time. At first I trusted him entirely. But of course, I had to go through what every police officer's spouse goes through—spending sleepless nights asking myself: why couldn't he tell me? Surely he could tell *me* where he was, what he was doing.

"But he couldn't. And the little time he spent at home, he spent explaining to me that he couldn't. Then he stopped explaining altogether. Who could blame him? More nights went by. And then I didn't trust him entirely anymore. *Who* was he with?

"Then, he didn't come home at all. Days went by. Weeks. I had nobody to turn to. His boss wasn't going to tell me what was going on, was he? I wasn't going to call up other officers' wives for commiseration, was I?

"One day, when I was at my wits' end, I opened the back door to let out the dog, and—God help me—I found a box with Matt's hand in it! And you know what,

Ellis? You know what my first thought was? My first thought was that it had to be criminals who had done this and not another lover and I was grateful—do you understand me? *Grateful*! I was completely berserk . . .''

"William, please . . .'' I was sick of sad stories and this was another one. But it was only part of the truth. He was no innocent bystander. No ignorant "cop's wife."

"Ellis," William went on, stammering out his words, "I've come here again and again, trying to get up the nerve to ask you to help me. You used to help people all the time. You were known for it. So why, I asked myself, would you who helped so many strangers refuse to help me? Besides, you of all people can understand both sides.''

"Both sides of what?''

"The law.''

It took me a minute before I realized what he was getting at. My years on the skids had taught me that there is a certain place in the subculture of crime for disgraced lawyers, men who know the law from the inside, but are outlaws, too. No matter how low I had sunk, I had never reached the level of these disbarred attorneys with shady practices conducted out of their "offices" in alleys, doorways and jail. I wanted to tell him to go to hell.

But he was so upset I was afraid he was going to be ill. If he was, I'd be stuck with him. There was a strong storm coming, and once it started, getting out of the ravine would take more stamina than either of us was likely to have.

"William, pull yourself together. I've known for a while that Matt disappeared and that the ring on the hand was his. Nonetheless, you have no reason to expect my help. But if I do help, you're going to have to answer some questions. You and Matt were responsible for sending a little hooker named Moonstar to Second

Chance hostel. She swore something illegal was going on there. She tried to solicit my help in finding out what it was. And for her pains, she died.''

His face was so white, it seemed to glow in the semi-darkness. ''Ellis, I swear, everything was legal and aboveboard with Moonstar. She lost her baby because her pregnancy was complicated by her heavy use of drugs—which did not cease even while she was at Second Chance. Her baby was a full-term stillborn. After the delivery, she was asked to leave because of the drugs. That's it. That's all there is to her story.''

What he was saying was more logical than Moonstar's accusations. It still didn't make sense that someone was selling babies and killing their mothers. So why wasn't I satisfied with his explanation? I had that gut feeling I always had when a witness was holding back. The whole truth and nothing but the truth.

''William, you know how lawyers feel about clients who won't tell the truth. Tell me or get out.''

He drew in a ragged breath. ''Ellis,'' he said, ''I swear I did nothing to Moonstar, but . . .''

''But?''

''I sent other girls to that hostel. Most of them did well, got their lives back in order. Many returned to their parents and their schools.''

''But some didn't return? Some were never heard from again. That's what Moonstar told me. And I think maybe she was right. Where are *they*? What happened to *them*?''

''I don't know. So help, me, Ellis, I don't know. I wasn't even aware there was anything unusual about Second Chance for a long time. I had a simple deal. It was a courtesy to Stow. All I had to do was refer a certain number of young female clients to the hostel.''

I thought about that for a minute. On the surface, it was a way of doing troubled girls a favor—setting them up in a comfortable halfway house away from the pressures exerted by their disapproving parents. On the surface.

"But Second Chance is a charity," I challenged. "Anybody could get in . . ."

In the gloom, I saw William turn away, "Not exactly. There was always a waiting list. And there were what we called 'enhanced services'—extra programs to raise funds. The idea of helping certain girls was presented to me as a sort of scholarship thing. Extra attention with all fees paid."

Abruptly, William stood—or tried to. He banged his head on the roof of the hut. But he stayed standing. "Do you think I haven't asked myself over and over again what was going on at Second Chance? I still haven't figured it out. But one day I was there for a meeting of one of the subcommittees of the board. I usually took public transit. But on this day, I'd had a prior meeting in the West End, and I drove directly to the hostel."

He rushed on as if afraid I would break off his narrative. "After the meeting, I took transit home. It wasn't until after midnight that I remembered the car. I decided to take a taxi back to get it. I didn't want to leave the car overnight and risk having it towed or broken into.

"It was about one when I got to the hostel. I walked down the alleyway toward the parking lot. Before I got all the way to the back, I heard voices. I kept to the shadows and watched. I saw a large, late-model unmarked van in the lot. And I also saw a stretcher with a body on it being loaded into the van. There were two people in addition to the driver. Both stayed near the stretcher.

"The transfer took about two minutes. The two beside the stretcher looked like doctors or nurses. I could see that the patient's face wasn't covered. I mean I didn't think the person was dead . . ."

"Maybe it was an ambulance," I said.

"No. It was, as I said, unmarked." He paused to catch

his breath. In the still, heavy, damp air, I felt clammy, so I wasn't surprised when William shivered.

"William, who *were* those girls at Second Chance? Weren't they pregnant like Moonstar? If so, why would it be so unusual for one to be taken away for private care?"

"Once in a while, the board accepted a street girl like Moonstar just to appear to be giving poor girls a chance. But most of my referrals were from well-to-do families—girls whose problems were an embarrassment to their parents . . ."

"Why would Stow choose *you* to refer clients like them? Your practice had nothing to do with the legal problems of teenaged girls."

"*Exactly,* Ellis," he said, with a return of contempt, as if I should somehow be able to figure all this out. It made me feel he was hiding as much as he was saying.

"From that night on, I began to be increasingly uneasy about the halfway house," he continued. "I wasn't a board member—just a volunteer—so I had no access to financial records, correspondence, files. I had no way of checking on anything. I longed to be able to tell all this to Matt, but I hadn't seen him in weeks.

"It had been several months since I'd referred anybody, and I knew Stow would soon call me in for one of the little 'meetings' we always had right before I chose a new batch of girls to be sent to the hostel. At these meetings, I presented the case histories of girls, and he made a selection of those he thought would be appropriate for Second Chance."

"Where did the girls come from?" I interrupted. He didn't seem to hear me.

"After I saw that van, I needed to find out more," he went on. "I took to monitoring the streets around the hostel—on foot, always after midnight. One night, I saw the van again—headed toward the hostel. By the time I got to Second Chance, it was there. I stayed out of sight and watched. I expected to see a repeat of what I'd seen before, but that's not what happened. Instead, I saw them wheel a stretcher *into* Second Chance. There was a patient—or a body—on that one, too.''

He dropped his face into his hands. His shoulders began to shake, and I thought he was becoming hysterical. Then I realized with a start that he was fighting nausea. With difficulty he continued his story.

''I waited. An hour went by. When the driver finally left the van and went toward the rear of the lot, I didn't waste any time; I headed for the door of the building. I could see that it was propped open so that the lock wouldn't engage, I guessed to make it easier to bring a stretcher back out. I pushed it open and slipped in. Just then, I saw a stretcher being wheeled down the hall toward the door. I jumped back into a recess near the door. It was so dark I could hardly make anything out, except that there was again someone on the stretcher. And protruding from some part of the person's head was a tube. It was connected to a clear bag, suspended above the stretcher, and one of the medical attendants was walking alongside the stretcher, making sure the bag and the tube stayed in place. There was something in the bag, something suspended in liquid. But that was all I could see.

''As they left, they reset an alarm on the door. I had no choice but to trip it as I left, but I wasn't caught.'' William swallowed several times in distress, but I urged him on.

''A while later, Stow asked to see me for one of our meetings. He said it was urgent that he speak to me at once because there had been a change in the situation. He was vague, but I didn't question him. I told him I'd come. But I couldn't force myself to go. I waited nervously for him to call—or even show up at my office demanding to know why I hadn't shown up. Nothing happened for several weeks. Then I got the box on the porch.

"That was a month ago. I haven't seen or heard from Matt since. I did what I promised. But I'm still done for."

"*Stow,*" I said. "You promised *Stow* you'd supply those girls?"

"I promised Stow I would do as he asked, but now Matt may be dead, and Moonstar *is* dead, and so will I be, and you, too."

"Me? Why me? Why have you dragged me into this? And don't tell me you came looking for 'The little man's friend.'"

William smiled, finally. I could see his white, perfect teeth. I used to have white perfect teeth like that, too, when I could afford them. "Ellis," he said, again in the old voice, condescending, insulting, "surely you haven't forgotten. I have come to you for the same reason that Stow came to me."

And he held up his hand so that the heavy gold ring he wore caught the bit of light that remained and shot it back toward me like a bullet.

CHAPTER

THIRTEEN

WILLIAM TOLD ME THAT AFTER FINDING MATT'S HAND HE sat in his house unable to move, even to think, until he pulled himself together enough to phone his office and tell them he'd been called away on family business. But that was the extent of his activity. He couldn't remember moving at all, couldn't remember eating or sleeping until he left the house carrying his awful burden. He drove around for several hours, eventually ending up near the river. That was when he decided to come to me in the valley.

"How did you know where I was?"

"Tim Garrison told me a long time ago. We belong to the same ornithological society. I used to come to this ravine often before I knew you were down here. I know it like the back of my hand. Since Tim told me about your being here, I've avoided it—out of courtesy to you."

Was he really such a gentleman or was he a liar?

"But as soon as you got in trouble, William, you came back and back and back? Come on . . ."

"Please, Ellis, I know how all this must sound. But I have been at my wits' end for a month—torn between begging for your help and risking having you go to Stow. I haven't done any work since this happened. You know how powerful Stow is. And once he's sworn in on the Supreme Court, his power will be greater still."

"I, on the other hand, am powerless and therefore disposable?" I shot at him.

"Right. You have nothing to lose if you help me."

Neither time nor tragedy had taken the polish off his arrogance. He regarded me as little more than subhuman, a slave to his wishes.

"Except my freedom. That's not 'nothing,' as you may soon find out for yourself. Why didn't you just go to the police?"

"Because of what I've done at Second Chance."

"What, William? What exactly have you done wrong?"

"That's the worst part of the whole thing. I don't know for sure. Stow told me that out of the girls I sent to Second Chance, one or two each year would be chosen for a special task for Harpur. He said he was unable to be more specific because he had made a personal commitment to honor Harpur's confidentiality, as he put it. It just sounded like one of the charitable things that rich people like Stow are always doing without attracting attention to themselves. But . . ."

"But?"

"But Stow was so particular about the girls he wanted me to refer to that place. For one thing, they had to be really young. He wouldn't even consider anybody who had gotten pregnant after the age of sixteen. He preferred girls who were completely estranged from their parents. He said those were the ones most in need of help. And the girls had to be healthy. He had his secretary arrange for them to be tested for all manner of things."

"Finding these girls made heavy demands on a man with a law practice and a teaching position, too," I couldn't help but observe.

"Yes. And he got more demanding as time went on."

"I don't get this, William. Why would Stow be collecting pregnant teenaged girls?"

He became agitated again, trying to stand in the center

of the hut, failing to get upright as much because of his own state as because of the limited space. "I don't know. But Matt might have found out. Moonstar, too. When I heard that her body had been discovered, I came back here. That's when I saw you were sick and called Garrison. I knew he would be able to get you out. When I saw the photo of the rescue in the paper, I knew you were out of the valley, so I came back for the hand. But I couldn't find it." He shuddered in distaste. "I can't afford to spend time out in the open. I can only conclude that Stow is after me, too. Except for the times I came here hoping to find you, I've been in hiding."

"Where?"

He smiled an odd smile. "Here," he said. "Here in your ravine. You're not the only one who knows how to survive in the wilderness."

"Except for the day that you went back to Second Chance . . ."

A look of shock passed over his features. I realized I'd been wrong about his seeing me the day I'd been eavesdropping beside the patio at the hostel.

"I had to see Mrs. Campbell. I had to find out whether Stow had sent anybody after me. But she was busy . . ."

"Where is the ring that was on Matt's hand—the ring you stole from my box?"

"I have it. I went back for it that first day. You saw me. You thought I was just any birdwatcher. You avoided looking at me and walked on. I followed you. I saw you go to the river. Then I saw you go to the rock. Through my binoculars, I saw you put the ring away. I waited until you were gone. I had to wait a long time, but no matter. I got the ring on the first try. It was Gleason's ring. Then it was Matt's . . ."

He began to cry again, harsh, gulping sounds like strangling. I was torn between pity and loathing.

"I had the inscription filed off just after Gleason died," he said finally, sounding far away. "You see, as

Gleason was dying in my arms, out on the road, in the snow, he asked his favor of me. He asked me to love another man as I had loved him. It was the worst moment of my life, but it was also the moment in which I knew what it was to love someone so much that you make an impossible promise."

There was a long silence. The wind had calmed. I couldn't hear it at all anymore. I also couldn't hear any birds.

"What do you want, William? What do you think I can do for you?"

"I want you to go to the police. I want you to tell them that you found the hand and then it disappeared. I want them to find out what happened to Matt."

What he was suggesting was the first thing Aliana had suggested a month before. There was no way the police would believe I was some innocent vagrant who had happened upon the remains of a victim.

"I can't do that, William—the idea is useless."

"You mean you think Matt is dead?"

"I don't know."

Once more, I went to the door of the hut. When I looked out, I was surprised to see that the black clouds that had given the sky such an angry, tortured look were gone.

Which is not to say that the sky was clear. In fact it was a uniform dull light gray, as it sometimes is before the weather settles into a steady, unrelenting rain. I wasn't used to seeing the summer sky in the valley look like that. Spring and fall are the rainy seasons. Nonetheless, it looked so much better than the angry sky of only a little while before, that it gave me an idea.

"Listen, William, I want you to go home."

"But it's not safe there."

"It's not safe here, either. You just never know who's watching—even who's taking pictures. If a person can target me with a telephoto lens, they can target us with a gun.''

''But . . .''

''Go now. I'm used to rain in the ravine. I'll sit it out. Then I'll find a way for you and me to go to Stow together.''

''How can we?''

I took his arm. ''Come on, there's a break in the weather now, but from the looks of it, it might rain for a while. I think you should get out while you can. I need to think things over . . .''

''Ellis,'' he whispered, ''you've *got* to help me. I can't go on like this. I never intended to hold you to that old promise, but now I find I must.''

Exhausted by my confrontation with William, I lay down, intending to rest for a little while.

I was startled awake by drops of water falling onto my face.

It was pitch black in my hut, and everything was soaked—my clothes, the new clean blankets and sheets of which I had been so proud, the book I'd been reading the previous evening. In the dark, I could only feel these things, and when I came upon a sodden mass that my fingers couldn't recognize, I realized with a start that I had left my judge's robe unprotected. Now it felt slick— almost slimy in my hand.

I smoothed it as best I could and laid it flat on the bed. Then I made my way toward the door. This wasn't easy. It was so dark that I had to feel the wall, my hand catching on the rough scrap wood before I could find the opening.

The din of the rain against the tar-paper roof of the hut was nothing compared to the noise of it pelting the packed earth, crushing the thick vegetation. It smacked the river with a sound like an open hand against flesh.

Once outside, I could tell it wasn't really night. I

found myself in some sort of eerie half-light. But despite
the devastation to my bed and my judicial robe, I welcomed the rain. I took my shoes off and put them under
a rock. I removed my wet clothes—peeling them from
my soaked body with difficulty. I held each garment out
in turn, letting the rain pound the dirt, the sweat out of
them.

Naked, I stood in the matted grass, the pelting drops
kneading every muscle, and I wondered why I had never
thought of an invigorating shower in darkness before. It
would have been so refreshing to have showered in the
dark of the marble perfection, the astringent cool of our
house.

But the rain was so hard that I began to feel uncomfortable under its sting. So I put my wet clothes back
on. Either my eyes were getting used to the half-light,
or else the sky was becoming lighter as it released its
burden.

Without putting my shoes back on, I made my way
toward the river. The sound of the rain had masked the
sound of the river itself, which I now heard with shock
and a little fear. I could hear the water thrashing against
the bank the way a mental patient thrashes against institutional restraints.

I turned from the river and slowly made my way back
to where I had left my shoes. I sloshed into them and
hunched back into my hut, the rain following me in as
if we were animals out together in the night. Now it
made a steady drumming sound as it hit rock and earth.

Working as quickly as I could, and able at least to
make out the shapes of things in the gloom, I found the
plastic bags that I had hoarded for just such an emergency, and began to stuff one of them with my most
necessary belongings: my glasses, my judicial robe. I
walked back out into the storm, intending to head for
Aliana's office—or, if I could remember how to get to
it—her house.

I was stunned to see that the river was now only a few feet from my door! Fighting the rain—and the wind, which had risen again—I got away from the river and turned in the direction of one of the paths that led out of the ravine into the suburbs. I had to fight to keep my eyes open. Though the weather wasn't cold, the rain felt like the freezing rain of early spring, each needle a stinging incentive to keep going, to get to shelter.

There were no caves in my ravine. There were no solid structures of any sort. The public washrooms in the parks were miles away, as were the cubicles that held the equipment of the electric company. It would have been useless to seek shelter behind rocks or in trees. I could hear the river clearly now, and what I heard was a roar.

The trees swayed and creaked, and branches snapped all around me. The woods were full of dead limbs just waiting to come crashing down. I quickened my steps.

Suddenly, in the distance I heard a sound that I at first mistook for traffic. Then I realized that in this storm there'd be no rush of traffic. Even if cars could make it down onto the parkway, they'd have to move slowly.

I looked up. Coming toward me along what was usually nothing more than a gully, was a great, dirty wall of water ripping up trees and bushes in its rush. Frantic, I reached to snag any branch I could grab. The last thing I saw before the water closed over my head was the green inner ring of a broken branch from which a drop of sap oozed like blood.

I was drowning. My life was flashing before my eyes. I was Gelo. I was Ellis. I became a lawyer. I married. I held my little children in my arms. I became a judge. I stopped being a judge. I read a book by the river in the long light of June. I ate lunch with Aliana Caterina. I saw William sitting in my hut telling me his awful tale.

Then the water was gone, and I discovered that I hadn't drowned after all. My first inkling of this was the feel of cold wet plastic hitting against my arm. Dangling absurdly from my wrist was my plastic bag.

Up on the street the devastation was worse than it was in the valley because the wind was so much worse. When I managed to look around, I saw that debris from the storm already covered many of the suburban lawns. The air seemed to be full of flying objects: branches, bits of plastic and wood, paper that slapped up against anything it encountered, including my face.

The best I could hope for was to find shelter in some-body's garage, but I had no luck finding one that was open. I was about to start looking for garden sheds, and even dog houses, when I was surprised to hear the sud-den rush of air-brakes above the sound of the wind.

Startled, I turned toward the street. Just behind me was a city bus, the driver holding the door open and beckoning me in.

"The mayor has declared a state of emergency. We're taking all buses off the road, but I'm giving any pedes-trians I find on the way a ride to the next subway sta-tion—if I can get there . . .''

I stayed on the subway all the way to Queen Street. I decided to try to find Queenie to make sure she was okay.

Once I came up out of the subway, I could see an additional problem—downed wires. Lying across the streets, sometimes letting loose with a blue arc of elec-tricity, they were everywhere. In an eerie patchwork of light, some buildings had power while others were blacked out.

It was hard slogging through the streets. The side-walks were slick with rain where they weren't com-pletely submerged by murky water. When I got to Queenie's house, it looked deserted. And the main door at the front was locked. I couldn't think of anywhere else to go except Kate Martin's community center. If

Queenie wasn't home, that was the place she'd most likely be.

When I finally got to the center, I was ready to drop. I didn't even stop to reflect that I'd been barred for life because of the Thanksgiving dinner fiasco.

I peered through the glass door to see whether any of the counsellors were in the lobby. An old wooden counter, gouged, kicked, scratched and worn away by countless destitute impatient fingers and feet, cut the room in half. Behind this counter were the helpers—their exasperated social-worker hearts risking burnout in the service of the poor. In front of the counter were the poor, and ordinarily they were pretty exasperated, too.

Today, however, a sense of excitement and urgency seemed to buzz right out to me as I stood on the steps judging how much trouble I'd be in if I went inside. None, I guessed. It was so crowded in there that I figured even a *persona* as *non grata* as I would probably go unnoticed in the throng.

I opened the door, displacing a few people who were leaning against it. One of them turned, and I saw the familiar face of Johnny Dirt. He looked even more ragged than usual, as if he'd been in a fight or had a hard time making his way through the wet, windy streets. He also didn't seem particularly glad to see me.

"Hello, John."

"Hey, Your Honor, long time . . ."

"Yeah, Johnny, long time. What's everybody doing here at once?"

"Ain't you heard?" He leaned toward me. He smelled like the street. A smell beyond dirt. A dark, rank, moldy smell, a strong smell of unwashed human combined with the pollution of the city and the day of rain. And beneath that smell was another. Alcohol.

"Big storm. It's headed right for the city, all right," he said. "Only a matter of time."

We moved away from the door, even though we had

to shove the people ahead of us a little. This was risky. Push too hard, say the wrong word, step on somebody's foot—it could start a chain reaction in a crowd like this.

But nobody seemed to mind. The feeling in the room wasn't angry, it was light—almost like a party or a fair. Sinking ship.

I eased myself onto my toes and tried to see where the crowd seemed to be headed. Beyond us, at the far side of the building, visible through a wide door that might once have been the door of a ballroom, I caught a glimpse of the center's largest room, a sort of auditorium. Usually it was used for sleeping mats, but now one side had been set up like a soup kitchen. On the other side, boxes of clothing had been set on the floor, and people were digging into them, scattering garments in a great circle around themselves.

"Yeah," Johnny was saying. "It's gonna be a hurricane, all right."

"This is too early for hurricanes," I said.

"You're always such a damn expert on everything, aren't you?" he replied belligerently. "Just have to be right all the time. Okay, *Your Honor,* so I'm wrong. So it's not a hurricane. So sue me . . ." He staggered away.

I was so hungry and wet and glad to be inside that I decided to stay in the line, which was moving slowly but in a very orderly fashion. I slouched down a little, just in case any counsellors were nearby. Being in the auditorium now reminded me of the last time I'd been there—shouting at the top of my lungs that I didn't care whether they threw me out or not because their lousy food wasn't worth coming back for anyway. I glanced at the clock on the auditorium wall. 9:00 P.M. It had been quite a day and I hadn't eaten once during the whole stretch.

I could smell people, bleach, forbidden cigarette smoke (which I think has a different smell from allowed cigarette smoke). I could smell wet hair, ungraced by shampoo but not necessarily devoid of hairspray. I could smell coffee. I could smell the sour odor of old clothing.

And I could smell stew.

I felt a tap on my shoulder. "Your Honor," the familiar voice said. "Thank God you're okay. They say all the roads into the valley are washed right out."

Queenie! I turned to look at her. She wasn't wet, like so many of the others. In the bright fluorescent light, her thick silver hair shone, and her clear dark eyes were suddenly the eyes of Moonstar, at once too young, too old, too innocent and too wise.

"I've been looking for you, Queenie. Thank God you're okay, too."

She smiled and touched my shoulder again. "You been soaked," she said. "You're gonna land up in that hospital again."

"Yeah," I said truthfully. "The thought has occurred to me. How come you're not wet?"

She gave me a long look. "I can read the sky and the heat. I knew this was coming. And it's a bad one. I been here all day, since right after I seen you this morning."

A social worker handed me a tray with a sandwich, a bowl of stew, a bottle of juice, a cookie, and an apple. I didn't know when I'd been happier to see a meal. Queenie and I found a corner where we could hunker down and eat.

I was so intent on the food that I didn't even notice that somebody was suddenly standing in front of me. I looked up and saw two long legs, like the bars of a jail. I heard Queenie make a soft noise, and I looked all the way up.

It was Kate Martin, the executive director of the center. Her territory straddled the gentrified neighborhoods of the upwardly mobile on one side and the vast stretches of assisted housing on the other, cut right down the middle by the city's most politicized gay community. She served them all. But she wasn't keen to serve me.

I put down my spoon. I wasn't going to fight her. Or anybody. I was tired. I was finished with fighting.

"Good evening, Queenie," I heard her say.

"Evening."

"Ellis?" When she said my name, I put aside the remains of my meal and got to my feet. Kate was a tall woman, and her eyes were only a little lower than mine when I stood face to face with her.

"When you finish your supper," she said in her authoritative voice, "come into my office."

I nodded, and she moved on. I squatted back down. "I'm going to be ejected again," I said to Queenie.

"I don't think so," she said. She ate the last of her apple with delicate ladylike bites. "She's got something else on her mind."

"You read minds, too?" I asked with a smile.

"Always have," she said softly. "Except for Margaret Louise's."

I got up and made my way through the auditorium. There were hundreds of people sitting on the floor. Most of them were done eating, but social workers and volunteers were passing out coffee. I wondered how the social workers could keep working hour after hour when they must be worried about their own families and homes. The thought almost made me feel tender toward them.

I stepped carefully over the hands and legs and laps of people, taking care to avoid knocking over anybody's coffee. The scene reminded me of pictures my father had shown me when I was a small boy—pictures of people like our relatives, sprawled on the floor just like this, awaiting processing as immigrants. Those people had crossed difficult seas in crowded ships. Heaven only knew how many rough seas the people crowding the center had crossed—and would cross again.

Kate Martin was seated at her desk, bent over some papers. I wondered at the formality of her summoning me into her office to tell me I wasn't welcome, but I didn't question it. The longer it took to throw me out, the longer I would stay dry.

"Before you throw me out, Kate, I need just one favor. Let me call Aliana Caterina to make sure she's okay . . ."

When she glanced up, she didn't even look surprised at my mention of Aliana. Her desk, like the desk of so many busy people, looked like a windy day at the recycling depot. She dug in a pile, picked up a pink telephone message slip and handed it across to me.

"What is this?"

"She called a couple of hours ago. She was afraid that you were trapped down in the valley with all this rain. Every road down there is washed out. A couple of the bridges are gone."

"Where's Aliana? Is she out there? Is she following some story in the middle of this?"

"Yes, I think she is. And I'm concerned. I know how well you know the valley. I'm just wondering whether . . ."

"You think she's in danger?" Aliana was a big girl. And she'd covered a lot of dangerous stories. Including walking into a lion's den in which I was the lion. But the thought of her wandering around in the valley in this storm was unsettling.

"I don't know. I don't want to alarm you, but I thought that if there was anybody who would know what to do if she *is* in danger, it's you. She told me—and a couple of clients here have told me from time to time— that you know that valley well enough to negotiate it in the dark.

"Aliana's not out looking for fallen trees and downed electrical wires," Kate said. "She's looking for people in trouble. The most dramatic action is going to be in the valley, considering how the river is flooding. Aliana

is probably in the thick of it. Do you think you could
find her?''

"I can try . . .'' I thought about what I'd need. "Get
me a good pair of trousers—jeans if you can. I'll need
a shirt and a sweater, and also a jacket. And a pair of
boots. Can you manage that?''

"Certainly,'' she answered, as if taking orders from
me was the most natural thing in the world. Without
another word, she leaned over, pressed her intercom and
summoned the janitor to her office.

"I'll be back for those things in a minute,'' I said. "I
want to talk to Queenie before I leave.''

"What's up, Your Honor?'' Queenie asked as I hunkered down beside her. "You ain't been thrown out?''

"No, Queenie, I haven't been thrown out, but I do
have to leave.''

"Why?''

"A friend of mine's out in this storm and she might
be in trouble. I'm going to go looking for her.''

"So are you stuck on her or something?''

I laughed. "No, Queenie,'' I said, "I'm stuck on
you.''

She smiled her beautiful, broken-toothed smile, and I
leaned over and kissed her still-smooth cheek. She didn't
smell like the street, she smelled smoky and sweet, and
I wondered whether it was part of Cree ritual—as it was
for some natives—to burn sweet grass. Maybe the ritual
was intended to abate the effect of the storm—or to help
one keep calm in the face of it.

"I have to ask you a favor, Queenie.''

"Shoot.''

"I want you to look after something for me.'' I
reached into the bag and pulled out my judge's robe.
The silk had mostly dried, but it was a wrinkled mess.
Queenie looked at it as if she knew that a treasure is a
treasure because of what it means to the possessor—not
because of how it looks, or even what it is.

"I want you to keep this for me, Queenie," I said. "I'll be back for it."

"Don't worry. It'll be here. Just make sure you *do* come back."

CHAPTER
FOURTEEN

I WALKED NORTH UP PARLIAMENT AND EAST TO THE Bloor Viaduct, the biggest and most travelled bridge over the Don. Beneath the bridge, one of the busiest sections of the Don valley highway ran along the east bank of the river. I figured the viaduct was a good spot to search for Aliana.

Through the rain, I could see red, white and yellow lights, and I figured that the police had set up some sort of rescue station. As I approached the lights, I could make out people on the bridge shrieking, "Come back up!"

"No!" somebody else shouted. "You've got to stay down there. You can't just let them die. Keep trying!"

I made my way toward the crowd. Could Aliana be here somewhere trying to get close to the action?

The wind at the top of the bridge was so strong that I was pushed to my knees. "Easy," somebody said. "Take it easy." It took me a minute to see who it was who had helped me up—a cop, a man not much younger than me.

"Can you help us here, sir? We need all the men we can get."

I tried to look beyond him, to see whether any media were on the scene, but I couldn't make out faces in the mist.

"Sir?"

"Okay. Sure, I'll help. What do you want me to do?"

"The highway flooded during rush hour. We've got hundreds of commuters trapped in their cars. And others are trying to crawl up the riverbank. We're trying to get them all to safety. Can you get down that path?"

He made a broad gesture toward the western edge of the bridge, where, in good weather, adventurous children were always being plucked from a beaten path that was a fast, though potentially deadly, way to get into the valley from the street. To climb down that path could be fatal in this rain.

Within seconds of beginning my descent, I could no longer hear the voices of the people on the bridge. But I could see that the white light I'd noticed earlier came from powerful searchlights trained on the river. When the wind blew strongly, the rain was a pale sheet blotting out everything but itself.

Intermittently, I caught sight of the shocking state of the river. And I saw what the people on the bridge had been screaming about.

The highway was completely submerged. Hundreds of cars trapped by the rapidly rising water floated in the murky darkness illuminated by the startling white beams of the searchlights. Other cars, washed up onto the flank of the steep hill on the valley's east side, were trapped between the rising river and the flooding streets at the top of the valley.

Everywhere there were people struggling. Clinging to the roofs of the cars, crawling out of windows, climbing up the hill on hands and knees. The rain and the wind washed away any human sound, but I knew those people were screaming. Their lives and the lives of their families and friends were in extreme peril.

"Come on," someone shouted from below. "We need a hand here . . ."

I could see the vague outline of a snaking file of human figures, a chain reaching from the top of the slip-

pery path down into the depths of the valley. I stepped
close to the chain and felt my boots sink into the mud
of the path. From somewhere far below, I heard the intensified screams of the drowning.

Digging my feet further into the drenched mud, I
reached out my left hand. It was immediately snatched.
"What are we doing?" I shouted, feeling the words
blown back into my mouth.

"Ballast," the person next to me said. It was the voice
of a woman, and not a young one, either. Her grip was
strong, though, and I tightened my hold on her hand.

Another gust of rain-soaked wind reduced visibility to
zero. It was only by a painful jerk on my hand that I
was alerted to the fact that something was happening.
No matter how hard I dug my heels into the mud, I
couldn't stop sliding. The hand that held mine broke
away, and my right foot went in a different direction
from my left. I was about to be torn in half by my own
awkwardness and ill luck, when I felt a strong push
against my bottom that had the unexpected result of giving me back my balance. "You okay?" asked a voice
breathless with cold and effort.

"Yes."

"Hang on then. We've got somebody. We're bringing
him up."

I pulled when the others pulled, until my hands felt
as though they were about to come away from my
wrists.

Then, suddenly, the line went slack. The hands holding mine dropped away. I could make out a short figure
being helped up the slope, passing from hand to hand. I
extended my own hand. It was gripped at once by cold,
trembling, bony fingers.

I felt a sudden surge of joy to be holding the hand of
a person in whose rescue I had had a part. But I was in
for a surprise. On top of the bridge, the streetlights were
on, and in their glow, I saw that the person we had saved

was somebody I knew. The terror of his experience had distorted his face, but there was no mistaking Pete the Shears. My first ridiculous thought was to wonder whether he had managed to hang onto his precious scissors.

But then another thought occurred to me. How had he ended up here—miles away from where he lived in the valley? It seemed impossible that he could have been literally washed down from the upper reaches of the river—six or more miles away. Even if he could have survived such a trip, how could fate have been so quirky as to deliver him into the hands of one of the few people he knew?

That was the first of a long night of mysteries, most of which could not be solved.

It was a mystery how we managed to save more than thirty people before the last of the cars was swept away.

It was a mystery how we kept going for more than seven hours without leaving the riverbank.

I kept looking for Aliana among the increasing number of reporters on the scene that night, but I never saw her. I knew she would rather have had me help with the rescue than look for her, but every time there was a pause in the action, I searched the bridge for her, and I asked the other reporters if they knew where she was. Nobody did.

In the middle of the night, we saved a man who was frantically trying to tell the rescuers that his little girl was trapped on a ledge between the still-rising water and one of the supports of the bridge. This man knew only one language well enough to tell us exactly where the little girl was. Italian. I was able to speak to him—and eventually to the child herself, calming her while police from the marine detachment secured one of the members of their unit by a cable screwed into the bridge strut and suspended him out over the river, where he plucked the child from the water. I hadn't spoken Italian in more than a decade, but I didn't miss a word.

By the time our rescue mission was complete at 5:30 A.M. and everyone had come up off the slope and onto the bridge, the rain had lightened to a drizzle.

I was exhausted but still determined to find Aliana. I caught a glimpse of one of the police officers gesturing toward me, an eager reporter beside him glancing in my direction. I supposed they were looking for some sort of local hero-type story. I shook my head "no" and got off the bridge as fast as I could.

I wondered if Aliana might be on one of the other bridges. There were four others that crossed the river south of Bloor: Gerrard, Dundas, Queen and Eastern. None would now be accessible from the valley itself, so I was left with the lengthy task of walking from one bridge to the next by going through the streets of the neighborhoods that lined the east rim of the valley.

The rain stopped and the sun struggled to rise. I was stunned at the destruction I saw as I walked the streets of the neighborhoods that bordered the river. Running and shouting, some inhabitants carried bundles of clothes and blankets; others clutched papers, briefcases, handbags; still others seemed to think that food and water were the most important things to salvage from their threatened homes.

I saw neighbor assisting neighbor—those without children helping those with, the young helping the elderly, the able helping the disabled. And the calm coming to the aid of the hysterical.

Every emergency crew in the city appeared to have been mobilized. Police vans herded families with children inside. I realized they must be headed to shelters.

On the Gerrard Street Bridge, I ran into a reporter who told me that the Don Jail had opened its gym to the public as a rescue station. He told me Aliana was covering the story. I didn't allow myself to think about the

last time I'd been in the building. I needed to see for
myself that Aliana was okay. And I needed to tell her
about William at the first opportunity. Now that the dangerous night was over, we needed to get to work.

The chairs set up in the gymnasium were filled with
sleepy, scared families. Volunteers went from family to
family offering blankets and coffee and cookies. Though
it was the middle of June, the wet and the wind had
made everybody cold, and the scene reminded me of a
group of people who had just come in from a game of
ice hockey.

I didn't want to sit, didn't want to stop looking for
Aliana, but I needed coffee. I stood beside one of the
servers and held out my hand.

To my amazement, she turned, handed me the whole
tray and said, "Thanks. I really need a break." Then
she walked away.

And—splashed with mud as I was—I ended up
spending the next half-hour serving coffee. As I went
from family to family, I felt dizzy with fatigue. I swayed,
and a cup went flying and spilled on the head of a small
boy who was sleeping on the floor. The coffee wasn't
very hot, but the child woke up with a blood-curdling
scream.

"What are you doing, you fool?" the child's mother
shouted.

She wiped the head of the boy with impatient hands,
and he began to cry. It was as if the fears of everybody
in the room—in the city—were in that cry. I put the tray
on an empty chair, got down on one knee and stroked
the head of the boy. His mother's anger dissolved as the
sleepy child looked up at me and smiled. It had been
many, many years since I'd comforted a child, comforted anybody, really. It was so simple. The touch of a
hand. The soft, reassuring word. I thought of the
thousands of people who had stood before my bench.

And it occurred to me that to most people, a judge in the criminal court is an object of terror.

The thought made my fingers more gentle, and beneath their touch, the little one fell into a deep sleep. I pulled away, I looked up.

But instead of the boy's mother, I saw Aliana smiling down at me.

"Ellis," she said softly, "thank God you're okay."

I stood and without thinking took her in my arms. "Your friend Kate sent me after you," I said lightly.

"Just a polite way of kicking you out," Aliana joked, drawing me away from my task as a waiter. "Do you want dry clothes or food?"

I looked around. "There's not much here, and I wouldn't want to take anything away from the locals."

"There's no way we can get back across the river into the center of town," Aliana said. "There's a roadblock on the Bloor Viaduct and the other bridges are closed—except for Eastern. It's gone."

The scene of the flooding cars under the bridge popped into my mind's eye with sickening intensity. "I've been out all night," I admitted to Aliana. "I guess it's starting to get to me . . ."

"Come on," she said, leading me to a chair. "Sit down."

I sat and she took the chair beside me. "You must be trying to get a story in," I said.

"It goes right from my laptop to the desk these days. They've got it already. Except for the pictures. I'm sure my regular photographer got plenty of good stuff, but I want to take a few shots of my own just in case." She hesitated. "Want to come? I've got my car. We can't get back to my place because of the bridges, but we could go east. I figure we could get some good shots of the upper reaches of the river—nearer to your place . . ." She hesitated, and I could see that she was embarrassed.

I saved her the trouble of explaining what was running through her mind.

"It's all right, Aliana. I've already faced the fact that my place is wiped out. What difference does it make anyway? It was nothing but a shack in the wilderness—somebody else's wood, somebody else's land."

"But it was your home!"

"No," I answered. "This is my home." I gestured past the sleepy crowd on the gym floor, toward the street beyond the open door where the sun's cheerful glow seemed to mock the wreckage of the night.

Aliana looked as if she were about to cry. "Hey," I said, touching her arm. "Don't feel sorry for me.

"Okay," she said softly. "I won't."

Since the highway was still under water, we had to make our way uptown by a circuitous route. The further we got from the river, the less obvious the effects of the storm, though there were plenty of trees down. Awnings, shingles, shutters and signs littered the street. Garbage was strewn everywhere.

"I heard you were involved in the rescue mission under the viaduct," Aliana said.

"Yeah. I went there searching for you. I figured you'd be wherever the action was . . ." I changed the subject. "Aliana, yesterday when the storm broke I was on my way to tell you that I found William Sterling. Or rather he found me. Ever since Queenie told me about seeing those rings on the two men who sent Moonstar to Second Chance, I had a hunch. And I was right. William *is* the lawyer and Matt *is* his partner—or was. William is also the person who brought the hand to the valley and has been harassing me ever since."

Her eyes were trained on the slippery, obstacle-strewn street, but I could see her stiffen with attention. "You've talked with him? He came to you in your ravine?"

"Yesterday. And several times before that. And I saw

him at Second Chance, too.'' I filled her in on everything William had said. She listened in stunned silence.

"He didn't tell you where the girls came from?'' she finally asked.

"No. He evaded the question. Before I could repeat it, I saw that the weather was getting critical. I convinced him to leave the valley.''

"We've got to get to him. He must know more than he told you.'' She hesitated. "I still don't see how Moonstar fits into all this.''

"Whatever Stow is doing with those girls, I think Second Chance must have clients that aren't involved in the scheme. There must be a number of regular clients that come to Second Chance to have their babies and get their lives back in order. As a cover to distract attention from the other cases, maybe. William swears that Moonstar was truly a charity case and not one of the girls he supplied to Stow.''

"Supplied—the word makes me sick. What can it mean?''

"I don't know. But we have to find out exactly—and put a stop to it. At the very least, we can prevent Stow's elevation to the Supreme Court.''

"And at the most, we can find out who killed Moonstar—and possibly Matt.''

I didn't want to point out that our own lives might be at risk—and William's too.

Aliana read my thoughts. "Are you and William in danger?'' she asked. But there was no time to answer. She negotiated a sharp corner on the wet street, and we found ourselves overlooking the valley.

"Ellis, I can't let an opportunity like this go by. I've got to get some pictures. It won't take long, but I've got to get down to the river. Help me find a good spot. As soon as I've done that, we'll try to get back to my place. You can clean up and rest, and when I get back from the office, we'll go to work. We'll set down everything we know, and then we'll follow every lead we've got.''

I helped her guide the car down a paved, winding path toward a lookout point that had been constructed by the conservation authority specifically for birdwatchers. I remembered my promise to William that we would confront Stow. I still had to talk to Aliana about that.

Before we got halfway to the lookout, we had to get out of the car. Water sloshed up against the doors and started to seep in at the bottom.

Undaunted, Aliana, who like me was wearing rubber boots, just hopped out, grabbed her camera bag from the back seat and kept going.

She seemed very sure-footed, and I had a hard time keeping up with her as she dashed for the river. "Look at it!" she yelled against the rushing of water. "Oh, Ellis, just look at it!"

The day before, the willows at the river's edge had been at the fullness of their summer green, the valley grasses thick and soft. Wild carrot had covered the river meadows. Black-eyed Susan, bladder campion, pink clover and white had dotted the upland reaches of the ravine with little spots of color. The purple-flowered milkweed had thrown its heady perfume into the hot evening air.

But it was gone now. Now there was nothing but the anger of the river, wiping out all before it as if it had some sort of right.

I turned to say something to Aliana, but she was already running down the water-slicked path straight toward the river.

"Stay back!" I yelled.

She scrambled over the huge concrete chunks that bolstered the river bank in her effort to get closer to the natural rock at the edge of the river.

"Wait," I called out. My heavy boots weighed me down as I made my way toward her. I slid and slipped and hopped and ran toward the bank, and when I got there, I saw Aliana poised on the very edge of a long black slab of rock that jutted out over the river. She was at work. She held her camera to her eye and waited in tense, perfect stillness until the right picture flew before her lens, the way I had often watched the grey heron wait for the right fish to break the mirror surface of the water.

I could hear the river clearly and what I heard was not good. I had to get Aliana off the rocks, back up the path and into the car. I moved slowly. She was crouched, almost hanging over the edge, aiming her camera into the maelstrom whirling toward and away from the base of the rocks. I saw clothing, and for a sickening moment, I thought she was about to take a picture of a body. But it was just a jacket that had snagged on the rock, then swiftly shot away. Keeping my balance as best I could, I moved to a spot about ten feet away from Aliana.

I was just about to say her name when I saw her abruptly stand upright and stagger backward on the rock. In the same instant, I saw what she had seen. Rushing downriver with all the power of the speeding water came a huge uprooted tree, complete with all its branches. It was so close to shore that the outspread limbs were sweeping debris off the bank and into the river. Aliana was directly in its path.

I lunged for her. I yelled for her to jump toward me and safety. In an instant, the uprooted tree flew by the ledge on which she stood. Its branches touched her hair. For a split second, she teetered, almost lost her balance. Then she righted herself.

"Aliana, please," I called out, "step away from the river."

"Whew—that was close!" she said bravely, but I could see her hand trembling as she clasped her camera.

She crouched down again and started snapping pictures of the tree that had almost got her.

"Aliana, come on. I'm going back up . . ."

She raised her hand. Maybe she wanted to let me

know that she heard me. Maybe she wanted me off her back. Maybe she wanted me to stay away because of the danger to myself.

For whatever reason, she waved.

And as she did, she lost her balance.

I watched as she swayed, slipped, and went toppling over the edge of the rock into the sucking streams at its base.

She didn't scream. She didn't cry out. I couldn't even hear her thrashing. When I caught sight of her, I saw she had hit her head. A small trickle of blood ran down from a wound on her temple. She was floating quite motionlessly, half in the water, her shoulders resting on the edge of a little pool formed by the base of the rocks.

Any sudden move would dislodge her and send her downriver with the same careless abandon with which the giant tree had gone down.

I stretched full length on the overhanging rock and reached to where she lay.

I managed to touch her, to brush her hair with my fingers. She didn't respond. Without her cooperation, there was no way I could drag her back up onto the rock.

For a heart-stopping moment, the thought occurred to me that her injury might be fatal, but then I saw that she was still breathing. "Aliana, can you hear me?" I saw her eyelids flutter, and I felt a flood of relief. But it was short-lived. She didn't open her eyes.

I figured that if I could lower myself into the water by hanging suspended from the ledge of rock, I might be able to get the river to swing me in exactly the same way that it had swung Aliana—depositing me in the same place.

If I was successful at this, I would land right beside her. I didn't even think about failure. I took off my boots and in a few minutes, I found an indentation in the stone large enough to cradle my fingers and substantial enough to bear my weight.

I let myself down. It was harder than the trick I used to mount the rock in the river where I kept my treasures. My fingers strained with the weight, but I hung on.

I had nearly got to the point where the soles of my stockinged feet were touching the water, when I heard her groan and call out my name. I tried to let go of the rock one hand at a time, but I slipped. I braced myself to feel my legs crushed beneath me against the sub-merged rock.

Instead, the water received me—eagerly. Debris rushed toward me: tree limbs, tires, clothing, paper. A plastic bag came bobbing along and covered my face. I had to duck under to free myself.

As I had hoped, the current caught and buffeted me and tossed me toward where Aliana lay. When I finally managed to reach her, she seemed more alert, though her eyes were glazed.

As clearly as if she were completely herself she said, "Ellis, the rock is unclimbable and the water is still rising." Then she closed her eyes again, and her breathing became so soft, so shallow, that I could hardly hear it at all.

I knelt on the edge of the pool beside her. My pur-chase on the rock was steady enough for me to lift her away from the water so that at least she wasn't sub-merged. She felt so light, just another small piece of flotsam in a city that seemed as if it were slipping piece by piece into the river, the lake and after that the sea. It seemed the river was getting even. It had given me a few brief moments of heroism, then decided to take me back.

I had made a deal with the river long ago. It could have me if it wanted. But why Aliana? A memory I'd never had before flashed into my mind. I was in the mental hospital. I looked up to see her framed in the doorway of my room, and I felt so overcome with shame and guilt that I hid my face in my hands. Aliana walked up to me. She took my hands from my face. "Judge Portal," she said, "I'm here to help you tell your story because I think you want to tell it. I think people want to know . . ."

Carefully, I eased her down until she was lying flat on her back on the narrow rock. As I did this, a few inches of water crept along her soaked body, but her face was well above it. I realized with a shock of thankfulness that the water was clearly receding.

I lifted her head and arched her neck. I put my fingers to her face. I lowered my lips. I breathed into her mouth.

After a night's observation at Pleasantview Memorial by the same doctor who'd treated me the last time I'd been rescued, we learned we had been spotted by police helicopters searching the river for survivors. As we sat together in the lounge of the hospital, Aliana told me she had felt as though she just couldn't breathe anymore when suddenly she felt me helping her. Her injuries, she said, were minor. Mine were non-existent. My only problem was exposure.

"More exposure than you realize," she said with a smile.

"What?"

"Look . . ."

She held up a newspaper and I was shocked to see myself leaning out over the river, coaxing the little Italian girl up off the support of the viaduct.

"You media types are everywhere," I teased, "taking pictures in the middle of every crisis . . ."

"Mitch the stringer got this one."

"He deserves a Pulitzer. He's not American, is he?"

Before she could answer, we were both startled to hear a commotion and to see someone come flying across the lobby: Tim Garrison in mud-splattered army fatigues. "Thank God!" He glanced from one to the other of us. "You both look awful! But don't worry. I'm here to take you home. I'll take Aliana to her place, then, Ellis, you come back to mine. We'll be honored to have you stay. Let's go."

I didn't have the strength to argue. Neither Aliana nor I said anything until we got to her house. "We both need rest," she said. "Then we need to put our heads together. The time has come to put a stop to whatever Stow is doing . . ."

CHAPTER

FIFTEEN

I WANTED TO CALL ALIANA FIRST THING THE NEXT MORN-
ing; we were losing time. "Let her sleep," Tim said.
"Besides, Ellis, I need you. The city has asked me to
spearhead the restoration of the valley. There's a lot of
healing that needs to be done after the devastation of the
storm. Among other things, we need people familiar
with the vegetation of the valley so we can replace it.
I'm assembling a special team for that. I want you to
head it, and I can pay. The city even paid the university
to give me leave."

I wondered if the city was being so free with its
money because the deal to sell the valley to the consortium was on, but I kept my mouth shut.

I spent the morning in one of the offices that City
Hall lent Tim, poring over aerial photos of the damage
and helping Tim match them to pictures of the same
areas before the flood. Across the city, rescue teams
were beginning to clear debris—including bodies. The
grim task of identifying those who had drowned was
proceeding slowly.

I went back to Tim's place with him when we finished, and I used his phone to try to reach William
Sterling without success. The phone at William's office
was out of service. Which didn't mean anything; a number of neighborhoods had lost service because of the

storm. William's home number *was* in service, but unfortunately, it was unlisted.

The next morning, I heard from Aliana.

She was at her office when she called, and remarkably I was at mine, a cubicle next door to Tim's cubicle at City Hall.

"Ellis," she said, "you're working for the city now . . ." There was a hint of laughter in her voice, but I couldn't help noticing that there was a hint of hope, too. "That's great news."

"You know, Aliana," I said, matching her light tone, "it's been more than four years since I was on the welfare rolls. Putting me to work isn't saving the city any money. It's costing them."

And she laughed again. "Can you come down to my office?" she asked. "You and I have a lot to talk about. I'll buy you lunch at the Press Box."

I was so deep in thought that, despite my vigil at a table in the Press Box, I didn't even notice her until she was standing in front of me.

"Ellis," she said and held out her hand.

The formality of the gesture, the fineness of her clothes, the little change she'd made in her hair since I'd last seen her, the gold at her wrist and on her fingers, even her perfume, which today was not lemony but astringent and French, told me that the closeness we'd shared during the tragedy of the storm was gone.

"I've got a whole hour," she said, "and I've brought my notes. I want to go over everything we have so far . . ." She flipped open a large loose-leaf notebook.

"First," she said, "we've got the hand . . ."

"Yes, the hand of a black man on which is a ring that is one of only five in the world. We know that the hand was the hand of Matt West, the long-time companion of William Sterling, who also has such a ring. We know that the ring in question once belonged to another lover of William Sterling's.''

''Right. And we know that Matt West is a police officer and that he has been missing since the beginning of the summer.''

''Yes. We know also that William Sterling is an attorney who has arranged for pregnant girls to spend time at a hostel called Second Chance. We know that John Stoughton-Melville and his wife Harpur are on the board of that hostel, and that Stow is its president.''

Aliana took over. ''And we know that when William Sterling stopped making the referrals, violence ensued. To Matt West. And to Moonstar.'' She paused. ''Have you had any luck getting in touch with William?''

I shook my head. ''Is there anything more we can do on the Moonstar angle?'' I asked. ''She died the night she told me the hostel was a front for some sort of clandestine operation. She thought it had to do with the sale of babies . . .''

''Her own baby,'' Aliana said softly, raising her pen from the page and holding it poised for a moment over the paper, before she set it down without writing anything more.

The waiter brought our lunch. My Press Box special of hamburger and fries, though less healthy than Aliana's salad, looked good to me—a feast after the storm's adventures.

''I keep going over these things in my mind, but I just can't figure out how they're connected,'' she said. ''Obviously the rings mean something. They're the best clue. And you've got one, yourself. What does it mean to you—that ring?'' She pointed to my hand.

''It means a lot of things—among them that I promised William I would help him confront Stow and demand to know what happened to Matt West.''

''What else do the rings mean?''

''The past. The promises. It all seems so old, so irrelevant. Originally, the rings meant that we knew we could call on each other if things went wrong.''

"Then they must still mean the same," Aliana answered. "Everybody owed everybody else something . . .''

"I still owe both Harpur and Stow. I still owe William. But I don't think this is getting us anywhere. Because any way you look at it, neither Moonstar nor Matt West owed anybody with our rings, and look what happened to them.''

"What *did* happen to them?" she asked.

The question shut both of us up for a while. As we sat there eating, the noise level in the Press Box kept rising. Aliana's colleagues were a loud, swaggering lot, and I felt a strong sense of dislocation, the same sense of dislocation I felt around Tim Garrison and *his* colleagues. They had their own way of swaggering, tossing around the names of marsh insects, the way reporters dropped the names of politicians. I wasn't a part of either group.

"I just thought of something," Aliana said. "Something we left out in the list of things we know about. You asked me to check the street name Solomon. I couldn't find anything on it, remember? Didn't Moonstar say he was a smart, black pimp? Didn't she say that somebody like that was hanging around Second Chance?''

"Yes. What are you thinking?"

"Maybe this Solomon is working for Stow. Maybe he's the clean-up man.''

"The what?"

"The person who gets rid of the girls when Stow is finished with them. Remember that list I showed you the first time we went over this? There *were* girls missing from Second Chance.''

"But even if their disappearance were linked to Solomon, even if he's our killer, that doesn't explain Stow's involvement.'' I had no choice. "Aliana, I'm going to his office.''

She reached across the table and gripped my wrist. "No, you're not. Go back to Second Chance instead, and this time get inside. I know you said William Sterling was pretty distraught when you talked to him, but we can't assume he was hallucinating. He saw bodies being taken in and out. There's *something* there. You've got to find it.''

She tightened her grip, as if she were going to hold me captive unless I agreed with her plan. "As for Stow, *I'll* go to his office. I have the perfect excuse. I'll tell his secretary that I'm profiling the newest judge-to-be of the Supreme Court.''

The last time I'd been near the hostel, I hadn't been dressed like a vagrant, but something of the street and the ground had clung to me. Not now. I had a job, a new set of clothes, and the reputation for being a hero. I didn't know how long the job would last, but I figured I'd make the best of things while I could.

I walked up the front steps of Second Chance, announced my presence to the receptionist in the foyer, and asked for the Director of Fundraising. Having called ahead, in the guise of one Angelo Portalese, contractor and philanthropist, this time when asked whether I had an appointment, I answered truthfully, "Yes.''

Over the receptionist's desk was a portrait large as life. It was done in soft colors, interrupted by a ripple of paler shades, so that the effect was of a beautiful red-haired woman stepping out of shadow into a gentle bath of light. The woman was simply dressed in what looked like cream-colored silk—an evening gown of stunningly elegant plainness.

"That's Mrs. Stoughton-Melville,'' the receptionist said.

No, it's not, I thought. *It's her mother.*

Before I had even sat down in the fundraising direc-

tor's office, she had glossy brochures spread in front of
me to show how giving to Second Chance was an investment in my own future as well as in the future of
the girls. I could see the hand of Stow in her sales pitch.
It had his polish and his boldness.

"What I have in mind," I said, "is a manner of man-
aging the estate of my elderly mother in a way that re-
spects her wishes as well as providing a modest return
for my own children. Naturally, they will be well provided for by me. But we'd like them to share in their
grandmother's wealth without taking away from others
who are also deserving."

I'd thought a long time about the speech. It sounded
arrogant and charitable at the same time.

"How very thoughtful of you and your mother to consider those less fortunate as equally deserving as your
own dear ones."

She was as good at fake speeches as I was.

I pretended to study the brochures. They were carefully prepared, showing only the backs of clients' heads,
so no one could tell who any of the girls were, though
the bright, smiling counsellors looked right into the camera as if to invite questions and, of course, contributions.

"Would it be possible to have a small tour of the
facility?" I asked.

"Certainly," the woman said.

She led me through tidy corridors, past clean, spacious, public rooms. Second Chance looked like a good
club. But beneath the fragrance of lemon polish and
fresh flowers and rich fabric, I smelled a trace of something else. Disinfectant or antiseptic.

When we got to the girls' rooms, all the doors were
closed except two. She pulled them closed with a click
and led me to another door that swung open to reveal
an empty model suite. The pretty room looked uncannily
like my daughter's own room long ago, and I suddenly

remembered that like the girls here, my girl was now a mother.

"This is a typical room," the fundraiser said brightly. "We like to think that our girls deserve the best. Except for one or two exceptional cases, they're not girls from the street. They are young ladies from good families, like your own for instance, who have simply made a few wrong choices. They come here because they are ready to change their lives. Even if they don't make it all the way through the program, the fact that they have spent some time with us means that they have taken steps toward making their lives and the lives of their children a little better."

We stood in the room a moment longer, as if she were giving me the opportunity to see just what a good investment my donation would be. Then she gestured toward the door and preceded me back into the corridor.

As we passed the first door, I saw that it hadn't clicked shut after all. It had swung ajar a tiny bit. On impulse, I pushed it, fully expecting to see the typically messy room of the average teenager.

The door swung open a few inches wider. Its hinges gave a creak.

The fundraiser stopped in her tracks. "That damn door," she hissed. She stepped past me, grabbed the handle and gave the door a good slam.

Then she seemed to remember there was a potential benefactor present. "Would you like to see the library?" she chirped, as if she were positive I had not seen what was behind that door.

But I *had* seen. A judge trains himself to notice in a split second what another person might not notice at all.

Behind that door was an operating room. And it looked fully equipped for surgery.

Happy Hour at the Press Box. Aliana nursed a white wine and I nursed a Coke. "To perform surgery in a residential facility like Second Chance has to be illegal in itself.''

"That's just one more thing to go on your research list, Aliana. We need to know what the law says about the maintenance of medical premises. That alone might be enough for charges. When we confront Stow, we're going to need everything we've got. More than one criminal has been brought up on a conviction for a minor offense and then put away for a major one.''

"Any luck reaching William?"

"No. I checked at the Faculty of Law, but they had no idea where he might be. And I also thought of calling members of the ornithological club William belongs to, but the secretary refused to give me any phone numbers. What did you learn at Stow's office?"

"The receptionist told me he wasn't giving any interviews, but when I told her my name and the paper's, she let me in to see Stow's secretary—a Mrs. Campbell, who said Stow was out of town, in Ottawa to meet with the Justice Minister. He's not expected to return until Friday.

"All the time we were talking,'' Aliana said, "there were people packing boxes, moving furniture, making lists of art objects—it's a very fancy office. Mrs. Campbell was so busy, she hardly stood still, but when I got a good look at her, I realized she fits the description of the woman you saw on the patio the same day you saw William at Second Chance—when he claimed to be hiding. 'Do you know William Sterling?' I asked, as casually as I could. Campbell got a little edgy. 'Of course I do. He volunteers legal services to Second Chance, one of Mr. Stoughton-Melville's favorite charities. Perhaps you might like to ask Mr. Stoughton-Melville about it when an interview can be arranged,' she said. 'He's always happy to give it publicity.' ''

"Hardly what you'd expect if Stow's involvement were a secret,'' I commented.

"Exactly," Aliana answered. "At that point I was sure I'd completely wasted my time. Then I remembered you never got an answer from William when you asked him where the girls came from. Obviously Moonstar was not your typical client at Second Chance, so most of the girls came from somewhere besides the street. And they certainly didn't come from among William's students at the Faculty—all of whom would have been too old for Stow's purposes. Needless to say, a lawyer with an exclusively gay clientele, as William claims to be, would also not be likely to have access to pregnant teens."

"No."

"So how did William find the girls? I figured that if you saw Mrs. Campbell interviewing a girl and William watching, it might mean that the two of them were engaged in the selection process that William mentioned. You said you saw actual children at Second Chance, and that some of the girls are clearly pregnant. William said Stow used one or two girls a year. So not everybody at the hostel is chosen for whatever Stow does."

"Right."

"So if Campbell helps select the victims, she might know as much as William—and know where he is. I asked her whether William Sterling volunteers anywhere besides Second Chance. She got downright hostile. She said, 'I thought this interview was to be with Mr. Stoughton-Melville.' I hit her with one more quick question, just to see what would happen. I thought about what William saw—the body on the stretcher. I took a guess. 'Mrs. Campbell,' I said, 'how many abortions are performed at Second Chance every year?'

" 'None that are any of your business,' she snapped. Then she ushered me out. But why would she be so defensive?" Aliana asked. "Abortion is legal . . ."

I thought about that. "Not in an unapproved facility, so far as I know. Not under duress. Not if the patient is underage. Not if parental permission is required but is withheld . . .

"And not," I added, "if the baby is less than full-term but is taken from the mother's body against her wishes before natural birth can occur."

CHAPTER

SIXTEEN

"COME TO MY HOUSE FOR DINNER," ALIANA COMMANDED, closing her notebook with a decisive snap and twisting closed her gold pen. Before I could reply, she was out the Press Box door.

I'd promised Tim Garrison I would meet that afternoon with a group of naturalists to discuss whether the plants re-introduced into the valley should be only those that had first grown there or the many "foreign" species that had made their home in the valley for two hundred years.

I made my way back to City Hall, and while I waited for the naturalists to show up, I took a closer look at the brochures I'd picked up at Second Chance. There was an extensive bio of Stow. He was on a lot of different boards. This wasn't a surprise, of course. Most of the boards had to do with his various business interests.

But in among the list of business boards, I noticed five directorships of charitable organizations. One was Second Chance. The other four included an organization that aided the families of victims of Alzheimer's Disease, a hostel for the victims themselves, an institute for research into the disease, and a scholarship fund for young doctors wishing to specialize in its treatment.

From the bio I learned that Stow devoted not only money to these organizations, but personal time and attention to their work. I wondered whether one of his parents had the disease.

It was past nine-thirty by the time I got off the bus and walked up Aliana's block toward her compact little house. I saw that lights were on in the kitchen and the living room. It was the third week of June—just a few days before the solstice, and the sky was not yet totally dark. Had I remained in the valley, I'd just be turning in after a long evening's read. A little flush of nostalgia warmed me. Already my life in the ravine was beginning to feel like the distant past. As for the future, that felt distant, too.

Aliana met me at the door and took from my arms the parcels I'd brought. She poked her nose in each bag and exclaimed with delight at the modest groceries I'd provided: a bit of meat, a bud of garlic, fresh tomatoes, a small bottle of perfect olive oil.

"You're going to cook?" she asked.

"Yes."

Then she added softly, "Were you ever able to do that in the valley—cook properly, I mean?"

"Yes, Aliana," I answered her, "as a matter of fact I did. And you're going to see that I haven't lost my touch."

And I hadn't. The sauce and the pasta came out perfectly, and we sat and ate in eager silence. We both seemed to be starved. It wasn't until we'd finished coffee and some pastries that we got down to our discussion.

"This would all be a whole lot easier," Aliana began, "if we could just get back to William Sterling. I tried Kate Martin again. She *did* have William's home address. He's done volunteer work with young gays at the community center. When she sent one of her volunteers to knock on his door, the next-door neighbor came out and said he thought William had gone away for the summer."

"He must still be hiding out. He seemed pretty petrified when I saw him, but I was sure I'd be able to get in touch with him."

"We're just going to have to proceed without him." Without another word, Aliana led me down a hallway toward the back of her house and into a room I hadn't seen before.

"This is my home office," she said, flicking on the lights. In the corner sat her computer. She drew up a chair for me to sit beside her. Then she turned on the machine and began clicking away.

A dizzying array of images flashed across the screen, but Aliana seemed to know exactly what she was doing. "Okay," she announced. "We're on."

"On what?"

"The Internet. First we check out the regulations concerning the operating room at the hostel . . ."

I watched as the images on the screen rapidly changed, Aliana reading and clicking faster than I could follow. When she finally stopped, I was looking at a headline that read, "Free-standing abortion clinics."

"I've linked to the data base at the law library," she said. "I started with abortion. Legal or illegal, it strikes me as the most logical reason for an operating room at a halfway house for pregnant girls."

Together we read as Aliana scrolled through the screens. "The thing is," she observed, "Moonstar could not have had an abortion. She told you she was seven months pregnant when she was sent to Second Chance. She also said that she woke up *in the hospital*."

I thought about the three times I'd been to Second Chance. "There's something else about Moonstar that always bothered me, the fact that she was so different from the other clients of Second Chance. They all seemed like healthy middle-class girls. I know Second Chance claims to help girls like her once in a while, but I didn't see any others. And I can't imagine the hostel using the help of girls like her for public relations or fundraising. Moonstar was a street person—not just someone temporarily down on her luck, but a girl who lived off the streets all her life.''

''But she *had been* a client at Second Chance. And she *is* dead. And Moonstar's baby definitely disappeared, one way or another, though I don't think anyone believes the child was sold. That gives me an idea,'' Aliana said.

I watched as she worked away at the computer. She kept her eye on the monitor, and when she had apparently reached the screen she was looking for, I saw her type in ''babies and selling.'' In a fraction of a second, two new words jumped into view. They were ''Sacred Goods.''

''Sacred Goods? What does that mean?''

''It's a legal term.'' She smiled ruefully. ''I guess it's one that's come into use in the last few years—otherwise you'd know it, Ellis. It's what you call parts of the human body that are being bought and sold as commodities.''

''Oh, Aliana! Surely Stow isn't marketing body parts!''

''Listen, it happens. About two years ago, I got a letter from a woman saying that she'd seen a piece I'd done about the illegal world trade in endangered species. She said she had recently returned from a trip to East Asia. She claimed to have proof that endangered animals were being brought right into Toronto for illegal sale to collectors.

''After talking to her for only a few minutes, I realized I'd made a mistake. She didn't have any new information about animals. 'Listen,' she said, 'you've got to help me. I have an infant son who needs a new heart. I have a donor already. I need you to write about me so that I can get enough money to pay the donor.'

''I was confused—I'd never heard of anybody paying

donors for organs. I asked a few questions. Finally, the
woman told me that she had arranged to adopt a child
in Cambodia. She was desperate to raise enough money
to fly her own sick child to that country so that the heart
of the adopted child could be used in her own natural
child . . .''

I was too appalled to speak for a few moments.
''What did you do?'' I finally asked Aliana.

''Nothing. I told the woman that what she had in mind
was murder. Then I tried to get my editor to assign me
an investigative story on the subject. He said nobody
would believe it.''

''I can't believe Stow would have anything to do with
the selling of babies for parts!''

''Yet what could a pregnant girl possibly have that
Stow would want?''

Neither of us had an answer. The computer screen
flashed impatiently.

As if she were talking on a different subject altogether, Aliana finally said, ''Once, when I was little, I
saw a purse made out of the skin of an unborn calf.
Later, when I started to wear makeup and use cosmetics,
I learned that some lotions contain the placenta of ter-
minated pregnancies . . .''

''What?''

''Think about it, Ellis, what is the one thing—the only
thing—that a pregnant girl has that nobody else can supply?''

''A baby?''

''No. No, of course not. A pregnant woman doesn't
have a baby. A *mother* has a baby. A pregnant woman
has a *fetus*.''

''Yes. So?''

''So maybe what Stow needed from those girls depended on their being pregnant, but not giving birth.
Maybe what Stow was after was fetal tissue.''

''Fetal tissue?''

"Yes."

She got back to the computer. "Here—here's something."

She read, "Because fetal tissue is not fully developed, the recipient body does not reject it. It grows at a much faster pace than post-natal tissue. Fetal brain cells, for example, quickly reproduce and quickly take over the work of sick cells. In such circumstances, a fetus can save the life of a human . . ."

"Fetal brain cells?" I remembered the list of boards that Stow was on. "Can you get anything more on that?"

Without saying another word, Aliana highlighted the words and clicked. Instantly, a long list of titles filled the screen.

"Look at this, Ellis! There are dozens of articles about harvesting fetal brain tissue. We've got to read these."

So we took turns. Aliana's twenty-years-younger eyes could stand it much better than mine. I felt I was slowing us down, but taking turns was the only way. While I read Aliana made coffee and took a shower. While she read, I napped.

It was 4:00 A.M. when we finally found what we were looking for.

"Ellis," Aliana was shaking my shoulder, "look at this . . ."

I read, "The transplanting of fetal brain tissue for the relief of Parkinson's disease has been carried out in private clinics for some time. Its use for other degenerative conditions, most notably the dementias, of which the most well-known is Alzheimer's, is more controversial. Doctors claim that success is most probable when the fetal tissue is from young, very healthy mothers and is removed from the host at precisely the correct stage of pregnancy. Most claim that any fetus older than eight weeks is too old. To be most effective, the fetus has to be alive at the time of the transplant. Optimum conditions call for double surgical procedures: the removal of the fetus from the donor and the nearly simultaneous injection of the fetal tissue into the brain of the recipient.''

William's grim description of the stretchers being wheeled into and out of Second Chance leapt to my mind.

"Ellis, are you still with me?''

"Yes. I'm just wondering whether a procedure like this would require a more complex set-up than the operating room at Second Chance.''

We were silent. It took a minute for this to sink in. Aliana was the first to speak, but her thoughts echoed my own. "If Stow's behind this as president of the board of Second Chance, the real question isn't 'How?' It's 'Why?' I don't think this is about money at all. John Stoughton-Melville is about to reach the pinnacle of his career—a career that has always depended on the quality of his mind. If he has Alzheimer's, everything would be over. He might well take extraordinary measures to remedy a desperate situation.''

"And,'' I added, "whatever measures he took, successful or not, his reputation would depend on his maintaining absolute secrecy—even to the point of shutting up anybody who might know, or even suspect . . .''

"Yes. He would certainly have to shut up selected clients of Second Chance—and a loud-mouth street hooker. He might even have to take care of a cop who figured things out. Stow might balk at actually killing a police officer. But what if he gave him a good scare—then bought him off?''

How far would Stow go to save his reputation? Would he even dispose of a life-long friend? Or two?

"Aliana, William would have been able to come to these conclusions. Maybe we can't find him because Stow took care of him, too.''

She clicked a few more times, and the computer

screen went blank. "What do we do now?" she asked quietly.

"It's time for me to fulfill my promise to William," I told her. "The old deal was no questions asked, all risks taken. I'm going to see Stow."

Her lips parted, but before she could remind me that I risked being jailed—or killed, I added, "And I have to go alone."

CHAPTER

SEVENTEEN

"BUT CAN YOU HANDLE IT? DO YOU KNOW WHAT TO SAY? Do you understand what we're after?" Aliana wondered.

"What we're after is simple, Aliana. The truth."

She offered me a shower, breakfast, a ride to Stow's office. I refused all three. She went to bed and I hit the street.

I needed to clean up a bit. It was 5:00 A.M., too early to impose on Tim. I went into an all-night drugstore and bought some deodorant, toothpaste, a razor, a toothbrush, and a comb. Out of habit, I used a washroom I knew would be deserted, and I groomed my body.

Then I went to a coffee shop and sat there for half an hour grooming my mind.

For the past five years, I'd been a beggar to Stow. He'd gotten me out of the Don Jail and into the mental hospital. And he'd arranged for me to *stay* out of jail. All I had to do was keep away from him and Harpur—permanently. A single call to the police would put me behind bars for breaching the conditions of my release from jail.

But the shoe was now on the other foot. Stow needed to convince *me* that he shouldn't be locked up. He was a sick man, about to destroy himself.

Or was he truly immune?

If that was the case, he still had the power to destroy me—what was left of me.

I finished my coffee and took my time getting to
Stow's office. I hadn't forgotten Mrs. Campbell had said
that Stow was in Ottawa. I was taking a chance on finding him there, but instinct told me I would. He had always been in the habit of using trips out of town as an
excuse for putting people off. And when he *was* in town,
he always began work early. It was almost as if I could
feel him waiting for me.

Stow's firm occupied the top stories of Blane Tower,
located near the main intersection of the downtown core,
Yonge and Bloor. The building was named after Harpur's father, and its silvered-glass surface caught the
eastern sun.

As soon as I approached, I could see activity. A moving van was parked outside and a stream of professional
movers was ferrying boxes of files from the main entrance on Bloor to the curb. At this hour of the morning,
they had the street pretty much to themselves. A burly
security guard kept one eye on the parade of movers and
the other on the front door.

Just as I was thinking that I might have to go around
the block to try the rear entrance, a second van pulled
up. Without catching sight of me, the guard approached
the van and demanded to see identification from the
driver.

I saw my chance. I shot into the lobby and just kept
going until I got to the elevator.

Blane Tower had thirty floors, the top five, I remembered, occupied by Stow's law firm. I saw that one of
these floor buttons had no number. I tried it. To my
surprise, the door closed instantly, and the elevator sped
upward without making any other stops.

The elevator was panelled in oak and had a red carpet
on the floor and a bevelled mirror running along the
top—too high to look into, but throwing back soft light
from bulbs hidden in the ceiling.

The doors slid soundlessly open and I found myself

in the reception area of an executive suite. I was astonished. Once a person got past the main door, it was easier to get into Stow's domain than it was to get onto the upper floors of the *Toronto Daily World*.

But then, such access was typical of Stow. Why should he depend on locks and keys and passcards and electric eyes? He depended on his own power. He had always been quite sure that it would keep him safe.

On the way up I had contemplated the possibility of having to tussle with Mrs. Campbell but there was nobody in the outer office, which was like a museum. There was no metal, no vinyl. Everything was wood, marble, rich fibers—silk wallpaper, expensive hand-knotted carpets in subtle, intricate designs. The painting over the receptionist's desk was one I recognized as a minor masterpiece from the Italian Renaissance. In glass cases, other art objects were highlighted with small intense bursts of light from hidden sources: a bracelet of heavy stone set in thick gold, also Italian, this time medieval; a wooden Madonna from the same period; a goblet. Were Stow's treasures now so varied and so many that he could make even the office of his receptionist look like the Uffizi? I doubted these priceless objects would be hustled into vans the way the boxes and bins of files downstairs were being carted away.

I was sure someone would have heard the elevator door open, so I was surprised that nobody seemed to notice my arrival. Maybe I was wrong after all. Maybe Stow really *was* away and I had come in vain. I considered turning back.

Then, from behind a partially opened door, I heard his voice.

It was the same controlled, cultured voice that Stow had always used. If he was under pressure, you certainly couldn't tell it from his assured tone. He was giving instructions to Mrs. Campbell—something simple and ordinary, about a letter he needed sent, a phone call he needed made.

I crept closer to the door. The carpet was so thick that no sound came from my feet. I leaned toward the opening and I glanced in.

Mrs. Campbell's face was toward me. As she had been the first time I'd seen her at Second Chance, she was impeccably dressed in an expensive, tailored suit. Her red hair was perfectly coiffed. Everything about her was as it had been except for her face, which looked as if she'd missed a night's sleep. I couldn't tell whether she was sad, scared or tired.

Stow was not looking at her. I realized that he was such a well-bred man that if an employee came to work looking under the weather, he would pretend gracefully not to notice. His back was toward me. Like me, he was a man of fifty-five, but his shoulders were wide and muscular, and his bearing was perfectly upright. If he were ill, it certainly hadn't affected his posture.

I knew I had to get into that office before Mrs. Campbell saw me. I didn't have a second to lose. I felt a sudden plunge of fear as I pushed the door fully open and stepped in.

The noise startled them both, but especially the nervous Mrs. Campbell, who jumped violently.

Perhaps she looked shocked, I don't know. It wasn't her face I was watching. It was Stow's. It mocked his posture and his voice. He looked wretched. I had never seen him so dishevelled. His charcoal pin-stripe suit was rumpled, as if he'd slept in it. He wore his characteristic dark-patterned silk tie, but it was crooked, hanging at an odd angle as if it had been yanked from his throat. And, it shocked me to notice, the tie was stained.

He stared at me. His gray eyes narrowed. His strong jaw clenched so hard I thought he would break a tooth. He ran his fingers through his still-blond hair. I saw that it had not recently been washed.

"Ellis," he croaked, his voice now as rough as his appearance. "What the hell are *you* doing *here*? This is no time for any of your nonsense . . ." He took a step toward me. I couldn't possibly feel threatened by a man who looked to be in the same state as Johnny Dirt, but instinct compelled me to pull sharply away.

"Please leave, Mrs. Campbell. This is a private conversation. We'll let you know if you are needed."

It wasn't Stow who spoke. It was I.

Stow just stared at me. His secretary glanced at him, but receiving no other order, turned and left, closing the door behind her.

"Sit down, Stow, we're going to talk. Something tells me you don't have a lot of time. All this packing and moving—so much action, so much activity. Yet, when you come right down to it, no matter how fast a man moves to get away, he never quite outruns *himself,* does he?"

"What the hell are you talking about?" His voice was contemptuous. But there was a hesitation to it, too. "Is this about blackmail, Ellis? Is that what you're doing here? How much do you want—or more to the point, who do you think would believe anything a vagrant would have to say about me? How much, Ellis? How much?"

"I can eat weeds, Stow. I can sleep under trees. What do I need with money? I'm not here to blackmail you. I'm here to stop you from doing again what you've done to those girls at Second Chance."

He seemed to make an effort to pull himself together, but his face was unreadable, which didn't surprise me. Stow was genetically self-possessed. How many business deals, how many legal maneuvers, how many intrigues at his club, on his boards, maybe even in his bed, had depended on never revealing his emotions?

"I'm on the board at Second Chance," he said. "I don't see why that should cause you such alarm."

I thought about Moonstar. And I started to feel anger, not the helpless anger of before, but the calming anger of those who seek justice. "I'm going to lay it on the line, Stow. The other day I was at Second Chance. I saw with my own eyes evidence that surgical procedures are performed there. I had a little friend—she's dead now—who told me that something terrible was going on at that hostel. She told me that she personally knew of girls who had disappeared—but not before they'd given up their babies. And I don't mean for adoption. I think you used the clients of Second Chance to save yourself. If you're sick, Stow, I'm sorry. But I think you robbed your clients of their fetuses, then murdered them to make sure no one could find out."

I watched his face. I kept watching it. And what I saw now was a look of total astonishment.

I was taken aback. Was I wrong? Had Aliana and I made some awful mistake? Had I finally and irrevocably embarrassed myself beyond repair in the eyes of the man I had respected above my own father? My throat dried up like the river in drought. And I didn't feel any better when Stow's look of astonishment was replaced by a smirk.

"You amaze me, Ellis. What amazes me about you now is the same as always. That you are so incredibly naive, such a little child. Why do you think people become involved in charities? To help the poor?"

"Yes," I said simply. "Yes, I do. But even if that isn't the case, I don't expect benefactors to do harm."

"Is that so? And you're quite sure that in the many years during which I've served Second Chance I've done harm rather than good?"

His smile irritated me, his grace, his calm, his smooth facade. I wasn't about to be beat down by his suave arrogance.

"Forget it, Stow," I said with more bluster than I'd

intended, "I know what you've been up to. Infanticide. Murder."

He pretended to ignore me. He moved closer to his desk and sat on its edge, the picture of ease. But his face was strained. A muscle twitched in his cheek, and he smirked again to hide that little spasm. "Worried about poor little fetuses. You're such a good Catholic, Ellis," he said, "for an atheist."

"Do you deny that you had surgery performed at Second Chance?"

His expression changed again. Now he looked weary, the way a man looks when something has been on his mind for a long time and he is tired of thinking about it. "No," he said. "No, I do not deny that surgical procedures are performed at the hostel. But so what? If you had done your research, you would have found that the hostel is licensed as a free-standing abortion clinic—one conducted outside of a recognized hospital. That's legal here, Ellis. Even a man as out of touch as you should know that. You may object to abortion yourself, but you can't deny others the right."

I fought to control my rage at his contemptuous tone. "We're not only talking about abortion, Stow—we're talking about girls disappearing."

I had never seen Stow lose control like this, had never even imagined how he might act. Now I saw a bright red flush steal over the pale smoothness of his face. He didn't shout, but the clenched-jaw tightness of his voice was more chilling than a tirade.

"You over-emotional, stupid man. Will you never learn to leave well enough alone? What do I have to do to keep you away from me? Despite all my efforts to make things easy for you on the Law Commission, you worked yourself into a breakdown. Then you drank yourself sick and got arrested for physically assaulting my wife. You begged me to keep you out of prison, and I did—only to have you haunt me despite a court order.

I'm giving you one last chance. Get out of here now or
you will leave this building in shackles.''

"Put me in shackles, Stow. Do you think I care? Do
you think I've got anybody left to impress? Who would
I be embarrassed in front of? I don't care what anybody
thinks of me—not even you. Especially you. And you're
not the only one who can call the police. I can, too. I
can tell them what you did to Matt West.''

At the mention of that name, he slumped. For a fleeting instant, an expression crossed his face that I had
never seen there before. I thought it was guilt or grief
or some combination of the two. This momentary display of weakness impelled me to press him. ''What are
you doing there, Stow? What have you done to those
girls?''

He shook his head in the dismissive way one does
when rudely brushing aside the irrelevant fears of an
ignorant child.

"Yes. I admit, you're partially right. A number of
girls did disappear from Second Chance. They came in
unaware that their parents had arranged for them to have
abortions. They believed they'd seen the last of their
families, but eventually each of these girls came around
to their parents' view that terminating her pregnancy was
the best thing she could do to ensure her future. Girls
who entered the program received scholarships to study
in the States. Several have graduated. A few are com-
pleting their studies as we speak. And yes, each of those
girls has been wiped from the record of Second Chance.
As if she'd never been there. Because that is what each
one of them wanted. A new start. A clean slate.''

"Paid for by you.''

"By my Second Chance Foundation. So what? What
good does it do to be wealthy unless you can help others?''

I wanted to smash his smiling, lying mouth. But I
couldn't lose my temper. If I had hoped to shock him,

to make him confess, I had misjudged him. Stow had admitted nothing. I decided to give it one more shot. "Stow, I'm here to give you one last opportunity to convince me that there is some reason why I shouldn't go to the police with what I know about fetal tissue transplant at Second Chance and the death of the girl called Moonstar."

I kept my voice calm, like a lawyer, like a judge.

Finally, I was too much for John Stoughton-Melville. He jumped up. He started to shout. "You know nothing! I didn't kill anybody. I've never killed anybody. You're a fool. You're simply beyond help. No matter what I've done for you, it's never been enough. Yet, I *have* helped. Well, you owe me a favor in return. You know you do. And what I want is . . ."

I waited. I waited for him to tell me that I was obligated to keep his dirty secrets. He had kept his promise to me by getting me out of jail. Now it was time for me to pay back. I had thought about this and discussed it with Aliana. She was prepared to go to the police herself. And besides, I didn't just owe Stow. I owed Moonstar and Queenie, too.

But words seemed to stick in his throat and in a moment, I learned why. Because the door to his office was open again, and the redhead was coming in. I saw her out of the corner of my eye, and I thought it was Mrs. Campbell back to announce the police were on their way.

But when I heard the lilting voice, still with its hint of teasing contempt, still as musical and haunting after all these years, I knew that the person who'd come into the room was not Mrs. Campbell. The redhead was Harpur.

"Stow, darling, I'm waiting," she said from behind me. "And I'm as ready as I'll ever be. Let's go now before we forget where we're headed." She had the audacity—or the courage—to laugh.

I turned and my eyes sought her face.

I was astounded. She looked wonderful. Though I hadn't set eyes on her since the night I'd ruined my life by getting drunk and forcing my attentions on her, then assaulting her when she'd refused my advances, she looked younger than five years ago. Her eyes seemed clear and bright—as alive as the eyes of a girl. Her skin was smooth, her hair was radiant, a sweeping bob that fell in a graceful curtain from her temple to her chin.

"It's you . . ." I said.

"Of course it's me," she answered with another rich laugh. "Darling," she asked Stow. "Who is this person?"

I thought it was a joke. I thought she was so bold, so sure of herself that she was taunting me once again, even knowing the violence to which her taunts had led me.

Stow put his arm around her as if she were a child and led her to a plush chair beside the window. For the first time I noticed there was nothing in his office but two chairs and a desk. The walls were bare. There were no files or other signs that business was conducted there.

Harpur sat in one of the chairs and stared straight ahead, a fixed smile on her face. Stow hovered, patting her shoulder, smoothing her still-vibrant hair, but careful, I noticed, not to disturb its style. It was as if I were seeing the real Stow and Harpur for the first time. They weren't perfect. They were not a god and a goddess. They were not immune from the terrifying things that life can do to anyone, rich or poor. Although prosperous, calm and polished, they also looked as if their dreams were dead.

I had to stare at them for a long time before the truth rushed over me like the Don. They had convinced parents and teenagers to barter fetuses for scholarships and other perks. But not for Stow's benefit. It wasn't Stow who was facing dementia. It was Harpur. And judging from the way she now studied the empty space in front of her, all their skilled trading had profited them nothing.

As always, Stow saw the change in me and saw his advantage. He knew how much I'd always loved Harpur, knew how realizing her fate would disarm me.

"In less than three months' time, Ellis, I'm going to be a judge of the Supreme Court. Nothing you do or say is going to stop me. For nearly six years I've hidden the fact that my wife has suffered longer and longer periods of instability, until now she is rarely lucid. I promised her the day she was diagnosed that I would do everything within my power to save her, and I have."

Again he smoothed Harpur's hair, but she no longer seemed aware that either of us was in the room.

"I don't owe you anything, Ellis, least of all an explanation, but I *am* going to explain because you're right about the fetal tissue transplants. You're right that I used Second Chance as a way to get the tissue. I needed healthy girls. I couldn't use street people or any other of the usuals from such places. That girl you mentioned—Moonstar—she was never part of the transplant team."

"*Team?* You have the gall to call your victims a *team?*"

"They were not victims. They all agreed to allow an experimental procedure."

"How can a sixteen-year-old agree to anything?" Before the words were out of my mouth, I saw that's where William had really come in. "William signed for them, didn't he? The parents would have agreed to routine abortions—but not the transplants. That was his part in the whole scheme. Under the child protection laws, a minor can sign for surgical procedures in the absence of parental consent as long as a lawyer co-signs . . ."

"Yes."

"But why William?"

"I knew he'd be discreet. But more than that, who would suspect that a lawyer specializing in cases of gay men would have anything to do with co-signing consent forms for experimental abortions? Neither Mrs. Campbell, who arranged with several schools to help with referrals, nor William knew about the transplants. As far as they were concerned, one or two girls a year, out of the dozens that we helped, would have the additional benefit of new procedures. To have William sign was a good cover. Nobody ever asked a single question.''

''Where did Matt West come into this?''

The smile left Stow's face, and that other expression returned, the one I couldn't quite name. I recognized it now: defeat. ''I had no idea Matt was an undercover police officer when he accepted the position of Harpur's bodyguard—another of the strong, smart men I've had to employ to control Harpur when she began to have fits of violence. She has always been brilliant, Ellis. Remember how she used to outwit you at law school? Her cleverness has not been completely obliterated by her illness. In the case of Matt West . . .''

He stopped to steady his breathing, which had become ragged. ''I am as guilty of loving too well as you are, Ellis. And my love has destroyed the life of Matt West.''

''Then he *is* dead?''

Stow seemed unable to respond. As if he needed to tell the story in his own good time, he continued. ''It wasn't until he had already been attacked that I found out from the police that Matt sometimes worked undercover in the guise of a pimp named Solomon. I now know that the police have had their suspicions of Second Chance for a long time. Though now that I've met with them . . .''

''Everything is fixed, I suppose . . .''

''I had to reveal everything,'' he said, ''to ensure that no charges could be brought against my wife.''

''Charges against Harpur?'' Whatever he was about to say, I didn't want to hear.

He cleared his throat. ''The first transplant, which was

done at a clinic in the States, was very encouraging. But the effects were temporary. In her lucid moments, Harpur laid the plan for continued treatment right here in Toronto. It was she who thought of the halfway house, who set up the criteria for the girls to be accepted at Second Chance, and for those further selected to be donors of fetuses. Harpur figured out how to convince the parents to consent to routine abortions. How to use a lawyer to get legal consent for experimental procedures on minors. She made sure that nothing done in the whole Second Chance scheme was illegal. And as long as she was able, she supervised the scheme herself.

"Love is blind, as you know, Ellis," he went on. "And it blinded me to a lot: the risks we were taking with people's health, the risk to my career, the risk to Harpur's failing mind. Love also blinded me from observing that Harpur was using her diminishing periods of stability to prepare for the future—for a time when her life would no longer be bearable. She took precautions. She managed to stockpile a supply of the powerful tranquillizers used to sedate the girls before the transplants. I think she planned to eventually use the pills on herself . . ." He fought to control his voice. "But something else happened."

"One night I heard a scuffle and ran to see what was going on. I entered our kitchen in time to see Matt subduing Harpur. I saw her grab at him hard enough to tear his shirt. I saw a flash of gold—a chain, I thought—at Matt's neck. But I think Harpur saw something more.

"From that night, she was like a different person—quiet, obedient. I thought we had finally found someone to watch over her who had gained her respect." He glanced toward Harpur, but she was miles away.

"I could not have been more in error," Stow went on. "One evening six weeks ago, while I was in Ottawa, Harpur managed to trick Matt into ingesting a quantity of the tranquillizers she had saved. It was she who mutilated him. Apparently she had seen his ring on the chain around his neck and had become obsessed with it. Over the years, we had sometimes discussed the ring and the old promises and wondered what had happened to Gleason's ring. I think Harpur decided that poor Matt West had come by the ring dishonestly . . .''

I remembered my own similar thoughts about the ring having been stolen, and I felt ashamed. I remembered how Aliana had once suggested that the ring was still a token of love. Of love and of loss.

"Perhaps," Stow said, "she felt she was somehow returning the ring to Gleason through William. She could have remembered what great friends the two men had been."

"If Matt wore the ring on a chain around his neck, how did it end up on his severed hand?"

"I don't know," Stow said with difficulty. "In her deranged mind, there may have been some logic to putting the ring back on the hand, but I think there may be a more tragic explanation. The police told me that Matt may have been awakened from sleep by Harpur. He may have been wearing the ring during his private hours. The police said that sometimes undercover officers wear their wedding rings when they think it's safe. It has cost more than one officer his or her life . . .

"It was some time before anyone in the household discovered what had happened," he went on. "I was summoned home at once, but when I got there, Harpur was missing."

"And Matt?" I asked. Had he bled to death?

Stow looked up at me for the first time since he'd begun this story. "Because of Harpur's condition, we had medical people on call twenty-four hours a day. They saved Matt's life, but, despite our recovering the hand from your ravine, it was too late to attach it. We still do not know how the hand actually got to William. Harpur was found wandering near his neighborhood and apprehended. Since no crime had been committed—Harpur was clearly incapable of criminal intent—I was able to call in a number of favors to keep this as quiet as possible. But there were a few things I couldn't control. The first was William. He knew nothing about Matt guarding Harpur. Understandably, finding Matt's hand put him over the edge.

"I also did not foresee the level of your involvement. The police traced William to the valley, but in the intense effort to recover the hand, William got away; perhaps he fled into the wild parts of the ravine. I did everything I could to find him. By then, Matt's partner on the Force had told me about the connection between William and Matt. I wanted to ask William's forgiveness. I wanted to assure him that Matt was safe at a private clinic and that everything possible was being done for him . . ."

"William was afraid you had killed Matt and would kill him, too . . ." *And me*, I reminded myself. But it was pity, not fear I felt now.

"If only I could have found William. I would have told him his refusal didn't matter. Aside from the unexpected side effect of making Harpur look years younger than her age, the transplants had stopped working . . ."

He put his hand on Harpur's shoulder, and she reached up to clasp his fingers, but it was a mindless gesture, like that of an infant who will wrap her fingers around anything that touches her palm.

"Stow, William convinced me his life was in danger. I haven't seen him since." A sickening thought occurred to me. Maybe William hadn't made it out of the valley the day of the flood.

"I never saw him again," Stow answered. He glanced at Harpur again, as if he didn't like to take his eyes off her for long. "Whatever happened to us all, Ellis? Remember how we used to be? It was such a long time ago, but sometimes I think about the five of us, and it's like thinking about the day before yesterday.'' Without looking at me, he said, ''You've been in love with her, too—all these years. So in love that when you thought she snubbed you, you tried to hurt her.''

''Stow, I was sick. I'd reached the end of a lot of ropes. I was burned out, and I was drinking. I wasn't the kind of judge you're going to be—dealing with nothing but the highest level of appeals. I spent ten years among criminals. I thought I could help them. In the end, I couldn't help becoming one of them.''

''But,'' Stow said, ''I helped you. And now you're going to help me. You're going to keep your mouth shut.''

''Of course.''

How could I not? And why shouldn't I? Harpur's scheme had been airtight. And now it was done. What threats and promises could not accomplish in thirty years, pity accomplished in an instant. I had feared that Stow was about to have me jailed, or even killed. Reality was more gentle, but somehow infinitely more cruel. I did not die in that room. But all my dreams of Harpur and Stow did.

Stow moved to the window. He stood there for a long time with no motion, no word. Harpur played with her fingers, like a child. I saw she wore no rings. I wished I could comfort them, but I couldn't find any words of condolence.

The last I saw of Stow, he was still staring out the high window of his tower, waiting.

On my way out the main entrance, I passed two burly men in white coats. They were not movers. I was glad I escaped before they tore apart the two people I had once thought were the luckiest in the world.

CHAPTER

EIGHTEEN

"ALL LOVE ENDS IN TRAGEDY," ALIANA SAID. "IT'S AN OLD Italian proverb.''

We were sitting on the patio of the Press Box sharing a late lunch. The sun was hot and soon we'd have to move indoors. Between us on the table was a copy of the *Toronto Daily World*. In it were the obituaries of seventy flood victims. One was William Sterling. Though I felt I should honor Stow's request to remain silent, I owed it to Aliana to explain everything.

"It'll be hard for him for a while," Aliana said when I was through. "But Stow will be okay. Despite everything—maybe even *because* of it—John Stoughton-Melville will be a fine Supreme Court judge. A person untouched by tragedy is unfit to judge others.''

"Maybe so.''

"What about you, Ellis?" she asked, putting her hand over mine. "What will you do next?''

"I don't know. But you can be sure that this is my very last case.''

"It doesn't need to be.''

I didn't answer right away. I looked across the patio. A little bit of the lake was visible from where we sat. A slight breeze was blowing the sailboats around the harbor like paper scattered in the street.

"Ellis, there's something I think you have to know. Last night when you were napping and I was at the computer, I started fooling around and found myself browsing through some matters of public record concerning judges who've been removed from the bench. I checked your name. It wasn't there. This morning I called the Attorney General's office. I have a contact there and he managed to access your file. In it he found an approved application for sick leave, effective since the day you were arraigned, which is the day it was filed. Ellis, you're still a judge—and not only that, you may be entitled to five years of retroactive disablity!''

I just stared at her. Finally I pulled myself together enough to ask, ''Who filed the application?''

She smiled. ''Your friend inside the circle—Stow. No doubt he would have told you, had you ever demonstrated you were well enough to handle the information, which ironically you now are.''

Her hand still rested lightly atop mine. I turned mine over and grasped her slender fingers.

But she pulled away. ''That's not all,'' she said. ''A judge is not the only thing you still are.''

''What else can I possibly still be?'' I asked, sure she was joking.

''Married,'' she said. ''You're still married. I checked that too.''

She was smiling, but it looked like a brave smile to me, though I tried not to flatter myself.

It was going to take a while for me to deal with what she'd said.

''What about you, Aliana? What will *you* do next?''

Now it was her turn to hesitate. A look that could almost be taken for sorrow passed her features. It made her look as young as she'd been the first time I ever saw her. ''I'm going away,'' she said so softly that I had to lean closer to catch her next words. ''I'm going to Asia on assignment, to do a series on organized crime in Hong Kong.''

Again I glanced at the lake. A mist obscured the boats.

It wasn't raining. It was me. I tried hard to keep Aliana from looking at my face. I wished for my old judge's trick of showing perfect impartiality. But it eluded me.

Without saying anything more, she stood. She moved close to me and put her hand on my shoulder. "Your Honor," she said, "you are the most worthy partner I've ever worked with. We're going to work together again. I can feel it."

I nodded assent. I don't know why. *I* didn't think we'd ever work together again. My cheek brushed her hand. She bent down and kissed me just beside my ear.

Raising a little wind of lemon and spice and jasmine, she breezed away.

I just sat there and watched the boats until darkness drove them into shore.

The answer to Aliana's question about what I would do next was quick in coming—at least for the time being. The week after Harpur was taken to Parke-Manning mental hospital, Tim Garrison quit his job at the university and committed to working permanently for the city on the valley restoration. Conservation experts from around the world seemed to be beating a path to his door, and foundations were actually *offering* him money.

"Ellis, listen," Tim Garrison said. If I had had a lapel, he'd have been holding me by it, he was that insistent. "This is a good offer and it's my final one. You can be my second-in-command. I can let you live at the headwaters in the old fish hatchery. And you'll have plenty of time to work on your research for the re-vegetation. We don't have to sell the valley, and it stands to benefit greatly if you take this on."

I had never found Tim Garrison persuasive on anything except the valley itself. I had never allowed myself to be swayed by his politics, his charming but overwhelming enthusiasm. But there was also the matter of my having nowhere to live except with him, which might become awkward if I turned down his offer. I decided to accept the job for one year. My old home in the ravine had been wiped out by the flood. This would give me an opportunity to return to a part of the valley that was still intact. And I'd have time to straighten out the other parts of my life that Tim Garrison knew hardly anything about.

"That's great!" Tim spouted when I said yes. "This is just wonderful, Ellis. Wonderful. Here, I'll get the map. Now, here's where the old Ministry lodge sits. I'm sure we can convert these outbuildings into greenhouses. What do you think?"

"Tim," I said, "sketch it out and we'll go over it. I've got a little errand to run for an hour or so. You can spare me, can't you?"

"Hey, Ellis. Sure. Sure thing." He shook my hand. "This is going to be *great*!" He beamed. Then he got back to the plans.

I took a chance in going to Queenie's room again without being invited. I knew it wasn't the polite thing to do, but I had to see her. I knew she was all right; I had heard it on the street. But I wanted to tell her about myself. About how my life was changing. And about how that meant that she and I could be better friends.

And I also wanted to tell her that no one had "stolen" her daughter's baby. The hostel's records showed that Moonstar had given birth in the hospital, and the hospital's records showed her baby had come to full term. She had been stillborn. Moonstar must have known this all along, but I didn't need to tell Queenie that. I couldn't tell her either who had killed Moonstar. I just didn't know.

As I made my way up the stairs and through the narrow corridor that led to her door, I tried to think of what to say. I knew that families often felt a tremendous sense of relief when the murderers of their children were brought to justice. But Queenie lived in a world where the concept of justice was different from that of the middle class. I was pretty sure that Queenie had made peace with the death of Moonstar a long time before.

Nonetheless, as I knocked on her door, I was afraid that I might say the wrong thing.

All plans for saying anything were wiped from my mind when she opened the door.

"Come in, sit down, Your Honor. I'll make tea. Boy, was I worried about you! But now you're a bigshot again, ain't you? I seen your picture in the paper. Gee, but it's good to see you."

She made me feel right at home. She said she just had to make a phone call at the pay phone down the hall, that it would only take her a minute, that she'd be right back and we'd have a cup of tea and a good long chat.

Which we did. I told her about the flood. I told her about Aliana. I had to be careful what I told her about Second Chance, but she got the gist. And when she asked me whether the people I knew there, meaning Harpur and Stow, had anything to do with the time I got in trouble, I told her the truth.

"I was bummed out, Queenie. One night I was drinking at one of the fancy bars in the shopping complex next door to the courthouse—the Eaton Centre mall. I looked up and there was Harpur—sailing out of one of the elegant shops like a vision. I was so drunk I didn't think she was real. I rushed out to her—just to say hello. But she ignored me. As if we'd never met. As if we hadn't known each other all our lives. Something came over me. I went at her. Before I knew what I was doing, my hands were around her throat . . ."

"They thought you were trying to kill her. That's what you went to jail for?"

"Yes, but only for two days. Because somebody helped me out . . ."

I didn't tell her the person who had helped me out

was Harpur's own husband, that I had found out that Harpur hadn't snubbed me at all. She'd had Alzheimer's, with periods of dementia, even then. She hadn't recognized me.

Even after all that had happened, even sitting in this small poor room, I still remembered rich, wonderful Harpur. I remembered the laughing girl with the strawberry hair and the magical horse. I remembered the young lawyer with the flashing green eyes. I remembered the careless laugh. I remembered that the heart needs no reason for love and the memory keeps what it cares to.

"She's the one you were sweet on all these years, isn't she?" Queenie asked. "Like a dream person. Like a movie star. Everybody on this earth loves someone at least once in their life way more than they love back."

"I'm so sorry, Queenie. I am so sorry about your girl."

"At least you found out for her what was going on at Second Chance, so no more girls lose their babies before they're born. I owe you, Your Honor."

"No, I owe *you* for being such a friend when nobody else was. As far as I'm concerned, we're even."

She nodded absently fingering her silver and turquoise necklace.

"Queenie," I said gently. "How did you get Moonstar's necklace after she died? Don't tell me it was the police who gave it to you. Nobody on the street leaves silver lying around long enough for the cops to pick it up. Who took it off her?"

She refused to meet my eyes. "The world has its own justice, Your Honor," she said. "A person lives a certain way, they got to expect to die a certain way."

"Who killed Moonstar, Queenie? Tell me."

"You put yourself on the line for my girl," she finally said. "I guess you got a right to know. One night I'm sitting here minding my own business. There's a knock and I go to the door. Johnny Dirt's standing there with my girl's necklace in his hands. Says he found it. I know right away he didn't find it. I call him a damn liar. He broke right down and told me how he fell off the wagon and needed money . . .''

''Are you telling me Johnny Dirt killed your daughter?'' I remembered how often he'd mentioned Moonstar. He always seemed to know where she was.

''No,'' Queenie said. ''But he found her in an alley, shooting up. She'd been beat all night; it must have been the worst beating she ever got. She didn't want any more. She always knew where to get a fix. Johnny saw her O.D. He saw her die. And instead of coming to me, he went to the paper and told a photographer she was beat to death.''

''But there would have been an autopsy. It would have shown how she really died.''

''So what? Somewhere in some medical report it says that my Margaret Louise died of an overdose of heroin. And in the papers, it said she was beat to death. Either way, it's shameful. And either way, she's gone.''

I sat in silence with her for a while longer. Neither of us had anything left to say. After what seemed an eternity, I heard the bell of St. Mike's Cathedral. It was three o'clock. I had to get back to work.

''Queenie,'' I said, ''I've got to go now, but . . .''

To my surprise, she jumped up and put her hand on my arm, as if to pin me to the chair. ''You can't go yet,'' she insisted.

''I'll come back soon,'' I promised.

''No. Wait just a little longer. It's so good to see you. Here, I'm gonna make you another cup of tea.'' She took the cup from my hand, reached for the kettle on her hotplate and headed out toward the hall. I heard the sound of water running a little distance away.

Then the sound of water mixed with the sound of

voices, and I heard Queenie say, "Thank God you got here. He almost left. You better get in there quick, before it's too late."

I couldn't imagine what this might mean. Why should anybody want to detain me? My heart started to pound, and instinctively, I looked around the room. It was on the second floor—too far for a man my age to jump. And the window looked painted shut.

But then I chided myself. Queenie wouldn't entrap me. She was a friend. We owed each other our lives. There wasn't anybody who could pay Queenie enough to hurt me.

I strained to listen, but Queenie didn't say anything, and neither did the other person. I relaxed.

A sound I had never found frightening before pierced the air: the wailing of an infant.

I jumped out of the chair. I grabbed the door. I bolted into the hallway.

A woman holding a chubby baby with dark curly hair and a big mouth stood beside Queenie.

"Dad!" the woman said. She passed the baby to Queenie and came toward me. But before Ellen reached me, I had moved quicker, and my arms were holding her and my tears were running into her hair.

And the little boy, little Angelo, was screaming at the top of his lungs.

"Railing against injustice," my daughter said. "It'll always run in the family."

"Is that a promise?"

"Yes, Dad," she said. "It's a promise."